"To look and pass" was

not enough for Dan Hendricks.

TAYLOR CALDWELL

To Look and Pass

A FAWCETT GOLD MEDAL BOOK

Fawcett Books, Greenwich, Connecticut

To Look and Pass

~~~~~~

If Dan Hendricks had been born thirty or so years later, things would not have happened as they did. He could have gotten away after his wife's death and begun again easily. Ease of transportation would have helped him. According to his means, he could have taken a train or a bus or stepped on the gas and let himself down over the horizon for fifty miles, for five hundred miles, for three thousand miles. In a restless and mobile nation, he could have lost himself completely, assumed another identity, without background or past. In an era that was born anew each morning, without roots and without sharp memory, he, too, could have been born anew, started at the first dawn again. But he was born too early, born when even cities thrust roots deeply and when every stranger in a community had to give an accounting of himself. Memory was

7

long then; things did not happen so quickly, and events did not tread feverishly on each other's heels as they do now. People remembered what they read and heard. Life was so quiet and static that even a distant thunderclap could be clearly heard.

This very quiet made it impossible for a man to forget. And this was the most important part of all. If a man lives in a forgetting world, he does not find it very hard to forget, either. Where there is so much change, all changes become equally unimportant. A quiet woman is remembered a long time for a few pungent words, but a woman who constantly chatters creates a psychic deafness in her audience, so that when she does speak with meaning, the very meaning is unheard.

Dan's tragedy was that neither he nor the world could forget, though what each remembered was entirely different. He could not run; the world's voice would have followed him down into his grave. Moreover, he did not want to run. There are men like that, foolish or heroic men, whichever your turn of character would have you believe. I prefer to think he was both foolish and heroic. But I do not see what else he could have done, the world being what it was then. It was only his attitude which made him seem to me both foolish and heroic. But that was before I understood him.

We went to school together, Dan Hendricks and myself, to the red schoolhouse of politically revered memory. Two little girls went to school with us, also. We remembered them best, for they became our wives. I've never really regretted marrying Livy, that is, not more than most men have regretted marrying the women they did. Livy was, and is all right, no worse than many women and a great deal better than most. We've lived forty years together come next Christmas, and we've never missed the children we might have had but didn't. There's a lot of foolishness written and said about the beauties of parenthood and the happiness children bring. I'm not so blind, and it seems to me that children bring you precious little joy and a whole lot of misery. No, we're not sorry we were

not "blessed" with children. We've had long years to ourselves, and very few sleepless nights, and countless hours
for reading and peace and learning understanding. Children do rob you of living; they're always on you, always
exigent, even when they're middle-aged and you're ready
for the grave yourself. They do more than merely deafen
your ears physically with the noise of their growing; they
deafen your mind, too. When you're a father, you're only
half a man, in spite of the pretty poetry and the Bible.
You can't strike hard at life when you're afraid that the
blow you deal might rebound and hit one of your children.
So life which is a yellow dog at heart, leaps at your throat
because you are afraid to use your whip.

But this history isn't mine, and I'm not going to tell too
much about myself. A writer or a historian must always
keep in the background, more for self-defense than for a
regard for real literature or history.

The other little girl we went to school with was the
daughter of a widow, the town seamstress. She was a good
seamstress, and there was some money, too, left by the
husband, Jacob Faire. Mrs. Sarah Faire and her little girl,
Beatrice, or Bee, lived very comfortably in their tight white
house near Big Bend. South Kenton wasn't really a town
in those days; it was just a sort of swollen village, though
I will say it had all of the orneriness and goodheartedness
of a town ten times its size. Thirty or forty years ago it
was just like any other village in the country, sleepy,
sunny, lazy, rambling, quiet, and "nosy." It seemed to
sleep all alone in the valley, wrapped in sunshine or snow,
living intensely only about every few years when someone
married or died or got put in jail. But, underneath, each
little life felt itself very important and exciting, just as
the ants do coming and going busily to their sandy hills,
when you watch them on a hot, still summer afternoon.

Mrs. Faire sewed for all the village housewives, even
the mayor's wife, who could have gone to Ripley for her
clothes. She also sewed for the farmers' wives, when they
felt the crops had been good enough so that they felt no
need to run up their clothes for themselves that year. She

was right handy with her needle and outlandish sewing machine, and could make a piece of woolen cloth look miraculously stylish even on a fat woman. In these days she would have opened a smart little shop, narrow and bright, with the word "Modiste" printed in gold on a beveled window, and charged ten times the price. She would have had her hair tinted and ridged, and used good perfume, and kept her hips down, and said "Madam." But she lived in the days before real civilization and was quite content. She was modern in a way, too; she adjusted her prices to her customers' purses. When Livy and I were married, she made Livy's whole outfit for a song, and I never did forget it. That was because she liked Livy. But then, most everyone did.

Sarah Faire was still young, according to modern standards. About thirty-five or so, when little Bee was twelve. But then she was considered old, or at least middle-aged, even though her figure was still good and her light red hair naturally curly and gay in spite of the nets and pins. She had a clear and creamy complexion, and a wide red mouth with dimples, and a soft neck. Her eyes seemed to dance all the time, as though she were having a joke with herself. That was funny, too, for living with Jacob Faire hadn't been any joke. It had been a sentence. He had been twice her age and had kept the general store. She probably married him for his money and because she was sick of teaching school. Perhaps the joke she always seemed to have with herself was that she found life so delightful when she was a widow. She never thought of marrying again. Life with Jacob Faire, who was greedy, sullen, and crafty, had cured her of matrimony.

Little Beatrice was very like her father, though, physically she was strangely like her mother, too. She was like Sarah, with the shine off. She was little and plump, like Sarah, and had Sarah's creamy skin and dimples and curly reddish hair. She even had Sarah's russet eyes. But Sarah laughed deeply and ringingly; Beatrice just sniggered. Sarah looked at you openly, with brown and yellow and red lights welling and shining in her eyes; Beatrice didn't look up often, even when speaking to you, and when she did, her eyes were just flat brown, with maybe a little sharp spark of malice in them now and then. Only malice could make her eyes lighten and take on expression. Sarah was always sympathetic and warm and ready with a cheerful word; but Beatrice was cold and sly and treacherous and mean of tongue. She's dead now; but I hated her then, and I still hate her. I'm sorry she's dead; I'd like to say all the things to her that I wanted to say but never got around to saying. The only thing I'm glad about is the way she died. That made up for a lot. Livy says one must never judge, that there are strange and secret currents and caves and abysses and fearful countries in every human being, and you can't judge unless you know all about them. But justice and courts and juries would be very funny things if they took all that into consideration. Why, according to that, no one would ever be convicted of anything! Sometimes, when I feel soft, I think of Beatrice and remember her father, and I wonder if Beatrice was entirely to blame, after all. Sarah Faire should have been careful about the man she picked out to be Beatrice's father. But then, what woman ever is?

Yes, I always hated Beatrice. Most people did at heart, I believe. Everyone in South Kenton knew what she was. Though folks laughed when I said it, I knew and believed that Sarah Faire finally hated her daughter, too. Folks are always shocked when they hear of what they call "something against Nature," as though nature has any niceties or bounds or set rules of conduct! They know that lots of brothers and sisters hate each other, and folks aren't too shocked; but when a mother or father hates an offspring, they refuse to believe that Nature could be so perverse. But Sarah Faire did hate Beatrice toward the end. She was an old woman when Beatrice died, but I remember the way she looked when we told her—

Livy has just glanced over my shoulder, and she tells me that I am rambling and not telling the story. And she adds, what is there to tell of Dan Hendricks, anyway, that couldn't be told in three hundred words? I tell her that even the story of Creation could be written in one hundred words, if necessary; that a man could tell all he knows in one word: "Nothing." But where would publishers and critics and authors be if stories were told in a few score phrases? Besides. though there are many climaxes and crises and excitements in the story of Dan Hendricks, there was what went on in his mind, which is worth a thousand volumes. But Livy now says that I have written enough for one chapter, and though there doesn't seem much sense in my ending this chapter, I will have to begin another.

It has always seemed to me that it is more important to tell what a man thinks than what he does, that the landscapes seen internally by only one eye are more significant and terrible and beautiful than the landscapes seen by a thousand. It would be a frightful but awesome thing to see, if only for a moment, the vast and formless country behind one blank human face, where the mind flickers like a dim flame in countless winds that never roved on land or sea.

Dan Hendricks had nothing physically to show why fate had picked him out to crush and rend and hurl and spit upon. I remember him well, how he looked when we were going to school together, a tall and lanky boy with a long face like a melancholy colt, and rather vague brown eyes. His hair was never fully cut; it clung at the back of his shaggy neck like a dull brown fringe, and one long lock was always falling over his forehead and blinding him. He would brush it away, vaguely, abstractedly, but never impatiently. It was just a nuisance to be borne. Life itself seemed to him just a nuisance to be borne without much thought of it, to be brushed casually aside in order that one might see clearly.

He was not a stupid boy, in spite of his apparent aimlessness of gesture and his slow movements and shabby clothes. He had a large, well-cut nose in his pale face, a very wide mouth, and high, clever cheekbones. There were times when he had a singular beauty of expression, soft and gentle and ironically kind. I never knew a time when he ever hurt anything or anybody. He spoke slowly, slurring his words, letting his voice die away toward the end of his sentences. He had big hands and bigger feet, but his knuckles were not large, and the fingers were slender, though fumbling. When he was a boy he had all the intrinsic gentleness and tenderness and stern integrity that he was to have when he became a man, but few besides Livy and Sarah Faire and myself seemed to know it. They never did know it, even when he was dead. To most of the folks in South Kenton, he was just a no-account, the son of the shiftless village blacksmith, living in a two-room shack behind the smithy. He wore galluses three-fourths of the time, even to church, and in the winter he merely wore a heavy, shapeless coat over them. He ran barefoot most of the time, too. He seemed to hate shoes, though I don't believe it was because he particularly loved the good, wholesome, rich feel of the earth under his feet. I think shoes simply seemed insignificant to him. I don't think he really loved Nature, either; he loved wild and stormy landscapes, bitter sunsets, and the dark calm before tempests. That was because he loved beauty, and loving beauty is very different from loving Nature though most folks won't agree.

Most folks believe that if a person is really good and honorable and high of heart, everyone will love him, feeling instinctively all his virtues. That isn't so. I knew what

Dan Hendricks was, and so did one or two others, but the majority of the people in South Kenton despised him and despised his father. Folks in the mass are very stupid and blind; they see only the mud on thick boots, the grime under fingernails, and the need of a shave or a haircut. They saw only that Sam Hendricks drank every penny he could lay his hands on, that he was godless, illiterate, and profane. They saw that Dan showed no more ambition than did his widowed father, and that Dan would sit slackly by the hour staring at the sky with his mouth open, the bucket he had been sent to fill, empty at his side. Like folks all over the world they believed that loquacity shows an active mind, and that feet that scurry are feet that are going somewhere.

My father was the old-time country doctor of popular memory. I will not add, "And may his tribe increase." It's a good thing for the country at large that the old-time doctor is disappearing; folks'll live longer for it. Not that my father was any more ignorant or superstitious or hide-bound than others of his profession in those days; but he did not know too much. My mother had been a "school-marm," and never forgot the fact. She, it was, who instilled what pride my father had in him. Therefore, they objected peevishly and harshly to my love and friendship for Dan Hendricks. Mother had inherited a little money, and we lived in one of the best houses in the village. I was never allowed to invite Dan there. I tried, awkwardly and blushingly, to explain why not to Dan, but he stopped me halfway with a slight, amused smile, as though he was surprised that I thought the matter important enough to talk about.

Livy, my wife, was the daughter of the town "reverend," and had two other sisters. Livy, too, was forbidden to play with Dan Hendricks, though she always disobeyed without any pangs of conscience that I could discover. She petted and pitied and teased Dan, and when we were youngsters I often suffered jealousy because of the evident affection Dan had for her. I wanted both of them to love only me. They knew it and laughed at me. But no one could help loving Livy then, for her smallness and darkness and plumpness and gay dimples and dancing braids of hair.

The children at school did not like Beatrice Faire, even though her mother dressed her exquisitely for those times, and she was always dainty and clean and had many pennies to spend for licorice shoelaces and molasses apples and hard, round lemon drops at the general store. She would spend the money lavishly on her schoolmates, not out of generosity, I knew, but merely because for a time she could buy the regard and respect of those she felt hated and snubbed her.

Yes, they hated Dan, too, as much as they hated Beatrice. They laughed at his shabbiness. For years they joked about the time Dan carried his shoes slung over his shoulder on the way to school, then sat down carefully in the dust near the door and put them on. But there was something good-natured in their dislike of Dan; they often included him, when necessary, in their games. But in their hatred of Beatrice there was something malevolent.

Dan, I found, pitied Beatrice. I thought, when I was young, that it was because the children snubbed her; I found out, years later, that he pitied her because of what she really was. He tried a few times to be kind to her, and gentle, but she repulsed him with such venom and loathing that he fell back.

Livy was kind to everyone. She was even kind to Beatrice, whom she really could not bear. Beatrice responded to this almost pathetically; she dogged Livy whenever she could, followed her constantly, was included in many things in order that the others could obtain Livy. "You'll ask Bee, too, or I won't come," Livy would say flatly. So Beatrice came. The little girls always walked hand in hand together, light red head bobbing beside dark head, ruffled skirts or plaid wool frocks mingling and blowing together. But what a difference in the faces beneath hoods or sun-bonnets or knitted woolen caps! Livy's face was so open, so smiling and fearless and generous, though not as pretty as Beatrice's. Bee's face, in spite of its pink-and-whiteness

and dimples and small red mouth and russet eyes, was so
sly, so crafty, so mean, that all its beauty seemed an
uncertain kind of ugliness.

Beatrice was always at Livy's home. The Reverend
Isaac Bingham and his wife, Livy's parents, were very fond
of Beatrice, in the blind manner of adults. They lauded her
pretty manners, her respectful manner of speaking, her
little curtsies, her spurious shyness, and soft voice. They
thought their tomboyish and rollicking little Olivia could
profit from the association. But I knew that it was only
Livy's inherent integrity and fine nature that kept her from
the pollution that Beatrice literally exuded from her whole
body. The reverend and his wife did not know that Livy
not only did not like Beatrice, but had a real contempt for
her, and that she only befriended the child because she
could not endure that even a mean thing be trampled upon.

The society of the little town-village was very tight and
close. Only about a dozen families were included in it;
mine, Beatrice's, Livy's, Dave King's, Bob Cunningham's,
Matilda Hughes's, Willie Williams's, Amelia Burnett's,
Mary Knowles's, Jane Mundell's, Susan Crawford's, and
Jack Rugby's. Dave King's father was an old man, though
Dave, at the time I speak of, was only twelve years old.
Endicott King had been married three times, the first two
without issue. He had married one of my mother's second
cousins, a young girl some thirty years younger than he,
and she had borne him this one child. Endicott was a retired farmer, comfortably situated and with extraordinarily
fastidious manners and luxurious tastes. They lived in a
large white stone house near Hamsville Pike and had two
hired girls. Bob Cunningham's mother was a widow; her
husband had been the owner of the shoe factory in Ripley;
and on his death she had retired to her old home on a comfortable annual income. Matilda Hughes's father was Ezra
Hughes, president, vice-president, secretary, and manager
of South Kenton's one and only bank, a shrewd and
miserly and pious rascal. Willie Williams's father was Tom
Williams, a lawyer of pompous appearance and sonorous
tongue; Amelia Burnett's papa was Mark Burnett, mayor

of South Kenton for ten years; Mary Knowles's widowed mother held half the mortgages in the county, it was said, and was a regular modern businesswoman who would have earned admiration even in these days for careful management and an eye for profit. Jane Mundell's and Susan Crawford's fathers were horse dealers of good income, while Jack Rugby's father was Mortimer Rugby, head of the South Kenton School Department and schoolmaster of its only school.

There were a few other families in South Kenton, also, in a sort of limbo between the despised stratum of nondescript townsfolk and farmers from the outlands and the snobbishness of our little circle. These included the constable's family and the undertaker's family, and the general storekeeper's family, and they were occasionally included in our refined little parties and other doings, though never completely accepted. The richest man in town was Ed Ford; he owned the brewery outside of South Kenton and the American House in town with its hilarious bar. But he was a man of such opulent appearance, with his plaid vest, white shirtsleeves, profanity, gold watch-chain and charms, and sleek, walruslike whiskers, that he was avoided publicly, though not privately, by the better element. He was also a foreigner; that is, no one knew exactly what his origin was, and besides, he tended bar in his "hotel." He gave lavishly to church funds, could always be counted upon for charitable donations, but he was too expansive of speech, too ready of friendly tongue and back-slapping hand, too loud and raucous of voice, to be included in our refined little orbit. His three pretty daughters were never invited anywhere except when absolutely necessary, and while I was still a child they traveled a good deal and finally married substantial gentlemen in other and larger towns. The good ladies of South Kenton were always suspicious of Ed Ford, and, led by Livy's mother, they were eternally getting up "crusades" against his wicked bar and brewery. However, the women were never too severe and thorough about them, because Ed Ford's generosity had to be depended upon, on not infrequent occasions, to pay

Livy's father's salary. When Ed, with a grand gesture, actually contributed half the funds to build a new parsonage, the crusades died a sudden and discreet death. Ed was no fool.

In the limbo was also included the family of Con Sturgeon, owner of the Opera House.

To all of the youngsters of the inner circle, the families in the limbo seemed brilliantly colored, romantic, enviably high-living, pursuing lives of mystery and excitement. Beyond the limbo, we knew nothing and cared less, imitating our elders' light scorn and head-turning. Even my father, the country doctor, kind and jovial and gruff enough when visiting farmers' wives and children, recognized his humbler patients with only a casual nod when he met them in town. Thus for early American democracy.

Some will ask why Mundell and Crawford, the horse dealers, and Sarah Faire were included in our solid inner community. Well, Mundell and Crawford were well off, and their fathers, and their fathers' fathers before them, had been first settlers, and of good family. Sarah Faire was not at first included, but eventually her charming manners, docility, fascinating voice, and unusual beauty endeared her even to the frosty-lipped ladies. She was very intelligent, and had the art of pleasing down to a fine point. Moreover, she was an accomplished musician for South Kenton, and could play the violin with extraordinary skill, though not, as I later discovered, with any particular inspiration. She had a select little class of pupils among us, and she handled this matter with a casualness, in conjunction with her dressmaking, which aroused admiration. She could always be called upon in an emergency, was also ready with a helping hand with her usual good nature and amiability. No one could help liking her. Perhaps that also accounts for Beatrice's later hatred for her mother.

Sarah Faire was the only one in our society who did not possess a carriage, but she had the choice of any of our vehicles on Sundays. We called for her, and she would climb lightly into the carriage, a dainty figure in her muslins or silks or velvets, exquisitely gloved and rosy of cheek, a parasol of many silken ruffles over her nodding plumes of chic little bonnet, her small white teeth flashing in a good-tempered and agreeable smile. She would be accompanied by Beatrice, a pretty little replica of herself in black boots, embroidered petticoats, and long fair curls. Sarah would laugh and talk gaily to her hostess, but Beatrice would sit in a corner of the carriage, smirking faintly, her little gloved hands primly in her lap. All the adults petted the child excessively; her manners were perfect.

We made a leisurely and delightful party, as we all drove up to the door of the little white Baptist church, our carriage wheels twinkling, our spanking horses fat and sleek, and calling out greetings to each other. The churchyard would be flooded with warm, quiet summer sunlight; even the gravestones looked festive, green and smooth and decked with flowers. There were few amusements in those days, and our social life centered about the church, with its small glass windows and scrubbed, bare interior. Life was placid and static, yet filled with a content and richness not found nowadays in the feverish coming and going of a life that lives only on the surface. We were not tired by headlines, by alarums, by movement that at last only resolves into inertia. We were not concerned with the doings of a febrile Europe; what the Kings and the Mundells and the Crawfords and the Rugbys were doing, were going to do, was excitement enough for us. We discussed marriages of two and three years ago with an avidity that did not tire until another marriage happened. Mrs. Hughes's new curtains furnished the ladies with conversation material for months; the Williams's new horse was a subject that could not be exhausted. For weeks, the ladies were in a flutter about the contemplated strawberry festival in the church grounds; the annual fair consumed the attention of all the community to the exclusion of everything else. Bourgeois women were not yet concerned with Art and Movements; in fact, they knew scarcely one book from another, and an artist seemed to them a monstrosity that would never cross the placid circling of their tight little orbits. When I became a young doctor, the pride of my father, I found no neurotic women in my community, found no inhibitions or complexes or psychopathic behavior. Livy says it is because these things had as yet no names. but existed just the same, as witness so-and-so and so-and-so. But I am of the opinion that strange and twisted behavior is the result of too much thinking, too much leisure, lives that are too crowded with exigent things that are worthless in themselves. Health lies in simplicity of thought as well as simplicity of living. When men become too concerned with their souls and their mental lives, trouble sets in. The more we emulate the animals in directness of simple purpose, whether that purpose is benign or cruel or barbarous, the better our health, mentally and physically. Excessive childbirth may have been bad in some few cases, but except for women like Livy, the childless woman is a whole lot sicker in her mind and body than the woman with six or more children. It seems to me that whatever mind or soul a woman has, she's better off if she ignores it.

Of course, we had our infrequent scandals and stupidities and cruelties. We wouldn't have been human if we hadn't. But even these things had a healthy lustiness about them. There was a sort of robust animalism in the way the people of South Kenton treated Dan Hendricks.

Dan and his drunken father did not go to church. The minister showed no wholehearted regard for their souls. The consensus was that they were not worth the saving. I confess that for a time I was troubled by Dan's godlessness, and each Sunday I resolved that I would cut off our friendship. Livy never had such thoughts; she was a total heathen, for all she was the minister's daughter. Livy has less religion and faith and more humanity than any other creature I ever saw.

I can stop now, and I can hear the little husky organ groaning in the soft hot silence of the summer Sunday; I can hear the leisurely singing of the congregation, following the music with individual interpretation. A bumblebee comes zooming through an open window, and, catching the sunlight on his yellow wings, he dips and soars over the flowered hats and bonnets of the women. Outside, through another window, I can see the quiet green fields and dusky purple hills beyond, and to the south, the white village houses in their nests of massive green. Mr. Bingham stands in the pulpit, lank and black-garmented, solemn and eyeglassed, his fingers between the leaves of the hymn-book; a sunbeam glistens on his bald head. Over everything is a shining and slumberous peace; heads nod here and there as Mr. Bingham begins to drone his long sermon. I see Livy and her mother and sisters across the aisle; Livy yawns, and mischief sparkles in her dancing round eyes.

Then, the huge Sunday dinner afterwards in a darkened dining room; braces of brown chickens and stuffing, roasted potatoes and greens, squash and yellow yams floating in syrup, golden pies and rich jams and thick brown coffee with cream, pitchers of warm milk, glass containers full of shining spoons, a tablecloth like a white board and napkins like small sheets. Then freedom, to run through the hot fields beyond the village, to go looking for wild blackberries and blueberries and, later, for nuts. Life, after Sunday dinner, seemed endless, full of shining sunlight, distant voices, white dresses, and sleepiness.

Dull? Yes. Perhaps. But when is life really not dull? It is all a very dull business. But it becomes duller when we expect vague richnesses and movements in the near future, when man cannot resign himself merely to exist and drink up the present moment, slowly and placidly, as cattle, standing in their own images, drink up satisfying waters.

∽∽∽∽∽∽∽∽∽∽∽∽∽∽∽∽∽∽∽∽∽∽∽∽∽∽∽∽∽∽

Sarah Faire's house was very popular with the children of South Kenton, even with Beatrice present. We liked to hear the whirr of her sewing machine. She was never hurried or cross. We could help ourselves to the contents of the huge cookie jar in the big, sun-filled kitchen, and then go and swing under the old trees in her front yard. Sometimes she would get out her "fiddle" for us, and play and sing sentimental songs, and then give us glasses of fresh rich milk and a slice of fruitcake or fresh, hot pie. She seemed as young as we; we liked to hear her laugh. We told her things we never told our parents. Because of her, we even played with Beatrice. She had an eternal youthfulness, joyous, laughing, generous, and gay.

We were all over there, about six of us, one warm spring afternoon after school, racing over the new green grass, shouting, dodging around the trees. The skies were blue as they are never blue now; there was a freshness to life, a newness, that never comes nowadays. Life was so young and untarnished and uncomplicated.

We trooped into the house for cookies and milk. We had smelt the cookies baking as we played; they added zest and high hysteria to our gaieties. We sat about the kitchen table with its turkey-red cloth, and stuffed our mouths with cakes succulent with raisins, and poured milk from a squat white pitcher with painted cherries on it. The early evening had turned cool, and the big black range, shining and clean, fumed with delightful warmth. We all talked as fast as we could.

Sarah stood over us, laughing, filling our plates. I can see, as if it were just yesterday, how her hair shone with reddish lights, how neat and trim her slender figure was in its dark blue dress with its white lace at the high neck. I was surfeited with content; I glanced about idly. A twelve-year-old boy is not particularly observant, but when my roving eye lit for an instant on Beatrice's face, I went suddenly very cold. The child's face, as she looked at her mother, was full of an elemental malevolence, still, held, yet ferocious. I can understand it now; she hated us as we hated her, and she hated her mother because she was good to us and liked us.

I looked away, uneasy. I felt that I could never come here again, and I was filled with sadness. I glanced at Livy; she was talking vehemently to Sarah. No one had seen but myself.

Someone knocked at the front door, and Sarah tripped away, humming. We paid no attention until Sarah reappeared with Dan Hendricks. Dan wore his usual galluses, was barefooted, shaggy, fumbling, and red with embarrassment. Though only thirteen years old, he stood an inch taller than Sarah.

We all stared blankly at Dan. To our knowledge, he had never been here before.

"Well, now, isn't this nice!" exclaimed Sarah vivaciously, as she shoved, rather than led, Dan into the kitchen. "Dan here just brought me Mrs. Mundell's red foulard, because you, Jane, you bad girl, forgot to bring it today. So now, Dan, you sit down right here, near me, between me and Livy Bingham, and help yourself to the cookies and the milk. Land, I almost forgot I've a fresh batch just ready in the oven!"

She ran to the stove, knelt before it, and produced from its hot depths a sheet of celestial circles. Dan did not sit down; he stood near us, not looking at us, his face very red as he wrung his hands together. A thick silence had descended on us, an uneasy and embarrassed silence. I tried not to look at Dan, coward that I was. But Livy at last held out a peremptory little hand and seized him.

"Didn't you hear Mrs. Faire say you were to sit by me, Dan?" she shouted. She literally dragged the agonized boy to the chair beside her; he fell into it, full of misery, trying to avoid looking at us. Sarah came back to the table with a platter of hot cookies, and poured Dan a large and foaming glass of milk, and tossed several of the cookies onto a small blue plate before him. If she noticed our silence, we were not aware of it.

The joy of the afternoon was gone for us. Two or three of the girls elevated small noses as though they had smelled something offensive. Two of the boys, in their embarrassment, began to scuffle furtively. But Sarah chattered gaily to Dan, continued to heap his plate in spite of his murmurs. Livy talked to him also, with a sort of fierce vivacity.

"I think," said Amelia Burnett in her high thin voice, "I'd best be going home. Ma'll wonder where I am."

As daughter of the mayor, she held the position of social leader among us children. She stood up, fastidiously brushing crumbs from her plaid gingham. She was a thin and spindling child, with light blue eyes and colorless straight braids and a somewhat shrewish expression. The others stood up obediently, and primly thanked their hostess for her hospitality. They filed out in a stiff and ludicrous silence. Livy and I remained behind, Livy because she wanted to, and I because I did not have the courage to do anything else. And this, in spite of the fact that I loved Dan Hendricks.

There were only four of us remaining, Beatrice, Livy, myself, and Dan. Sarah appeared to have noticed nothing wrong; she continued to urge us to eat her cookies. But in spite of Livy's chattering and Sarah's laughter, we were all miserable. Dan said nothing; I said nothing; Beatrice said nothing. Beatrice's face was full of loathing and detestation whenever she glanced at Dan, and she edged away from him, ostentatiously inch by inch.

At length Dan stood up and mumbled something to the effect that his Pa was expecting him, and he had to go home. His long pale face was quiet but not humble; his wide mouth quivered a little, but looked very stern. Livy was gazing at him frankly, and I was surprised to see tears in her eyes.

"Oh, come now," said Sarah lightly. "You've never been here before, Dan, though I've often wondered why. Wouldn't you like to stay a few minutes, and I'll play my violin for you all?"

In the little silence that followed this question, Beatrice sniffed, and Livy tried to cover up the sniff roundly. "Yes, he'll stay, Mrs. Faire. I bet he'll just love your fiddle." She bounced to her feet, dragging Dan with her. She literally hauled him out of the kitchen into the little gay parlor beyond, Mrs. Faire and Beatrice and myself following. At the doorway Beatrice glanced at me; she was smiling a secret and gloating smile, full of significance. I think, now, that Beatrice was far more intelligent and shrewd than any of us ever were, and that she had a subtle way—uncanny and disconcerting—of reading thoughts. I hated her more than ever. I felt, even then, that in her was something boundlessly evil, an alert and discerning evil that smiled viciously at all things and found no good in anything. I remembered, too, things I had heard my elders say about her father, that he had been a mean one who could look right through you and see all the worst things in you and none of the virtues.

Sarah's little parlor was not like our parlors at home, which were full of vases and whatnots and stiff curtains and brocaded drapes and horsehair and massive walnut and gloom. Her windows were wide open to air and sunlight, the shutters thrown out, the spring wind billowing the fresh little curtains. Her furniture was nondescript and inexpensive; she had painted one or two little tables herself, and one was a bright red and the other a milky white. She always had a bowl or two of brilliant flowers on these tables, arranged with a carelessness that was the height of artistry. Hooked and rag rugs sprawled on the whitely scrubbed floor, and on one wall she had hung a strangely colored shawl. Everything seemed to smell of soapsuds and flowers, and an odd fragrance like that of old rosebowls, always hung in the sunny air. I think that little house was about the prettiest I ever saw, and I have been in all kinds. Perhaps it was because the woman herself was so clean and scrubbed and freshly fragrant.

I saw Dan look about the room with a sort of dazed expression, as though he found it incredible. That was no wonder; he had never seen simple beauty before. He seemed afraid to move, and stood there until Livy pushed him affectionately into a chair. Sarah closed the windows and then lit a waiting wood fire in the little grate, and the dry sticks began to chuckle merrily. Her fireplace was painted a gleaming white, and on the mantel was none of that Victorian litter which afflicted mantels of other houses. Here were no hideous Dresden figurines or strangely twisted vases of gilt and violently painted roses, no black marble clocks with deathly and lugubrious chimes, no chenille draperies to gather dust and be a fire menace. On the chaste whiteness of Sarah's mantel stood two copper tankards and one large copper plate, glitteringly polished. Now the firelight leapt up, shining on the few pieces of daintily gleaming furniture and on the white floor. The last rays of the spring sun barred and dappled the fresh curtains; through the windows one could see the greening yard and the pale golden-green of the newly-leafed trees. Here was peace, and beauty, and a high-hearted love of living.

Sarah tripped out of the room in her tiny kid boots and tripped in again, all nods and smiles and rosy dimples, carrying her violin as tenderly as a mother carries a child. We children sat about awkwardly. Sarah stationed herself near a window and began to play. I can see her so vividly, now, with the late sunshine gilding her pretty hair, the outline of her breasts under the tight dark blue of her bodice, the creamy roundness of her throat above the lace collar, and the gentle softness of the sweet chin that lay on the dark wood of her violin. On her face was a dreamy expression, tender and absorbed, half smiling.

"This, children, is the 'Moonlight Sonata,' by Beethoven," she said as her bow began to move smoothly over the strings. We sat silent, listening. The notes began to soar serenely, effortlessly, ineffably, like a flock of pale doves rising through darkness with spectral moonlight on their wings. Then, there were chords that seemed to beat with mournful impotence on the heart, notes that brought tears to the eye, solemn phrases like the admonitions of an angel. Groups of notes like prayers; bars like groping hands blindly fumbling at a door that would open on celestial and terrible glory. The feeble cry of mankind full of a trembling ecstasy at a glimpse of the eternal.

I glanced about me, boyishly ashamed of the thickness of my throat, trying to assume a casual air. Livy was listening, round-eyed and solemn, her red mouth open. Beatrice was sitting primly in her chair, looking at her feet. She half-smiled—that secret and knowing smile I always detested. But on Dan's face shone the glory of the opened door, a reflection uplifted, startled and ecstatic, as though he were hearing a familiar and beloved voice he had almost forgotten. I stared at him, blankly, fascinated by what I saw, not comprehending it.

I did not know then, but I know now, that that thirteen-year-old boy had fallen in love with the thirty-five-year-old woman, that he loved her until the day she died, and until the day he died. Things like that do happen, skepticism to the contrary. And this love that burst in him that cool, green April evening carried in it the explanation of all the frightful things that happened to him, and all the beauty and the peace he was ever to know. It was not a mere childish infatuation and idealism. It was as if he knew even then her true goodness and sweetness, her gentleness and cleanliness of heart. In a world he knew to be ugly and bitter, cruel and sordid, dim and hopeless, she was the sound of laughter and hope, the falling of scented petals, fortitude, the iron of endurance and integrity. I know I sound sentimental, but there was nothing sentimental in that love. Looking back, I can see it explained everything, was the reason for everything.

The last note fell from the violin, and Sarah laughed softly. She looked at us all, beaming, innocently well-pleased with herself, and somewhat surprised.

"Why, it never sounded like that before!" she exclaimed. She looked at Dan, and she stopped smiling. "Did you really like it so much, Dan?"

He did not answer. He stood up, his head hanging as though he was confused. He was an ugly boy; the only claim he had to good looks was in his large brown eyes with the thick, short lashes. The lashes were heavy with tears. Sarah put her round, plump arm about his shoulders.

"Perhaps you are a real musician, Dan," she said gently. "Suppose you come to me twice a week and I'll teach you to play. I'm not very good, but I'll teach you what I know."

Beatrice had stood up and was standing near her mother. Sarah's eye touched her, and I saw again that rather troubled and vaguely frightened expression on Sarah's face that I had idly noticed many times before when she had looked at her daughter. There was something speculative and bewildered in that expression. Beatrice seemed to make her mother feel inferior. And again, I must repeat here that Beatrice was really far more intelligent than any of us, even her mother, not with the twisted intelligence of the neurotic or the psychopathic person, but with a sort of Satanic intelligence full of malicious humor. I have met a few women like her since, in bigger cities than ours, and such women were universally admired for their wit and their cleverness, but hated for tongues that never spoke any kindness or understanding.

"I'll come," mumbled Dan in a low voice, almost as though he was sealing a solemn covenant. "I'll come."

I'd like to write here that Dan revealed true genius during his lessons, that he became a famous violinist and composer, and shook the world with his colossal genius. Yes, I'd like to say that. It would be dramatic, the substance of a real novel. But the truth of the matter is that though he became fairly proficient in technique, and learned to play competently, he was never a great, or even a fairly great, musician. He played for me a hundred times, and I watched the lifted glory of his face each time with a certain uneasiness and bewilderment. Finally I understood that he really never heard his own playing, but only the great chords in himself of which his playing reminded him. He was like the intense but impotent lover of music who can endure even the bad rendition of a selection by an amateur for what it recalled to him. His imagination was too tremendous, and it numbed his physical fingers; it made it impossible for him to develop a critical ear for his own playing and prevented improvement. I am sure now that the greatest musicians and lovers of music can never learn to play a note, because of this imagination; genius in this, as well as the other arts, demands a certain salty flavoring of mediocrity.

We three children, Livy, myself, and Dan, went home together in the sweet and exciting coolness of the evening. Livy walked between us bouncingly, her head bobbing at our shoulders.

"Mrs. Faire is the nicest lady," she said to us in her round fashion. "Mama says she is a real lady. But I hate that Bee! She's the meanest thing!"

We smiled over her head in indulgent, masculine fashion.

"Well, you always let her hang around you all the time," I said teasingly. "Folks say you're her only friend, Livy."

Livy pouted, shook her head violently. "I feel sorry for her, kind of," she admitted. "She's so mean. Now, you stop that laughing, Jimmy Marcy! You can, too, feel sorry for folks because they're mean. They're—they're sort of like a bird that got its wing broken. They can't fly very high."

Dan glanced at her with a quickness and sharpness unusual for him.

"Yes," he said eagerly. "That's it. Bee's crippled; I mean, in her mind, or something."

I found this too subtle for my young healthiness, and snorted.

"Crippled! I'd like to cripple her!"

"Why?" demanded Livy, annoyed. "She never did nothing to you. She never does nothing to anybody. She's got nice manners, that's what Mama says. She never says much that you can get mad about. She's—just kind of quiet—"

"Oh yes," I jeered. "We all love little Bee!"

Livy tossed her head, poked me sharply, but answered nothing. We came to her home, a huge, rambling structure next door to the church, lowering under ancient trees. It was made of wood and covered with scrollwork, fretwork, and cupolas. A hideous house. Its interior was even less prepossessing than its exterior, and was full of all the ugliness of which the Victorian era was guilty. We left Livy at the gate, and went on together.

Darkness was setting in rapidly, and I hurried. The sky was like a dim opal, veined with faint rose and pale purple, quiet and vaguely sad. Lights from windows began to glimmer through crowding trees; the streets were practically deserted. Suddenly a flock of crows rose cawing and blackly stiff against the melancholy of the heavens. A wind lifted and a dimly transparent gloom settled over the world.

We came to the smithy. Dan's father had called it a day,

but a few glowering embers still burned on the hearth. I hung about as Dan pushed open the door of the wretched, two-room shack that he called home. He never invited me in, but over his shoulder I could see the bare and filthy floor, the bed in a corner, unmade and with dirty quilts, three broken chairs and a table loaded with chipped crockery. On a few nails on a wooden wall hung the shapeless balance of the boy's wardrobe; an ancient black range in a corner was streaked red with old rust and grease.

I was very young and tactless. Looking over Dan's shoulder, I said naïvely: "Don't look much like Mis' Faire's house, does it?"

I could have kicked myself for that remark immediately afterwards. But Dan did not seem to take offense. He studied the room beyond for a long moment Then he said tranquilly: "I don't mind it. It suits me."

I know now that there was no bravado or hurt in what he said. He really did not mind it. He did not see it with his inner eye, and that was the most important of all. Neither this squalor, nor life, was seen by that inner eye of his, but only something in himself that was infinitely calm and beautiful and satisfying, that no one else could see.

Mr. Mortimer Rugby's opinion as to the best way to teach the young mind how to function was somewhat on the order of the old saying: "A woman, a dog, and a walnut tree, the more you beat 'em the better they be!"

He had a strong, flail-like arm, our schoolmaster. He was extremely energetic and nervous; he twitched even in repose, and while sitting, watching us studying, he would continually pass a lean and corded hand over a lean and jaundiced face, and would keep one crossed leg constantly in a gentle and feverish motion. At the time of which I speak he was about fifty years old, with a long and straggling mane of grayish-brown hair which gave him a somewhat affected appearance. I imagine he thought he looked every inch the poet, to which high estate he aspired with more solemnity than humor. During the Civil War he had

written many bloody, ferocious, and ringing poems for the
newspapers, poems literally dripping with gore and patriotism, in which young men were urged in cantos and short
stanzas and even epics to lay down their lives for the Great
Ideal and Freedom. On the occasion of Mr. Lincoln's
assassination, he had written a blank verse play of some
ten acts, each act containing at least five scenes, and he
was much commended for it. In fact, a copy was elaborately printed (the only copy which ever was printed) and sent
with the tearful devotion of the whole county to Washing-
ton. In the town hall, heavily gilt-framed, hung the reply
of Mrs. Lincoln to this touching tribute, couched in words
that would melt the hardest heart, and expressing her appreciation and brokenhearted gratitude. I heard from my
parents that there was no holding Mr. Rugby down for at
least ten years after that; he sprouted poems of all kinds,
all becoming progressively more patriotic and sentimental,
with a decided leaning in the direction of the Sanctity of
Legal Love, the Hearth, Home, Fireside, Heaven, and
Mother. I remember one poem in particular, for my father
was fond of quoting it, not, however, with reverence and
appreciation:

> O little bluebird on the wing,
> O sing, sing for me!
> And raise this mundane, earthy Thing
> To all Eternity!
>
> I stand below with humble hands
> And muted voice, in tears,
> And listen to Time's hissing sands
> Run through the bloody years.
>
> But through my sadness, like a gong,
> There peals the message of thy song!
> Tweet! Tweet! So sweet!
> So sweet! So sweet!

This poem was much admired by the ladies. Miss Alice
McCall, our saintly and rather damp-nosed local virgin of

conjectured years, composed a little music for it and played it on the organ months on end. My mother used to say that it made even hardened sinners weep when Miss McCall played it on the church organ. Mr. Rugby was so grateful for this tribute that he honored the lady by making her his second wife, and her gratitude for this magnanimous act was so great that she spent the rest of her life in a sort of Greek Chorus to her husband.

But alas for the tragedy of a poet's life, and alas for all fame! A man might spend two-thirds of his life in devotion to a cause or a people, and let him slip just once and the populace leaps on him joyously and pounds hell out of him. The last third of his life is usually spent thereafter in spitting teeth and rubbing his jaw. I see a sort of justice in this: mankind suffers a lot from its saviors and poets and idealists, and its reaction in a moment of weakness is healthy, and continues to give hope for the ultimate civilizing of the race.

I suppose there were a lot of obscure things that led to the artistic downfall of Mr. Mortimer Rugby. He had been a widower for ten years; his first wife had been a wholesome, bustling woman who never considered her husband to be any first-class hero. It was even rumored that she had laughed at the Sacred Play written about Mr. Lincoln. (I believe it was called "Man—Crucified.") Her ridicule and laughter and healthiness had kept Mortimer's higher flights in check, for which a generation ought to be grateful. Her influence had been so great that for ten years of his widowhood Mortimer had not transcended any bounds to amount to anything. And then he married the Greek Chorus, Miss Alice McCall. Fate, which always lies in ambush with a club for a hero; leapt out joyfully, chortling.

Mortimer was intoxicated by his wife's adoration, by the incense she poured on his altars, by the worship in her big, calflike eyes. She was not buxom nor seductive, being at least thirty-eight years old and scrawny. I cannot imagine anyone less likely to inspire a love poem, but then, I was not privy to their bedchamber. Mortimer produced an erotic poem that would have put Lord Byron to shame, and would have made the lusty Shakespeare discreetly cover his eyes. Worst of all, it was a very bad poem, and because of this it was unpardonable. The man must have been mad, for even to the last he was bewildered, felt outraged martyrdom, and bitterly hinted that mankind always jeered at its artists and then revered them at their death. I don't believe he ever read his poem objectively.

For two years he was in terrible disgrace. He was removed as schoolmaster. He had not been in the war, and so had no pension, for, like all schoolmasters, his exercise of patriotism and worship of the soldier had taken place far behind the fighting lines. It was fortunate for him that Miss Alice's father had been a captain in the war and had been providentially killed, leaving her mother a substantial pension. The old lady, who admired her son-in-law, supported the little household of Mortimer and his wife and his young son, Jack.

Mortimer was so bewildered at the treachery of Pegasus that he seemed broken for two years. He wrote no more poems, and again I say that a generation ought to be grateful. He seemed to turn against his devoted wife, as though he obscurely believed that she was at fault. He attended church with great regularity, spoke little, carried his head as though he felt it bloody but unbowed. He had a colossal dignity of carriage and manner, and had an appearance so refined and wounded and spiritual that the ladies of South Kenton relented, and forgave him. The forgiveness of their husbands quickly followed. I am of the opinion that the men had enjoyed the erotic poem, for in later years I heard snatches of it around the bar and in barbershops. Yes, it was really very bad.

He was restored as schoolmaster. He accepted the position gratefully, yet with a dignified hurt which made the townsfolk feel vaguely ashamed. Thereafter he confined himself to writing pageants for the Sunday-school children, and eulogies at elections, with an occasional rhapsody upon a local wedding or a birth. But the wings of the bird of song were clipped, and it soared no more toward Venus and secret, sylvan vales.

We children hated him, and feared his terrible arm. I believe now that he took out upon us his frightened wrath and humiliation, made us pay for the recriminations of our elders. He was a very tall, thin man, always dressed in black of an artistic cut, with flowing cravat which mingled with his long and fastidious mane. He had a thin face, spiritually haggard, and languid eyes. The eyes belied him; he was constantly and jerkily in motion. Remembering his sonorous voice and stately periods, I believe that a politician–orator was regrettably lost to the nation. He would have caused the Honorable William Jennings Bryan some bad moments.

He was schoolmaster for twenty years. When he died, at the age of seventy-three, his sins were all forgiven, and a tombstone was erected to him with these touching words inscribed on it:

Here lies one whom God endowed.

If we children hated him, I am sure that he hated us. We were not more stupid than any other children, but he seemed to think we were. It was no use for us to complain to our parents of our frequent floggings, for in those days discipline and birch-rods were highly regarded as aids to education. He did not spare even his own son, Jack. The boy resembled his dead mother, being rosy-cheeked and mischievous, loud of laughter and generous, utterly earthy and unsentimental. In fact, I believe that Mortimer whipped Jack more regularly and thoroughly than he whipped any of us. But the whippings never took the amusement from Jack's round face, never made him yelp or blubber.

I do not think that Mortimer was entirely stupid, in spite of his poems. He showed discernment in that he was the only adult in South Kenton who disliked Beatrice Faire. The girl's deportment in school was perfect; her lessons were perfect. She was always prepared, always respectful and attentive. But Mortimer disliked her intensely, used to rag her continually, nag at her upon every occasion, and regard her with deep suspicion. And he was the only adult in South Kenton, with the exception of Sarah Faire, who liked Dan Hendricks. For this, I bless his memory.

Often he would shout at Dan: "You can do better, you whelp! You're just lazy and contemptible! Come here!" Then would follow a ferocious flogging that made even the hardened children uneasy. Dan did not seem to mind. He accepted flogging as he accepted everything else—indifferently and abstractedly. Mortimer tried to instill bodily fastidiousness in Dan, and there was a great deal of suspicion among us children that the cleaner shirts Dan wore came from Mortimer's discarded wardrobe, as did pantaloons obviously cut down and taken in. Mortimer had very little money, and less, after his mother-in-law's death, but we were well aware of the purchaser of Dan's winter shoes and socks and mittens. With great gestures of ferocity, Mortimer would tell Dan to remain after school for a real flogging, but one day when I came back for a forgotten book I saw Dan contentedly munching two solid sandwiches and a huge slab of cake, while Mortimer fumed at the blackboard preparing the next day's lesson.

Mortimer was our pretense to exalted learning in South Kenton. He knew several languages and had a tremendous library. He was an encyclopedia of knowledge and misinformation. If he did not know the answer to a question he never let anyone suspect it, though his ignorance could be detected in an increased pompousness and severity. There was something rather pathetic about the man, though he would have been enraged had anyone remarked on it.

One day there occurred something that had in it deep significance, the key to all of Dan Hendricks' character, though I was too young then to know it. Perhaps Mortimer guessed it, for he was not dull, and perhaps that was the reason he was always more gentle with Dan after that.

Dan had the run of Mortimer's house and was forever borrowing books from the schoolmaster's library. I did not know that for a long time, for children are not concerned with books. I was compelled to remain after school one afternoon, and Dan remained also, waiting for me, for we walked the same way home. Dan sat on his bench across the room, reading with a sort of steady fierceness. I scratched on a slate wet with my own tears. Then Dan carried his book to Mortimer, who was frowningly reading on his platform.

"What does this mean, Mr. Rugby, sir?" he asked. "This: *'Ma guarda e passa.'* It's in this book. It's a foreign language. I expect."

Mortimer took the book with impatient dignity and stared at the words. He cleared his throat, and the jaundiced tint of his complexion became touched with pinkish brown. It was evident that he was having difficulty in translating. Then he handed the book back to Dan loftily. "It means," he said, " 'Look and pass.' "

Dan looked dreamily at the book. "Look and pass," he repeated vaguely.

Mortimer passed his hand rapidly over his face, and swung his foot.

"Well, boy, do you know what that means?"

Dan seemed to ponder. All at once his face looked old, much older than Mr. Rugby's, though the latter's hair was turning whiter every month, and wore the half-petulant, half-bellicose expression of those who remark the passage of the years resentfully.

"Yes, sir, I think I do," replied Dan thoughtfully. His grimy finger moved over the words in the book. " 'Look and pass.' Maybe it don't—doesn't—mean the same thing to everybody, but to me it seems like it means—being born and living and dying. You—you just sort of—look and pass. That's all you can ever do in life. It don't matter if you work or don't work, or amount to anything, or don't amount to anything, or run about like you had a fever, or just set. None of us can do more than that: look and pass."

I remember now the peculiar quality of silence that followed his words, as though everything pondered them, the dusty schoolroom with the rows of shabby and dis-ordered benches, the sun at the window, the bright shining of the sky outside, and the deep October coloring of the wide country under it. Mortimer Rugby seemed to ponder it. He had started to draw his hand over his face again in his old, nervous, impatient gesture, but the hand never completed its journey. It lay as if violently arrested over the lower part of his face, hiding his mouth and chin but leaving the restless and pathetic fierceness of his eyes glinting out over it. For a long time the silence continued.

Mortimer's foot had stopped its incessant and gentle swinging, like a pendulum halted in its arc. He cleared his throat; he had difficulty in clearing it properly, for the harsh sound rent the silence several times before he could speak. I was surprised at the muffled quality of his voice.

"Well, Dan. If folks thought that all the time, kept it in mind, it would paralyze everything, y'see. Folks would realize nothing was worth trying for, or doing. We'd all just 'set,' as you say. But what about ambition, ideals, justice, trying to right wrong things, trying to make beauty out of ugliness?"

Dan smiled faintly. Again I was impressed by the fact that he looked older than Mortimer, who waited for the boy's next words with a kind of humble anxiety.

"It don't—doesn't seem to change it, sir," he said, as though he groped for the proper words. "Julius Caesar or Napoleon, Galileo or Darwin, Goethe or Shakespeare; all they could do was come, look, and comment on things, and then pass. Failure or success: they don't mean anything. You can't get any closer to life than a bug can, and when you're dead you have done just what the bug did, get born, look at something you can't understand, and pass —die."

A man's ambition and inherent passions are not always in exact ratio to his endowments. I know now that the zeal and the devotion and the aspirations of a Shakespeare had burned madly in our poor and mediocre Mortimer Rugby, that his comprehension of beauty and splendor had not been less because he had been able to cast only a poor and shabby shadow on paper. I know now that he must have suffered subjectively all his life, because his fingers and tongue had no finenesses, because he had been compelled to stare mutely at eternities and emit only a despairing squawk as he had tried to join in the terrible symphony. He had looked at colossuses standing in the ruck of time, hating himself for his little stature, but reverencing the pedestals on which he had been unable to climb. In this, he was much unlike our present-day artists who cast mud on the pediments they can never stand upon. And I think now that his poor and bewildered spirit was comforted by Dan's words, that peace came to him, that he felt himself a spectator among the gods who are themselves only spectators.

He was silent again for a long time after Dan had spoken. His hand dropped from his face, and it showed itself naked, stripped of little affectations and dignities that he had worn to shield himself against others. I think there were tears in his eyes, for they were suddenly filmed and obscure, as though he wept internally even while he was comforted.

He stood up and laid his hand on Dan's shoulder. He tried to speak, but did not. He began to pat Dan's shoulder inarticulately, over and over. Then he picked up his hat and strode out of the room on his long and wavering black legs.

I was amazed at my sudden release. I had not understood the conversation. Dan was always saying queer things. I shouted and threw my slate across the room, and leapt up.

"Old Daddy-long-legs must've got a bellyache!" I exclaimed. "Guess I can get out of here now. Looks like he forgot us."

"I expect he did," said Dan mildly.

We walked home together under the brilliant blue of the October sky. Maples burned scarlet on the hillsides; zinnias and asters clustered violently in every white-fenced garden that we passed. The very air burned, and tingled with poured light; the wind smelled spicy and exciting. We raced along the roads on carpets of hot dust, rejoicing in the heat of the sun on our faces even though we knew that winter was coming. Along the quiet streets the painted

trees were motionless; we pulled a surreptitious apple or
two that hung over the sun-hot stone walls. The last breath
of summer seemed more exciting, more delightful to us,
than July and August. It was as though we were stealing
grapes in a vineyard, with the pickers close behind us.

Dan had been taking lessons from Mrs. Faire for nearly
four years now; today was Thursday, so we stopped in at
the little white house under its great trees. The grass was
already brown, but still warm to our feet, and as we went
up the flagged walk, colored leaves fell from the fading
trees and crackled under our step.

To our dismay we discovered that Mrs. Bingham, Livy's
mother, was calling on Sarah Faire, accompanied by Mrs.
Burnett and Mrs. Knowles. I never did like Livy's mother,
who was a tall woman with a decided attitude and a prim
and bigoted manner of speaking. She always looked as
though she expected you to say something indecent, and
often, indeed, she prompted hapless wretches to say
appalling things which they had never intended to say and
perhaps had never even thought. She sat there in Mrs.
Faire's gay little parlor, stiff in black mohair, holding a
white handkerchief as she always did, as though preparing
to put it to her lips in horror. She had a preening motion
to her head, as if what she had said recently covered all
matters, and any dissent would put the dissenter in a contemptible position. Mrs. Knowles was a bright little body,
and her red merino dress seemed to add a sharper brightness to her small, pert face. Mrs. Burnett was constantly
aware of her position in the village as the mayor's wife;
she was a dull, stout clod of a woman with all the meanness
and malicious impudence of her kind. She curried favor in
spite of her airs; there was something cringing even in her
haughtiness, something defensive in the cold and lightless-
ness of her pale eyes. She could not seem to forget that she
had been only a hired girl in her youth, and that the
unexpected and fortunate death of a miserly uncle had been
the only thing that had turned the poor but ambitious eyes
of Sam Burnett upon her.

Sarah looked subdued as she always did in the condescending company of the great ladies, though I know now that this was sheer hypocrisy and she was only gently amused. I also know that despite Mrs. Bingham's bigotry and stupidity and Mrs. Burnett's vicious malice, Sarah really did not dislike them the way she disliked Mrs. Knowles. She could hold her own with them, with her sweetness, deference, and eagerness to please. But in the face of Mrs. Knowles's sharp pertness and intelligence and briskness she felt too feminine, too useless and ignorant. Mrs. Knowles made her feel untidy and planless, a sort of little painted butterfly who had no real use in a utilitarian world. She knew that Mrs. Knowles had contempt for her gentle femininity, that she watched all her graceful little ways with amusedly lifted brows and knowing slyness. Mrs. Knowles had a mind of her own, spoke of men with casual indulgence, and despised female wiles. In these times she would have been an active clubwoman, a businesswoman with men working hatingly under her. She was far in advance of her times, and because of her lack of charm, (though she was handsome in a wholesome and masculine way) she had never had a suitor after her harried husband's death.

Sarah caught sight of our dismayed faces at one of the parlor windows, and she laughed at us gaily.

"Come in, boys," she called. "No one's going to eat you."

We came in, shuffling our feet. The ladies looked at us with the frank annoyance most adults feel in the presence of adolescents. Sarah laughed and then looked grave.

"I'm sorry, Dan, but I can't give you your lesson today," she said with real regret.

"That's all right, ma'am," he mumbled. His face was red.

"But you must stay and have some cake and coffee," said Sarah eagerly. She never talked to us children as an adult, but as one of us, and she gave us the same courtesy which she gave those of her own age. "Bee's out in the kitchen now, cutting the cake."

I wanted the cake, and the coffee smelled overwhelmingly attractive as its odor curled insinuatingly into the little parlor. I tugged at Dan's arm.

"If you don't mind, Mis' Faire, we'll eat in the kitchen," I said. Sarah looked hurt; I knew it was not mere affectation. But Mrs. Bingham waved her handkerchief dismissingly.

"Run along, boys," she said loftily. We went into the warm bareness and brightness of the big kitchen. Bee was there, cutting cake as her mother had said. It was still warm, and, bursting with raisins, it smelled spicy. She glanced up at us as we came in and smiled her secret smile. She looked oddly like her mother as she stood at the white table, and Dan stared at her as though seeing her for the first time. She and Dan were nearly of an age, about sixteen, then, and she had all the gracefulness and prettiness of early girlhood. She really had beauty, I must admit that, with her bright hair and clear skin and lovely figure which all the bunches and buttons of the period could not hide.

"Your ma said we could have some cake and coffee out here, Bee," I said. I spoke boldly as I always spoke to Beatrice, for she made me feel inferior and uncouth as she did almost all of us.

She shrugged. "Well, don't drink all the coffee and eat up all the cake," she replied. "We've got to have some for supper." Her voice was light like her mother's, but did not have its music or tender inflections. She carried a tray out of the room, her shoulders set contemptuously. She had not looked at Dan directly; it were as though she had been unaware of his presence.

In spite of Beatrice, I ate immensely of the cake and drank two cups of coffee. The cream stood clotted in its little yellow pitcher, and I scraped it out with enjoyment. I liked the contrast of the blue plates against the red tablecloth; I basked in the warmth of the brightly polished range.

But Dan scarcely ate anything. He looked abstracted, and rolled a crumb of cake between his thumb and forefinger. He seemed to be listening; now I know that he was listening to Sarah's sweet laugh and happy voice. When Beatrice came back into the kitchen, moving with her silent correctness, he started.

"Ma says she wants you two to come into the parlor, if you've finished," she said indifferently. We shoved back our chairs; we had no desire to go into that room, but I think that Dan would have gone into a lion's den for a glimpse of Sarah.

The ladies were standing up, pulling on their gloves. They glanced at us severely and with absent disapproval, which seems to be the stock expression of adults in the presence of youth. Sarah put her hand on Dan's arm, and he looked at it as though bemused. It was such a little white hand, with needle marks roughening the fingers.

"Mrs. Bingham wants me to make you come to church, Dan," she said affectionately. "I've told her how good you are at music, and she thinks I ought to be a good influence on you. So, I've just about promised her that you will come to church next Sunday with Bee and me."

I expected instant revolt, but to my amazement Dan nodded silently. He would have done more than that to please Sarah.

Mrs. Bingham breathed deeply through her nose. "There, you see, Sarah, you were all wrong," she said severely. "Of course the boy will come. He needs Christian instruction and training."

Sarah said nothing; she continued to smile, and now she patted Dan's arm. But in spite of the smile her eyes were a little sad.

We stayed for a few moments after the ladies had gone. Sarah still seemed uneasy. She acted as though she felt that in some way she had betrayed Dan.

"You don't have to go to church if you don't want to, Dan," she insisted.

"But I do want to go—with you," he answered almost with the indulgence he would give a child. Still she did not seem satisfied.

"I never took church, nor religion, to be very important," she said gravely. "I go because folks expect me to. Not that I really care whether they like what I do or not, but it makes them happier for me to do like them, so it isn't very much for me to do."

"Besides, go to church, be respectable, and your friends'll see to it that you are comfortable," said Bee. She spoke so rarely that when she did speak it was as though an alien voice had suddenly intruded itself, and it startled us. We stared at her, blinking. She was smiling, and her pretty white teeth glinted between her lips. Her eyes glinted also, their brown flecked with dancing amber sparks of malice. Upon her whole face sparkled the sharpness of her intelligence, in which there was something gnomish and cunning. It was as if she understood all our obscure and fumbling hypocrisies and weaknesses, and found them acidly amusing.

"Oh, Bee, you mustn't say that!" murmured Sarah uneasily. The old shadow crept back over her face. "We don't do right things or kind things just to have people approve of us, or to get them to do nice things for us."

"Don't you?" Bee's voice was light and mockingly surprised. She turned to Dan and myself; we were both abjectly uncomfortable, which no doubt she well knew. "I don't know about you, Jim; you're a sort of lumbering calf, but Dan, here, reads quite a lot. I suppose you've read *Vanity Fair,* Dan."

"Yes," he mumbled. Bee laughed.

"Doesn't Mama remind you of Amelia, who could never find anything wrong with anyone, and who used to substitute a dimple or a blush for reason? Poor Amelia. But still, I think she got too much for what she was; Becky Sharp was really badly abused."

I know now that she thought of herself as another Becky Sharp, and conducted herself accordingly; Bee, too, was ruthless, amused, cynical, and avaricious. But Becky Sharp had had her moments of kindness and hard sympathy; Bee never had such moments.

Sarah, though she had not understood much of Bee's words, looked downcast and a little shrunken. But Bee was in a flush of high spirits, the first I had ever seen in her.

There was something elated and eerie about her rare good tempers, something gloating and incomprehensible to simpler organisms. If she made an amusing sally, and we laughed, I felt that she laughed at us and not with us, that she found something ridiculous in our slow gestures and less complicated minds. When psychoanalysis began to afflict the world, Livy asked me if there could have been some "complex" or "repression" or "inhibition" in Bee. But by that time I had had many years experience in doctoring sick minds and sick bodies, and I knew there was nothing sick about Bee's brain or body. If she was abnormal, so is a rattlesnake abnormal. Both are healthy specimens of their type. It is the comfortable custom for people to say that an evil thing is abnormal; but an evil thing or man or woman is just as rounded and complete in characteristics of its type as in a more normal creature. And I will say this for Bee: if the world were peopled by her type, there might be few loyalties and fewer kindnesses, very small compassion and smaller mercy, but there would be no superstitions, no monstrous ideals, no "righteous" wars. Perhaps a world composed of such as she might be a little interesting, at any rate.

"You are young yet, Bee," said Sarah hesitatingly, with the darkness in her eyes again. "You don't understand that folks at heart are all scared, scared of life and mysteries and all the things they can't understand. So they all bunch up like cattle huddled together, frightened, in a barnyard, and they like to feel the warm hides of their own kind pressing against them. It sort of gives them a feeling that they are safe from all those strange things outside the barnyard. But when someone comes along, and laughs at their scaredness, and threatens to open the gate so that all those strange things outside can rush in on the poor beasts, why, they start to mill around and snort and stamp, and they might hurt that someone with their frightened stamping. So you see, it don't hurt to pretend, at least, that you are just as scared as they are, and press yourself up against them, and pretend to believe as they believe. It's just kind of human, and sympathetic, and pitiful."

Bee shrugged, not with anything so robust as contempt for her mother's anxious words, but with indifference. Even at sixteen she felt the measure of her own intelligence; she felt that it was like steel with which she would like to slash. But Sarah presented no firm flesh for slashing; she had only cloudlike softnesses and little laughters. If she had been a strong antagonist, Bee might have spent much of her venom on her and would have had less left with which to poison other lives.

However, she was in good temper today and announced that she would accompany us a ways, as she wished to see Livy. Livy had finished school last June, and had not yet decided whether she would go to Ripley to the high school or stay at home with her mother for a year. Mrs. Bingham had had a miscarriage, which was bad at her time of life, since she was about forty-five. We younger people were believed to be utterly ignorant of Mrs. Bingham's illness, but like all children we knew more than we were suspected of knowing. Mrs. Bingham was never quite the same after her "inward complaint," as the ladies called it, and Livy stayed with her mother, not out of an excess of affection, but because she felt that it was the decent and indicated thing to do. The two older girls were at the Ripley High School, Marjorie in her last year and looking towards college (an outlandish and exciting subject of conversation in our town), and Lucille in her third year.

Beatrice had finished school when Livy had finished. There was no question of her going to Ripley High School. Mrs. Faire was always artlessly surprised when higher education for women was mentioned. Once she asked simply: "What for?" Of course, the answer then was no more convincing than it is today. If I had had daughters, I suppose I would have sent them to college, but that does not alter my belief that education for men is a necessity, but not for women. Men have the originality, the power and the fortitude, and education increases them, enriches their lives, hurls back horizons. But women have no originality, no power, and little fortitude in other than physical matters, and so education is an affectation in women, adding nothing to them except stupidity and arrogance. Women have always had great faith in words and formulae and the sound of their own voices; giving them an education only gives them access to more words and formulae and adds a shrillness and clamor beyond endurance to them.

I don't suppose Beatrice Faire ever argued with her mother about education, though I have reason to know that she desired to go to school in Ripley. It was part of her curious character that she rarely entered into an argument when her opponent had inferior equipment. That was because she would not waste her time. She was greedy for time; she snatched at it. Time to her was infinitely valuable. She seemed to think that it was something to mold, to bend to service, to use for personal aggrandisement. She was feverish about it, as though she must always be alert or something crafty would rob her of a moment or an hour. In this she was violently different from Dan, who did not believe in time, who really did not believe in anything or find anything valuable. He was convinced that all one could do was "look—and pass." Beatrice believed that one could, and should "look—and seize!"

As she walked between Dan and myself that brilliant October afternoon, we were both taken aback by the new side which she was showing us. We had always been somewhat afraid of her, and resentful, but today she laughed and chattered with only slight glimpses of dark waters under the foam of her gaiety. She seemed in exceptionally high spirits, and was affable even to Dan, whom she despised. Dan was sensitive about the fact that he was almost seventeen and still at the local school. He mentioned that Mortimer Rugby wanted him to go to school in Ripley after January, when he would be finished with our school. But he could not do that, he said. His pa was getting old and tired out. He could get a job in January with Mr. Riggs, working in the general store. Mr. Riggs had promised him two dollars and a half a week. Mr. Riggs's brother had sold out to him, the brother buying a large and prosperous farm near Ripley. The succeeding Mr.

Riggs was a bachelor with long walrus whiskers perpetually stained with tobacco, and had the reputation of being an atheist, if not actually a heathen. Dan liked him. The work would not be too bad, he said, mostly evenings and Saturday afternoons, because Mr. Riggs liked to visit Ed Ford's bar and chatter in the park with his friends, and play chess with the undertaker, and argue horses with Crawford and Mundell.

"I should think you'd hate to waste your time there," said Beatrice scornfully.

"Why?" asked Dan with indifference, as though her opinion did not matter at all.

"I should think you'd want to go to school, to amount to something."

"Why?" he repeated equably.

"Well, don't you want to amount to something?" she cried. "Don't you want to get anywheres?"

"Why should I? Getting somewheres keeps you from thinking. That's about all you can really get out of living, seems to me. Just thinking. Getting somewheres means, I expect, eating better vittles, and having more suits to wear, and maybe a horse and carriage of your own, and traveling 'round on trains and boats looking at folks who'd like to travel around and see the places you've come from. All that don't seem important enough to me to sweat for it, and give up thinking-time for it."

"I think you're just lazy!" exclaimed Beatrice.

"Maybe," he replied mildly. "Maybe. What if I am?"

"Mama says you've got what she calls a 'touch' on the violin she gave you. You could perhaps amount to something if you wanted to."

They had ignored me during this conversation. I was more than a year younger than Dan, and besides, I thought the argument so dull, when the sky was so bright and blue, that I could contribute nothing intelligent to it. But, as I glanced at Dan I was arrested by the sudden tightening of his face as though he had been greatly hurt.

"No," he said slowly. "I'll never amount to anything—playing a violin. I know it. I feel as though I—try to push too hard on it, try to make it say things it hasn't got all the strings for. I try to make it sound like all the drums and flutes and horns and things I hear, inside, and when it can't sound like all that, I sort of bear down on it, and it just sounds dull. It's no good."

A lady was coming through the opened gate of a pleasant house, her arms full of late flowers. It was Mrs. Burnett, leaving a friend after a visit. Her carriage stood at the curb, the old darky drowsing on his seat. She stopped when she saw us young folk approaching. She smiled at me with her cold mouth and eyes, and beamed at Beatrice. Dan, she entirely ignored.

"Oh, there you are again, you children!" she said. "Seems we are always running into each other! Bee, I forgot to ask you this afternoon, but Amelia wants you to come to her birthday party next week, Tuesday, and you, too, Jimmy. I do hope your mama finishes Amelia's blue challis by that time, Bee."

"I'll help her with it, Mrs. Burnett," said Beatrice sweetly. She put her head gently to one side, and her eyes swam in softness.

Mrs. Burnett was moved, and patted the girl's cheek. "Your mama is very fortunate in you, dear," she said. She entered her carriage, and waved her gloved hand at us, and drove away. Beatrice snorted as we went on.

"Horrible old woman," she said. "Horrible little Amelia. Toad! What I'd like to do—"

"If you think that about folks, why're you so nice to 'em?" I demanded.

She laughed. "Because if you know what they are, and are nice to 'em, and flatter 'em, and make 'em feel good, they can do a lot for you," she answered derisively.

We left her at Livy's. Livy came to the door, her plump little face somewhat pale, but still wearing her air of pert awareness and good sense. She did not seem overjoyed to see Beatrice, but greeted her pleasantly enough.

Dan and I walked on together. Suddenly he looked at me with amusement.

"I suppose you want to amount to something, Jim," he said. "What've you got in mind?"

"Well, I wouldn't mind being President," I said, half afraid of his ridicule. "Wouldn't you?"

"Yes, I would."

~~~~~~

Dan went to work in Billy Riggs's general store. Business there had been conducted with more or less laissez-faire and lofty nonchalance. It had nothing of the heat of commerce, the bustle of achievement; Mr. Riggs's favorite platitude had nothing to do with a daily "something accomplished, something done." He showed no impatience towards congenital philosophers who slumped in stupefied positions on his cracker barrels, contemplating what, had it not been for overalls, would have been their navels. No, Mr. Riggs was all for a gentle flow of spirit and peace in his store; in the winter he kept his iron potbellied stove in a genial fume and red glow, and showed no decent shrewdness in the prodigal way in which he handed out free mugs of cider on frequent occasions, and tossed in crackers, apples, and chewing tobacco to boot.

The result was that though he had the greatest good will of South Kenton, his books, if he had kept them, would have shown a steadily increasing decline in more practical assets. But so long as he was able to meet most of his bills, and Mrs. Knowles did not press him too regularly on his mortgage, and there was a good thick slice of salt pork in his beans each day, he did not worry a particle.

Then Dan came to work for him, and to share with him the three warm but musty rooms behind the store. Dan's father had injured his thumb one day some two months before Dan had taken the job; it had rapidly become infected, and within a week he was dead. The general disfavor in which Dan was held was not lightened by the fact that he showed "no decent feelin's." South Kenton failed to notice that Dan got the best possible price for the smithy and the half-acre of land about it, and so was able to keep his father's funeral "off the town." I think South Kenton would not have disliked paying for the funeral had an indigent son edified it by dramatic demonstrations of grief over the grave of a pauper father. Folks will always like their little Roman holiday of morbid emotion, I guess, and will even be pleased to pay for it.

Billy Riggs liked Dan immensely. He, himself, was profoundly and hypnotizingly lazy. He frankly asserted that only chickens and other brainless creatures really liked to get up at dawn, and that folks who followed suit, and liked it, didn't "have no more sense than a settin' hen." As far as Billy Riggs was concerned, you could have your nonsense about industry and dew-washed worlds and getting early starts, and early birds getting the worms. He preferred his good narrow bed and a long hour of drowsing before rising to confront the day. "Folks'll rush and rush," he would say, "and by and by, come the years, they'll rush around until there ain't anythin' more to do, and then they'll sit on their backsides and starve to death, seein' that everythin's all done and washed up and built up and made, and needin' about fifty million more folks than there is to eat up and use up what the hard-workin' folks piled up in their factories and silos." I have heard more learned discourse, and read more rhetorical and scholarly essays on the subject of depressions and boom periods and economic ebbs and flows, but I doubt that any of them had the uncomplicated pungency and clarity of Billy Riggs's elucidation of overproduction and unrestricted work.

He liked Dan because of the boy's easy-goin' ways, and lack of what he called "agog-ness." Billy had physical inertia, but Dan had an inertia of the spirit. He cleaned up the most flagrant dirt in the store, tidied shelves, kept accounts, and made indignant customers pay on the nail. He was leading a far more comfortable life than he had ever experienced before. Billy Riggs was a bachelor, but more than that, he was chaste. He never "sashayed after wimminfolks." It was not that he had a contempt for women; it was just that he had never needed a woman, and therefore found the exigency of them incomprehensible. A neighbor woman came in every day to clean up the three rooms behind the store, and prepare the meals and wash the few clothes, but Billy would never sit down to eat until the last flutter of her skirt had disappeared. He said his vittles didn't set right with a female "a-swishin'" around the premises.

Dan had worked for him about a year when Billy Riggs informed all and sundry that he was leaving his store and his possessions to Dan. "I ain't got no one but my brother's pesky younguns that I'd just as lief pizen as look at," he said frankly. "Dan, here, is like a son to me. He can have every blame thing I got."

The ladies of South Kenton were fond of speaking of Billy as "being quite a character." They found nothing outrageous in many of the outrageous things he did and said. That was because, I believe, he had a shrewd and dangerously candid tongue and a certain brutality of expression that was justly feared. But they did resent his wholehearted and well-published admiration for Dan and the fact that he had made the boy his heir. Mr. Ezra Hughes, president, vice-president, secretary, and manager of the First National Bank, knew that Billy had something like two thousand dollars in the bank, and he righteously resented the idea of shiftless Dan Hendricks inheriting that sum.

South Kenton's regard for Dan did not increase because of this, not even in the face of the obvious fact that the store was better kept than it had been, that all bills were paid promptly, books balanced, and larger varieties of stock kept on hand. Dislike is always increased, if anything, when unexpected virtues in the disliked appear; society must have its scapegoat and always resents its devil suddenly appearing in newly washed robe and fresh wings. I notice that preachers do not unduly emphasize the Lord's nostalgic grief for his "Lucifer, Star of the Morning," but prefer to keep up the stench of brimstone and refer to Satan's alleged ugliness.

It would be nice to write something romantic about Dan Hendricks' business career, something epically American. Think what rhetoric, what admiration and reverence, could be utilized to show how he built up a lowly little village store into the nucleus of what would some day be giant chain stores in giant cities. A charming story could be written about startling innovations he had thought up, built on the good old hypocritical foundations of Service, Value, and Courtesy. Perhaps, in such a story, I could tell how he invented some simple little sales trick which made him a millionaire with two yachts, a palace on the Riviera, dyspepsia, a swimming pool, and a bodyguard. But, unfortunately for the edification of youth and the support of educators and preachers, such was not the case. Beyond the simple and well-worn mechanics of making the store pay a little profit and keeping down the majority of cockroaches, mice, and rats, and using a broom with casual regularity, Dan accomplished nothing much.

He kept up his lessons with Sarah Faire. He knew by now that he would never be even a fair musician. But it gave Sarah pleasure to teach him. And only God knows what pleasure she gave Dan by her very being, by the sight of her, by the touch of her hands, and by the kindness of her sweet voice. I am sure that all the heaven he ever knew was in that little white house under its gnarled old trees. He would take her a slab of bacon, or a ham occasionally, insisting that it was payment for his lessons; or maybe he'd carry over a sack of potatoes or flour, or a bushel of apples. These are not romantic things like orchids and books and bits of gold nothings and furs. But no jewel was ever given with deeper passion and more atavistic love than that which accompanied Dan's prosaic offerings.

The last time I ever saw Dan taking a lesson from Sarah Faire was when he was nineteen years old, and she, past forty. It was during my summer vacation, and my last year at Ripley High School, and I walked over to Sarah's house one hot July evening. I watched Dan take his lesson; his fingers seemed to hold well enough, with gentleness and strength and power, but the sounds that he brought forth were confused, muffled, yet terribly strong. Sarah was distressed; she stood beside him, wrinkling her clear brows in the funny way she had, and automatically waving a finger. She could not understand it. At length she sighed in despair, laughed a little, and shook her head. Dan removed the violin from under his chin, and looked at her as she sat in her chair, smiling in bewilderment and affection. Sarah did not appear forty, though she was somewhat plumper. The bright patina which she wore was not of the flesh, but of the brightness within her. I thought she was prettier than ever, in spite of the silvery gleam of a few gray hairs in the mass of red-gold curls on her head, and the fine web of wrinkles about her apple-brown eyes.

"I expect it's no use," said Dan slowly. He still looked at Sarah. He had grown very tall during these past years, and though still shabby he was very clean. In recent years I saw a rare portrait of Abraham Lincoln when he had been a young man, and there was something about that portrait which reminded me of Dan Hendricks at eighteen. There was the same ugly and melancholy face, the mild yet somber eyes, the serene and tender mouth, the indefinable aura of crude beauty and strength. There is nothing paradoxical in saying that Dan had both ugliness and beauty, and that the ugliness increased the beauty, made it alive and full of splendor.

I had grown used to Dan's face, yet youthfully careless and unobservant as I was I was struck tonight by its expression. There was always something guarded about his expression, something held back and reticent. But tonight his guard was down, and his love for Sarah Faire was blazing so simply in his eyes that only one as innocent as Sarah could have failed to see it. Fortunately Bee was not there. But I saw, and I became hot-cheeked and frightened and embarrassed. I felt that I had come upon Dan when he was naked, and that I ought to retreat a distance and shout, thus giving him time to resume his clothing, and I, to pretend that I had not seen. But I really did not understand completely, and forgot it entirely within a year.

When we went home together it was already dark and moonless. Whippoorwills and katydids were shrilling in the trees; the stars were hot faint points above us. We could smell the burned odor of grass, the pungency of weeds and the warmth of the trees. Twigs cracked loudly under our cautious feet; once or twice a distant dog barked warningly. But beyond these was smothering silence.

I heard Dan sigh in the darkness. We had not been speaking for some time. He sighed, and sighed again. Once I heard a faint sound as though he had struck a hard fist into the palm of his hand, and something that oddly resembled a groan. These sounds embarrassed and frightened me, after what I had seen in Sarah's gay little parlor. I wanted to get away from Dan, away from his disquieting presence. After nearly a year I had very little to say to him, and even that little was held back by the disconcerting sight of his nakedness and the unmuffled sounds of his spirit.

I pitied him, and loved him, yes; but I wanted to get away from him, resenting my own embarrassment and the cause of it. I did not see him alone again that summer, and only at a distance when I did see him.

Chapter

~~~~~~ *Six*

I liked my first year of college in Pittsburgh, and also my mother's relatives, her sister and the latter's husband, and my two young girl cousins. In June, when I began to think of returning home for the summer, Aunt Mary invited me to go with the family to Atlantic City until September. I wrote my parents for permission, and receiving it, went with my aunt and uncle and cousins on their vacation. It was unbearably hot in Atlantic City, but the saltwater bathing was splendid and exciting. I wrote home only twice during the summer. I had hoped to be able to run up to South Kenton before school started again, but found it impossible. So, it was nearly two years before I returned home. I had not been able to return for Christmas, either. Father's parents were very old then, and had asked their son and his wife to go for Christmas to their home in Indiana; as Grandmother was very feeble and bedridden, and this would probably be her last Christmas, my parents went. It was too far for me to go, and my grandparents did not particularly care for young people. So I had a big box of things from home, and spent the holidays with my aunt. The second Christmas I developed scarlet fever and was quarantined in the dormitories with ten other victims.

It seemed to me when I arrived home that South Kenton had shrunk amazingly. I thought it a sleepy Rip-Van-Winkle sort of place, with the low white houses under the sleeping trees, the sun ruddy and motionless on their boughs, the green shutters pulled silently in against the warm midday, the gardens blazing with hollyhocks and delphinium and pansies and phlox and roses behind trim white picket fences. Father had met me at the station with the buckboard, and as we drove under the trees in the thick hot silence, clouds of white dust rose about us, instantly turning to warm gold as they caught the sun. We met scarcely a soul on our way home through the slumberous streets, and so hypnotic was the tranquil and static air that I drowsed for a moment or two, and forgot all the questions I was going to ask. Time had disappeared, had become a telescope that had folded together, bringing two years ago to yesterday. Despite my shiny new bag, my stiff collar, and satin cravat, and low-crowned brown bowler, very cityish, I was a cub again, returning after a short visit to Ripley. Even my new polished boots looked grotesque to my eyes, as though I had put on my father's. Only my new and very young mustache was fixed in the present.

Father avoided Main Street; he disliked the very semblance of a crowd, though heaven knows, even the Saturday farm crowd was very modest in South Kenton. He told me that there were two other stores on Main Street now, special shops carrying men and women's clothing, hats and boots. This was not so good, he said without regret, for Dan Hendricks.

"Was poor old Billy very sick before he died?" I asked. For a moment I disliked my father. Though folks often spoke of the kindness in his bluff and bearded face, I always thought, with all due respect to him, that he had very cold and narrow eyes.

"Yes. Pretty bad. I always did think he looked consumptive, and the way he was carried off in the spring with pneumonia made it positive for me. He had no resistance, no fight. Expect his lungs were riddled in the first place."

"Gosh, that's bad, Father! And Dan slept in the same room with him, lived with him. Have you looked him over to see if he might have gotten it?"

Father flashed me a derisive look. "Oh, you young fellows with your germ theories and folderols! I never did hold much to all that germ nonsense. I'm not saying there's nothing to it, but it's exaggerated. There's other things besides germs. I believe, like better men than you new young squirts think you are, that consumption is due to bad blood and humors in the system, and inherited. I laughed when you wrote home about folks being able to take consumption from infected cow's milk. Nothing wrong with our cows in this country. Folks are just born consumptive, and all your stuff about being able to cure it with fresh air and rest and good food and sunshine—" He shook his head humorously, and tugged at his beard. "When you've got the consumption, you're finished. Like cancer or diabetes. You'll never be able to do anything about 'em. Never. So, old Billy had it, I'm sure, though he didn't cough that I heard. Always something funny about him, anyways. I always did think so, and was convinced when he died. He left your precious Dan Hendricks his store, three thousand dollars in the bank, and everything else he had. On one condition, and that was that Dan wouldn't put a marker on Billy's grave, not even a piddling little stone or a piece of wood. And that he wouldn't bury him near other folks, but under a tree off in some corner. The grave was to be smoothed over, and covered with grass, no flowers mind you. Nothing to show there was a grave there. Folks were scandalized, especially Parson Bingham, who's an ass, if you want my private opinion. Anyways, it was done like he asked. Dan saw to that.

Folks were riled about it pretty bad, and for a couple of months hardly anyone went into the store. And now that there are two other stores, business ain't going to be so good for your precious funny friend." He chuckled.

Dull anger began to rise in me. "What've you got, all of you, against poor old Dan?" I demanded hotly. "Everything he does is wrong. You won't give him a chance. You hated his dad, and despised Dan when he was a kid, and now that he's trying to make good, and do things right, you try to stamp him down. Why? Why, in God's name?"

"Whoa!" said my father. He chuckled again, but gave me a nasty look. "Don't be so hot-headed, you young fool. There's things you don't understand about folks. I admit we don't think much of your friend Dan. Why? I don't know. I'm not interested in knowing. He's just different from all of us, and we don't like folks that're different. Simple. We don't need to explain to you or any other whippersnapper with a brand-new doctor's bag and polished boots and city doctor ideas."

There was no use arguing with him. I knew that my father loved me, was proud of me in his obscure way, proud even of my new ideas. But I had never really loved him, and now I actively disliked him, felt a sickness against him and all the others like him in South Kenton. I can't pretend I regret this; even fathers and sons can be antagonistic, naturally, and all the cluckings and head-shakings in the world won't change it. But we never hated each other the way Sarah and Beatrice Faire came to hate each other. My father had ability, integrity and solidity, and he always had my respect if nothing else.

My silence must have irritated my father. He gave me a side look. "When you take my place here, and before that when you're working with me, don't try to force folks to follow your ideas too quick," he said warningly. "Folks move slow, like the tides and the stars. No use trying to rush them. You just muddle them all up. Circumstances sometimes move rapidly, but people don't move rapidly. Slow, creeping, fumbling their way from point to point, learning slow and easy, and forgetting half they learn. You can't rush things. Science always moves in spite of folks, not because of 'em. That's why martyrs are always young; they rush in and start to shout and wave their arms, and kick the old slow ways in the backside, to stir them up. And that's why they get knocked on the head. Wise men try to feed things gently to folks, like putting peppermint and sugar into the castor oil you give children. They take it easylike, and first thing you know it works, without them knowing anything about it.

"You can't buck opinion openly. You won't do any good championing your friend Dan. Folks hate him, suspect him. You won't do any good. Him with his fiddle playing, and reading, and walking out in the country of nights to look at the stars! Humph."

I felt profound disgust, and even fear. The fear was like a premonition. I would not talk about Dan anymore to my father.

"And how's Livy, and Jack Rugby and old Mortimer, and Amelia Burnett, and Dave King and Willie Williams, and all the rest?"

"Oh. Livy's fine. Her ma dying made her take things hard. But she's keeping house for her pa, now that the other girls're married and living in Ripley. Fine girl, Livy." He gave me a shrewd side glance again, but I kept my face stolid. "Lots of good common sense, though she's a smart-talking piece when she feels like it. Talks too roundly, gets too excited. But time'll heal that. She does her duty. Won't marry, though Willie Williams, with his new law business with his pa, asked her a dozen times, they say, and Bob Cunningham's been sparking her. Maybe she's waiting for someone, eh?" He prodded me archly in the side. I still kept my face stolid, though I could feel it burn. "Dave King's quite a young country gentleman now, seeing Endicott's got senile. But Livy won't look at him. Your ma says she's bound to be an old maid, but I can see she's pleased. She loves Livy like a daughter. And there's Sarah Faire. Been feeling poorly this winter; I gave her some iron, but it's her age. Funny thing about Sarah; she likes your Dan, always has the boy hanging around there. Must be trying to marry Bee off to him. She don't show sense there, though I always did like Sarah, and thought she had a level head. Bee's one fine girl, and as pretty as a picture and smart as paint. Funny she's not popular with the young folks. Expect she's too bright for 'em. Independent, too, though with a good tongue in her head and nice manners. After Livy, expect your ma'd like Bee for a daughter-in-law."

I turned my head aside. I felt a sudden loathing for everything and everyone. I wanted to see Dan more than I wanted to see my mother or anyone else. Father rambled on with his relishing account of the townsfolk. He became spiteful and contemptuous about the farming folk, as he always did. Once or twice he spat. Having been born and raised on a farm, he despised country life and country people.

We had reached home now, and I went into the cool and shuttered dark of the house. Mother was delighted to see me. She was a cold woman naturally, and I do not recall any great manifestations of affection from her, but I know that I was the apple of her eye. She kissed me only three times a year, on my birthday and when I left home and when I returned. I thought she looked colder and paler and more upright than ever. But I was glad to see her. I felt a wave of happiness when I smelt the spicy odor of good cooking as it wafted in from the kitchen where the hired girl was sweltering over the stove. I whistled as I ran upstairs to my room with its smooth, white bed and sun-dappled curtains. Two years!

My parents gave a party for me, and there was a great deal of coming and going. So I did not get to see Dan for nearly a week after I returned. Then, one night, I sneaked out of the house and got out my bicycle. The twilight was warm and full of the smell of dust and trees and flowers and approaching rain. It was very dim and moonless. My wheel made no sound in the thick dust of the streets, but I could hear distant voices from vine-covered porches, and the twanging of guitars. It was good to be home. I had no ambitions for wider and bigger places. South Kenton was where I wished to live and work and die.

It'll be a lifetime job to educate these people to sanitation and prevention of infections, and hygiene, I thought. No use looking for a bigger place. There's all the work I can do right here. Better to save a few thoroughly than save a lot partially.

I was still very romantic. I'm getting along in years now, and it's only recently that I've come to the conclusion that you can't save people thoroughly or even partially. They always resist their saviors. Perhaps that's a good thing, too. Eventually, I hope, all fools will be killed off by bacteria, which really have more sense, anyway.

South Kenton had gas now, though it extended only to street lighting as yet. Several good wells had come in in the vicinity, and there was some talk of oil for awhile, but that talk petered out. The wells were good gas wells. A dim gaslight burned before Dan's store. But the store was closed. People didn't feel much like congregating in the warm evenings in front of Dan's store, as they had done when Billy was alive. No, they tipped their chairs before the American House, and talked to Ed Ford, going in occasionally for a beer or such like. The two new stores were brightly lighted across the street, and there was also an ice cream store, full of giggling young folk. Business seemed to have grown up across the wide width of Main Street, and there was quite a coming and going of buggies and bicycles and people, and quite a lot of voices and laughter. But this side of the street was almost dark. Dan's store was the only one on the block. Big old houses with shrouded porches and iron dogs and stags on well-tended lawns filled the rest of the street.

I saw that Dan had neatly painted his store. But behind the dark panes of well-polished glass his wares—saddles and pails and mops and dishes and overalls and tubs and boots and rakes and shovels and what not—looked forlorn and unwanted and lonely. There was a ghostly and spectral look about the place. My heart literally ached as

I saw this. I got off my bicycle and wheeled it around to the back. I could see a lozenge of yellow lamplight brightening the darkness, and could hear the muffled wailing of a violin. Poor Dan, young and strong, was yet deserted and avoided as though he had a plague. He should have been across there with the other young folks, laughing and eating ice cream, and joshing the girls. Yes, he had a plague, all right, the plague of a great mind. He was like a black and noble beast, strange and somehow wild, herded in with a flock of fat and comfortable cattle. There could never be any peace between him and them, never any meeting place, never a word passing that either could understand. I knew without proof that his store was never patronized when it could be avoided, and that any trade given him was given sourly and grudgingly. My angry melancholy increased as I leaned my wheel against the side of the house and knocked at the door.

The violin wailed on, sad and mournful, sustained and powerful. He had not heard me. I listened for a long time. Though the music was indeed powerful, it was yet subdued and hushed, as though a mighty voice was speaking in meditative accents. I could not bear it; I felt foolish young tears stinging my eyes. It seemed to me that Dan was thinking on his instrument. I knocked again, louder. The music stopped. I heard the scraping of a chair as it was pushed back, the sound of slow footsteps, and the door opened. Dan stood in the doorway, peering out heavily, as though bemused.

"It's I—Jim Marcy, Dan," I said. He stood aside without speaking, and I entered the room. I saw at once that it was a clean, poor room, sparsely and cheaply furnished, but somehow homelike with its globular oil lamp on a bare table which held only the lamp and a pile of books. The floor was scrubbed but carpetless. My eye was caught by a rack of pipes on the wall near the fireplace; old Billy's pipes. Dan did not smoke yet. Somehow the sight of those cherished pipes still hanging there affected me tremendously. It was all that Dan had left of the man who had been his friend.

I smiled heartily and turned to Dan. He was standing near the doorway, regarding me gravely, his violin still in his hands. He looked much older than his twenty-one years, and rather tired. His homely and beautiful face seemed less fitting to South Kenton than ever. His hair was still shaggy and dull, his eyes still somber and absent. He returned my smile forcedly.

"How are you, Jim?" he asked quietly. When I offered my hand he hesitated for a moment and stared at it as though it were a strange object. Then he shook hands. "Sit down, Jim. When did you get back?"

"A couple of days ago. Say, Dan, you don't seem very glad to see me!"

He smiled slightly. "Sure, I'm glad. Take off your hat; sit down. I've got a pot of coffee on the stove in the kitchen, and some pie Sarah—Mrs. Faire—gave me yesterday. It's good pie. Strawberry. Sit down there, and I'll bring it in. I haven't eaten any supper yet. I've got some good baked ham, too, and fresh biscuits. Mrs. Faire gave me them, too. I'll only be a minute."

He put down his violin hastily and literally rushed out of the room. I sat down, uneasy. He had not known what to say to me at all. I hated myself because I had not written to him. I thought at first I would explain that I hadn't written anyone except my parents and Livy, but that would make it too obvious. There are times when explanations only complicate things. I picked up one or two books and glanced at them. All classics, with old leather bindings, crumbling. There were strange names on the flyleaves, and old dates. Where on earth had he picked them up? He had read them, and handled them tenderly. There were many pasted leaves and repaired covers, and I saw that he had made a great many marginal notations in his fine small hand. I did not read the notes; I knew they were too private and it would be presumptuous. Somehow I felt that everything was very sad, and my anger made my mouth bitter.

He called to me from the kitchen, asking me if I minded coming there. I went out. It was a dark, clean little hole with its ancient range and dimly burning oil lamp. He had covered the table with a turkey red cloth, and set out thick white ironware. But the coffee smelled very good, and the half pie oozed rich red juice and lucious berries. The ham was pink and white and stuck over with cloves, and the biscuits were hot. He had put out his best, a comb of honey and a lump of butter molded to the shape of a beehive. There was also a white pitcher of rich milk. I had eaten my supper, but everything looked very good, and I had a young appetite. My spirits rose. He ate with me with very good appetite, too, and soon we were talking and laughing.

After awhile I asked him about poor Billy. Immediately the new light and pleasure went out of his face. It looked suddenly pale and sick, as though he had felt a stab of great pain. Billy had been poorly a long time before he died, but he would not let Dan call Dr. Marcy, my father. He didn't hold with doctors; all they did was poke around and look wise, not knowing a blame thing, and then they sent a bill and felt their duty done. No, he didn't want a doctor. A man knew when he was going, and having doctors fussing around only gave a man a headache when they didn't make him laugh.

"He was so—good to me, Jim," said Dan in a low voice, as though he was thinking aloud. "He taught me things. He talked about courage a lot. He knew what it was. He suffered so, but never whined or said anything about how he suffered. He said once: 'Have guts, Dan. Have guts and nothing can hurt you. Devils or men, they can't touch you, if you look 'em in the face straight, like a man. They might hurt your pore, miserable flesh, but they can't hurt *you*. Only yourself can hurt you by lettin' down, and havin' no guts, and lettin' them get at you that way.' Oh, he taught me lots. It—was like opening my eyes. He didn't believe in God, the way church folks do. He made fun of hymnbooks and sermons and preachers. Said they were just a loud noise in the presence of the Lord. Sort of deafened people to the voice of God. When he was dying, and Parson Bingham came to see him, Billy sat right up in bed and swore and shouted and ordered him out of the house. Said the parson made a stink in a room that was all full of flowers that only Billy could see. He hated almost everyone in this town. No, not hated them; he couldn't hate anyone. But they didn't matter to him. He was awful kind to everyone, though, and that's why they came to sit in the store and gossip. It was like coming to a peaceful place, to come to Billy. And when he was dying, he talked to me. I couldn't stand it, Jim. But after he talked to me, I was glad he was going. It was like hearing someone talk of going home after they had been away a long time. I couldn't even be sorry when he died, though it's been mighty lonesome." He paused. "But sometimes, I have a feeling he's come back to see me. I feel if I look around quick I'll see him, but if I see him he won't come again. So I just sit, and talk to him in my mind, and somehow, everything seems right again. I can just feel him, warm and close, with his old walrus mustache, and spitting in the fireplace, and rubbing his socks together as he used to do, warming his feet."

"Dan," I said awkwardly, "he must have thought a lot of you to leave you everything the way he did. Why don't you leave here, take what you have, and start up somewheres else? This—this town doesn't—I mean, I think you'd do better some other place." I could not bring myself to speak of the animosity against him in South Kenton, but he knew what I meant.

"Where could I go?" he asked simply, looking at me with candid and mournful eyes. "I don't know any other place. I couldn't get used to it. Besides, people are pretty much the same wherever you go. You can't get away—from what they think about you. And Billy lived here. I want to be where he was. Then I like South Kenton. Yes, I really like it. It's familiar to me, the town and the country, and I like the hills. I like familiar places; I couldn't get used to a strange place. It would take me years. It would just be a waste of time, getting adjusted, getting accustomed to strange faces and houses and work. I don't want to take that time up. Here, everything is known to me, and I don't have to think about it. And then," he paused a moment, and a deep wash of color rose to his forehead, "I wouldn't want to go, for another reason."

All I could think of was that he had fallen in love with some girl. Beatrice Faire? I sucked in my lips at the thought. I said nothing, and gulped my coffee.

"Well, but how is business?" I said at last.

He shrugged. "I make expenses," he replied. "That's all. Just expenses. But it's enough. I don't want any more. It seems foolish to me to want more. A waste of time. I couldn't eat any more than I do, or wear any more. I've got all the books I want, and newspapers, and a place to sleep, warm and comfortable, and I'm independent, and I have a few friends. What more does anyone want? Oh, I know you'll think I have no ambitions, the way Bee does. But ambition seems to me the consolation and hope of small minds. Get somewhere? Why? You can't leave the earth until you die, and where else in the world would you get anywhere? I don't want the admiration and worship of little people. Perhaps I could make a lot of money somewhere, and then people would respect me. But I don't want their respect. I'd know what it was founded on."

I was silent. I felt emptied and depressed, somehow deprived and resentful. He saw that. He touched my hand and smiled at me humorously.

"With you, Jim, it's different. You're going to be a doctor. You can do things for folks, relieve their suffering, prolong their lives—for what they're worth. Doing things for others, helping them, seems to me the only thing to be ambitious for. But, what could I do? All I could do would be to do something for myself, and I don't want any more than I have. I've got lots; I don't think you'd understand that, Jim."

Frankly, I did not, then. I do now. Dan is dead but I'd like to tell him that I understand. It took me a long time.

We talked of other things that night. He listened to my prattlings with grave affection and attention, like an older brother listening to a boy. And I felt in him a deep peace and tranquility that nothing could shake, nothing could touch. He was removed. He would always be removed.

When I left him, I did not feel anger against South Kenton any longer. South Kenton's meanness was like an accolade to Dan Hendricks, an explanation of him.

Chapter

ᴄᴢᴄᴢᴄᴢᴄᴢᴄᴢᴄᴢᴄᴢᴄᴢᴄᴢᴄᴢᴄᴢᴄᴢᴄᴢᴄᴢᴄᴢᴄᴢᴄᴢᴄ *Seven*

I had almost reached the dark street when I bumped squarely into a humped and spindling figure, very tall, moving with a sort of wavering furtiveness. We both exclaimed irritably. The street light was on my face, and the figure cried: "Why, it's Jim Marcy!"

"Oh, it's you, Mr. Rugby. Yes, it's Jim. I've just been to see Dan. Are you going in, too?"

He hesitated. I could not see him very well. I saw him drawing his hand over his face with the old familiar gesture. He hummed a moment or two. The dim lamplight made little glistens on his gray head under the shabby black hat. He gave me the impression of being very fragile and old and tired. I could hardly believe that this old man, cowed at last by life, could be the terrible schoolmaster of my school days.

"Um. Yes, thought I'd drop in a minute. Want to ask Dan something," he mumbled. "Yes, Jack said he went to your party the other night. Thought perhaps you'd remember your old teacher, but you didn't. Thought you might come in to see me."

I was embarrassed. I could not tell him that I had not given him a thought for years. But he was obviously ill at ease, and was talking absently, without really thinking of me, so I forgot my embarrassment.

"Oh, I'll come in, Mr. Rugby. I had to get things in shape at home, though. First time I've been home for two years." I paused. We were both silent, both longing to be rid of the other, but neither knowing just how to terminate the conversation.

"Oh. Ah. Um," said Mortimer at last. He cleared his throat. He half turned from me.

"And how did you find Dan, Jim? I haven't seen him—lately. Bad blow, Billy Riggs dying and all."

"Yes, it was. Dan's all right." Another wretched pause. Then I said impulsively, "Mr. Rugby, I wish there was something we could do for Dan."

He started, and turned to me with such a violent gesture that I was startled, and fell back.

"Eh? Do something for him? Do what? Listen here, young man, neither you nor anyone else can do anything for him. You can't help him; the least you can do is not to hurt him. That's all! Just don't hurt him; leave him alone!"

I was amazed. He was turned sideways toward me, now, and the lamplight showed his old and withered face to be blazing with a sort of terrified wrath; his eyes leapt and sparkled; he shook one finger in my face. His voice had startled me, so quavering and tremulous it was, but full of fierceness. My next emotion was one of anger at his words, but I could not be angry at this shabby old man, whom life had already mauled and torn beyond any human feeling except compassion.

"I wouldn't hurt Dan, Mr. Rugby," I said quietly. "Dan's my friend. Goodnight, sir." I turned and left him. He had not replied to my goodnight, but I had the feeling, though I did not turn, that he watched me wheel out of sight.

The next day was Sunday, and I went to see Livy. At twenty Livy seemed to me to be still the little girl with whom I had gone to school. She was small and plump, with a resolute little face and quick dark eyes, though the leaping braids were now primly pinned about her head. She had her old round way of speaking, definite and frank. I was very much in love with her; she was a constant delight to me. I wanted to kiss her very urgently. It seemed to me very wrong that there was no color in the courageous face, and that her hands were darkened with hard work. It was especially hard for me today to keep from kissing her, for she smelled of clean soap and starch, and the shirtwaist she wore with her plain blue serge skirt was stiff and glistening from a hot iron. At her throat she had pinned a cameo brooch, a hideous thing, rimmed with small discolored pearls, but the little firm chin above it gave even it a sort of beauty.

She looked tired and jaded. The house was very dismal and had a moldy smell for all her hard work and the constant scrubbing of the hired girl. Gloomy old trees shrouded every window; there was an odor of sanctity here that made me remember what Billy Riggs had shouted at the Reverend Bingham. I smiled, for all the latter was Livy's father.

I called her attention to the golden warmth and splendor of the July day. Not too hot, I said, but just balmy. Why couldn't she smuggle her bicycle out behind her pious father's back and come for a wheel with me? She smiled a little, tiptoed away to pin on her stiff straw sailor, and came back, glancing at the small gold watch pinned to her shirtwaist.

"I expect we can go for an hour or two, Jim," she said. I helped her wheel her bicycle out of the carriage house. We glanced fearfully at the study window; we could see Mr. Bingham's head nodding over his Bible. No doubt he was preparing or touching up his evening sermon. As we

wheeled away I thought I heard him call sternly: "Olivia!"
But Livy did not seem to hear, and I discreetly refrained
from telling her.

The only thing wrong with Livy was that she had a sense
of duty toward the most unlikely creatures. Just when I
was beginning to enjoy the bowling along the quiet streets
toward the open country, she had to say:

"Jim! Let's call for Bee and take her along, too. She
never goes out much. We—they—all seem to dislike her
just as much as ever, though I think she has improved a
lot. I don't know why people her own age can't stand her,
while the older folk think she is perfect, an example to
all of us. Do let's call for her, Jim! Jim?"

I scowled. I wanted to say something violent and negative, but her dear face was so pleading and sweet that I
grudgingly assented. But the whole day was spoiled for me.
I had had visions of getting her alone somewhere in the
quiet country, and sitting down with her under a willow tree
beside the creek. I was going to ask her something that
needed no asking, but I wanted a definite date fixed in the
still distant future. I wanted to talk to her; I had so much to
say. And now she had to drag in Beatrice Faire.

"Well," I said spitefully as we turned towards Big Bend,
"if you get Beatrice to chatter and giggle with, I'm going
to get Dan Hendricks for myself."

She nodded delightedly. Was it my imagination, or was
the exercise and fresh air or something the cause of the
quick light color in her cheeks, the sudden flood of illumi-
nation in her eyes? Perhaps it was because she always
found pleasure in giving others pleasure.

When we arrived at the Faire house, little and white
under the old trees, Beatrice informed us that her mother
was lying down, resting. Beatrice wore a white apron over
her skirt and shirtwaist, and looked competent and smiling. She glanced from Livy to me and back to Livy again;
I thought there was something gloating in her smile. The
old secrecy and knowing mannerism were still hers. She
seemed pleased at our invitation. I had had a last hope that
she would refuse, but her consent put the last touch of

gloom upon me. When we three rolled out to get Dan Hendricks, I tried to be pleasant. The girl laughed and chattered to Livy; beside her, Livy's wholesome prettiness faded, became commonplace. For Beatrice at twenty was a real beauty with her reddish-gold hair and gleaming brown eyes and extraordinary complexion. Too, she was taller than Livy, and finely made, with an exquisite figure that my youthful eyes hung on reluctantly. When she wished, she had a sweetness of manner that was mesmeric, and nothing could be more musical than her light and flexible voice. She spun along without apparent effort, seeming to float on the wheel, turning to us brightly when we spoke. Yet her sweetness was poisonous to me, like the sweetness of some deadly flower that I had read grew in sinister jungles. I know my friends would find absurd this description of a country-town girl who had not been beyond the confines of her birthplace in all her life. They would think me exaggerating, or too imaginative, and a little funny. But she affected me so, and I believe that she affected others in the same manner, though they were not articulate enough to say so.

I tried to like her that day, or at least endure her without irritation. But I could not get rid of the feeling about her, that there was something completely evil in her, and noxiously sophisticated. Yet so secret was her inner life that nothing she had done, to my knowledge, bore out my suspicions. If she laughed at her mother in the presence of others, her laughter had a note of affection and good temper. If I had not seen the distressed and dimly anxious expression on Sarah's face at these times I would have laughed at my own thoughts, myself. If she never said a kindly thing of anyone, she never said a very bad thing. It was only her voice that betrayed her, for all its musical inflections. It was her eyes, lighted with cunning and malice, that made me uneasy. I think now that she was born too late. She would have made an excellent Borgia, or the astute and subtle mistress of some unscrupulous king. She, too, in her way, was a victim of time and circumstance.

She seemed to be sincerely attached to Livy, and so I almost forgave her, even though she made me fumble and feel uncouth whenever she glanced at me. She had made no objection to the inclusion of Dan into our party, but only nodded indifferently.

Dan was in his garden behind the store and living quarters. He was tying up a rosebush when we appeared at the gate, and he came towards us slowly, blinking. He smiled at Livy, nodded to me, and greeted Beatrice with a stiff reserve, though I noticed that his eyes kept returning to her grudgingly, as though fascinated. I know now that it was her resemblance to her mother that held him, but I did not know then, and my heart sank as I remembered all the rumors that he was "sweet" on her. But I do not think that Beatrice was ever really deceived; I think she knew from the start, and that is why she could make Dan's life the red hell that she did.

He was willing to go with us, and seemed grateful that we had remembered him. He got out his bicycle, locked his door, and the four of us wheeled away, the girls in front and we behind. He still was not a great talker, but there was infinite peace and content to me in his presence. We rolled out into the country, laughed when the girls squealed at some deep rut in the country roads. The sun shone warm on our faces, the green and growing fields of corn and wheat and rye shimmered on each side of us. The trees bent over us, pungent in the sun, their leaves motionless in the heat. Birds laced the hot air before us, calling in startled notes, and cows looked at us mildly from behind fences. The Sabbath peace lay on everything, and we met no one on the roads, for which Livy was sincerely thankful. It would never do for people to see the minister's daughter breaking the holy Sabbath this way. We were young; we did not mind the choking golden dust that made us cough as we stirred it up; we did not mind the burning heat. We laughed and sang, and when far from some farmhouse, we whistled and shouted. Even Dan was merry.

We approached the hills, which had darkened from

distant violet to thick greenness. At the first foothill we
dismounted and left our wheels. We climbed up the hill,
the girls shrieking when some briar caught at their long
and heavy skirts, and professing to be much outraged when
they displayed a neat ankle to our boisterous masculine
admiration. Their shirtwaist collars were looking a little
wilted for all Livy's and Bee's perkiness, and our own
collars, stiff and tall, were softening about the edges when
we reached the hilltop. But it was cool up here, and there
was a cluster of young second-growth timber to sit under.
A breeze was blowing. We could look down at the floor of
the valley dancing in heat waves, at distant white farmhouses, at trees golden in the sun. The lowing of cattle
came to us in the shining stillness. In the distance we could
see the dark and tufted irregularity of timber that followed
the hot blue glint of the creek.

I had never seen Dan animated before to any extent.
But today there was a sort of fugitive wildness about him,
a gaiety that had in it something feverish and reckless.
He exuded vitality as a great stone hot in the sun exudes
vitality, an immobile strength, a living power, not to be
moved, but eternal. The wildness and gaiety he showed
was like the dancing of sunbeams over that stone, the
shadow of summer lightnings, the patterns of fluttering
butterflies. They did not affect the static vitality underneath, the motionless peace. He laughed easily, lightly, at
everything we said. Only his eyes remained as they were,
mournful yet placid.

Livy was more carefree than I had seen her since my
return. Her girlhood seemed to return as she was released
from the pressure of her father and his house. She became almost frivolous. She appeared bent on drawing
Dan out; almost all her remarks were addressed to him,
and the two laughed continually as if at some private joke.
She made foolish gestures, tossed her head, giggled and
shrieked. About her, too, I felt a feverish gaiety, as if she
were making merry in the face of something that she knew
was about to overwhelm her.

Beatrice was more sedate, though she never stopped

smiling. She would let her russet eyes wander minutely in turn from each of us. They roved in a circle, never missing a face, a gesture or an expression. Her white teeth glittered between her red lips; the sun brightened her already bright hair, threw golden shadows on her white flesh. She leaned against a tree trunk, her hands, beautiful hands, in her lap, her shoulders square and erect; about her was an air of serenity and poise which made me reluctantly admire her. I, myself, laughed and joked with all of them, but I still felt uneasy. There was something here I could not understand, though I had an obscure and discomfited feeling that there was much I ought to understand, and that the understanding would not bring me much happiness. I tried to find the answer in Livy's glowing face and aimless gestures, in the quickness of her always quick tongue, in the sense of release and energy that I felt about her.

She was talking to Dan eagerly, when Beatrice stood up, brushed mold from her skirt, and then, letting her hands fall to her sides, stood on the windy hilltop and looked over the valley. Somehow, I knew that she saw not only the valley, but the world and all the things that were in it. The wind blew her clothing backwards from her figure, so that she seemed like a figurehead at the bow of a ship, the line of breast and hip and throat and leg caught in the carving of the wind. She had removed her hat, and the wind blew back her hair also, and I thought grudgingly that nothing could be so pure and clear and lifted as the outline of her profile against the shining blueness of the sky. The others looked at her and stopped their laughing and chatter. I glanced at Livy; her face had lost all animation, and it was somewhat pinched and withered, as though she were consumed by a mysterious anxiety and pain. She was gazing at Beatrice searchingly, with an intensity that was compelling.

"What are you looking at, Bee?" she asked in a voice that had something forced in it in spite of its apparent lightness.

Beatrice continued to look over the valley to the wall

of hills beyond it. She turned to us after a moment, laughing, smoothing down her reddish pompadour with her slender hands.

"I was just thinking what a fool Jesus was," she said.

An embarrassment fell upon Dan and myself, and we peeped furtively at each other. I had discarded all religion youthfully, in the laboratory and schoolroom as did most young medical students. Dan, I knew, had no religion. Yet, with masculine inconsistency, we felt embarrassed at any blasphemy uttered by the so-called gentler sex. We also felt embarrassed for Livy, a minister's daughter, and after that one peep at each other, we peeped at Livy. To my surprise and rather obscure annoyance, Livy did not look shocked.

"Why?" she asked casually.

"Why?" Bee raised her clear brows and laughed lightly. "According to the story He was offered the world and refused it. The world! Yes, He must have been a fool!"

I waited for Livy to utter some grave platitude. God knows she had heard plenty at home. She would not have to make a conscious effort to recall one; it would have welled automatically from memory. I would have felt much better had she quoted something pious and sedate, however much I would have smiled internally at it. Even the most villainous atheist, I believe, likes to think that his wife prays regularly. But Livy uttered no platitude. She merely continued to regard Beatrice thoughtfully.

"I've thought that myself, sometimes," she said slowly, as though thinking over each word she said. "The world is very beautiful. We in South Kenton don't know much about it. But perhaps He was like Dan, here. Perhaps He knew all the world by a sort of instinct, and didn't find it worth the wanting."

I was astounded. What did she know of Dan and what he thought? More than I, it seemed. I was whipped by an unreasonable annoyance and anger. I did not understand it myself. This was still in the nineties, and such loose, free talk on the part of women outraged some part of my mind that had not been touched by theory and science and schoolbooks. I think it was that part of my mind that whipped up the anger. I don't know. I still don't know, and I don't want to probe into it too much. I am getting old now and want peace, even peace that is based on something that does not exist.

"You girls don't, know what you're talking about!" I burst out irately. Even in my irritation I noticed that the glance Beatrice gave Livy was unfriendly and bitterly cold. "You talk like children! You haven't been outside this piddling little town, yet you try to assume wisdom and understanding you don't possess. Jesus knew what wonders there were in the world, and what glories and powers, but He would have none of them, not one of them! They weren't worth it!"

"Worth what?" Beatrice's voice was cool, like an uncomfortably cold finger laid hard on a sick hot forehead.

"Why, worth anything," I stammered, angry at the heat in my face and voice. "Worth giving up—I mean, worth abandoning—peace and comprehension—for. Besides, He could have had the world if He had wanted it. He didn't need Satan to offer it to Him. He had other things, love and—and—well, everything."

I was humiliatingly conscious that I had not expressed myself, and more humiliated that I was not clear about what I wished to express. I could have murdered Beatrice for her light laugh, her humorously glinting eyes.

"What a lot the little boy knows!" she exclaimed. "He's been everywhere and seen everything! He knows what it means to be bad, and feel sorry. He's seen all the tinsel and knows that home, sweet home, is the best thing after all."

I hated her more than ever. Her allusion to "the little boy" was not mere rhetoric and humor, I knew. My stature, shorter than that of most boys my age, was always humiliating to me. She had the uncanny ability to touch the sorest spots with an acid-tipped finger. Livy gave me a gently pitying glance, for which I confess I was not at all grateful.

"I think what Jim is trying to say can't just be put into

words," she said. "It's something you know, without being able to say. I know what you mean, Bee. I don't agree with all of it, but with some of it." She turned to Dan, and her face seemed to melt and glow. "You know what we all mean, Dan. But what do you think?"

He grinned. During all the conversation he had seemed to be detached and vaguely interested, without being touched in the slightest.

"Well, here's what I think," he said, and quoted:

> Waste not your hour, nor in the vain pursuit
> Of this and that endeavor and dispute.
> Better be jocund with the fruitful Grape
> Than sadden after none, or bitter fruit.

I was too young then to understand that completely, and I believe that Livy, though she understood more than I did, still felt the quotation somewhat obscure. But Beatrice understood. She shot Dan an evil glance, though she continued to smile.

"I expect you ought to know all about the 'fruitful Grape,'" she said.

He looked at her tranquilly, though his brows twitched as though at some twinge. "Why? Because I take a drink occasionally? Or because my dad used to see pink crocodiles once in a while?"

She shrugged. Her thrust had not hit him.

"You're pretty dull, Dan. That's not what I meant, and you know it."

Suddenly I felt something unclean and menacing in the atmosphere. It disturbed me. I have always detested undercurrents. They always seem about to suck under all clearness and cleanliness. But Dan merely lifted his shoulders and his brows. He put a blade of grass between his teeth and began to hum tunelessly. Livy looked from Beatrice to Dan, and kept on looking. She had a somewhat frightened expression. Then, as though her innate propriety and tact came to the rescue, she changed the subject, though I could see that she was distracted.

"Did you know, Jim, that Amelia Burnett is engaged to Jack Rugby?" Beatrice asked. "Mr. Burnett wasn't for it at all until that little strip of land Jack's stepmother owned came in with three big gaswells. The other wells don't amount to anything. Now, she's just flooding in money. She's gotten to be rather stingy, and old Mortimer doesn't get much. I expect, though, that he wouldn't know what to do with it, anyway. But she is awfully fond of Jack, and so he will come into the wells. She just loads him down with money. Well, old man Burnett isn't making any more objections, and Amelia and Jack are going to be married in September."

I was interested. I talked about the engagement to Livy and made some silly and laughing remark. I glanced at Dan and Beatrice, expecting their laughter, also. Dan smiled idly. But when I looked at Beatrice, I was startled. Her face had become black with fury, not with the violent and explosive fury of other natures, but with a fury that was pent and dared not burst forth. She was staring at Livy, and then I knew that she hated Livy with a homicidal hatred. I was so startled and frightened at that that I did not stop to wonder then why she should feel her evident fury. She saw me look at her; I could see the visible efforts she made to control herself as she caught my eye. By sheer force of will she smoothed her face, made it bland and secret again.

"I expect the money is the only reason why that little greedy toad of an Amelia looks at Jack Rugby," she said lightly. "Ugh, with her green eyes and green-white face and washed-out hair! Mealy-mouthed little beast, all new dresses and mincings and bangles." She smiled, though there was murder in her voice.

"Oh, I don't know," said Dan casually. "Amelia's not so bad. And Jack's a fine boy. Looks like John L. Sullivan; lots of muscle, but brains, too. I always thought old Mortimer didn't appreciate him. Jack'll make three dollars bloom where one bloomed before. I thought, though, that he had his eye for awhile on Mary Knowles."

Beatrice laughed gaily. "Mary Knowles! Her mama has

made her half a man already! Did you see Mrs. Knowles since you came back, Jim? Wears boots like a man, now, and they say she smokes like an old trooper, and swears, and rides her horse astride as she goes over the country to see that her mortgages are coming along all right. She even cut her hair short, and they do say that one of these days she's going to sprout whiskers, even if she is an old woman now. And Mary's just as bad; she's taller than her mother and hasn't a woman's figure at all. Jack wouldn't marry her any more than he would marry a man."

I thought I had caught the drift now, and was greatly relieved, for Dan. I had a score or two to pay Beatrice, and prepared to pay it.

"If Jack wants Amelia it's because he believes that no other girl in South Kenton's as good as she is," I said smoothly. "He's a fine fellow, as Dan says, and has all the money he wants. He has an eye, too. If he likes a girl it's because she's worth liking; if he doesn't look at a girl, I expect it's because she's not worth a look."

Yes, I thought with enjoyment, I must have gotten the drift, for one moment a baleful light flared across Beatrice's face as she looked at me. But the next instant the balefulness had gone, and she was smiling sweetly.

"Well, let's hope they will be happy," she said, and there was such a convincing ring in her voice that I became confused and wondered if I had understood after all. Beatrice had retreated once more into her secrecy and blandness; behind it, she looked out at us as from a dark room, unseen, while we stood in glaring light exposed to sharp eyes.

The red sunset was burning through the trees on the hill across the valley, and we all stood up, brushing ourselves free from mold and little blades of grass. Livy exclaimed mournfully when she discovered a stain on her skirt. Poor girl, she had few clothes enough in those days, and this stain was a calamity. Beatrice was instantly all solicitude; with sisterly concern she rubbed Livy's skirt, shook her head, and exclaimed. "Now, Livy, don't take on so. Just rub it lightly with a mite of soap and a little cold water, and it won't affect the color at all. Then hang it up to dry. It'll be all right afterwards." She smiled, her beautiful head on one side as she looked at Livy, and patted Livy's shoulder. If I had not seen that one appalling and unguarded look, I would have softened. But all I wanted to do now was to take Livy away from Beatrice's proximity, to run with her as from some noxious gas.

We went down the hill, the girls slowly because of the high heels on their ribbon-tied slippers. We were almost at the bottom when Livy shrieked faintly and lurched forward. Dan was closer to her than I, and he caught her in his strong arms. She must have been enduring a strain during the last hour, for even while she laughed apologetically, tears rushed into her eyes as she looked up into Dan's face, and they spilled over her cheeks, which had suddenly turned white. He held her gently and kindly. Beatrice took her arm, and, greatly disturbed, I came back to them. Livy seemed to be in great pain.

"I expect I've turned my ankle," she stammered, smiling through the tears that did not seem to want to stop. She accepted my arm; I was astonished to find that she was trembling. She half turned her face from me, and I could see the fine violet veins distended in her pulsing throat.

"Here, Bee, you'd best let me take her other arm," said Dan gently. "Jim and I'll help her down the rest of the way." Beatrice released Livy slowly, and Dan took Livy's arm. I said something to him about being careful. Beatrice had withdrawn a step or two from us, and I was arrested in mid-speech by the look upon her face. It was gloating; her eyes literally danced, and they were dilated as though with an inner and satanic glee, almost inhuman, as if she were enjoying an obscene joke beyond our comprehension.

She thinks all pain is funny, I thought with hatred. With great tenderness we helped poor white-faced Livy down the rest of the hill. She did not limp much; her pallor and trembling and agitation seemed all out of proportion to her injury.

"How on earth are you going to pedal back to town?"

asked Dan with concern as we reached the bottom.

"Oh, that's all right," I said importantly, being an embryo doctor. "The thing to do with a sprained ankle, if it isn't too bad and the ligaments aren't torn, is to use it actively. That keeps the blood circulating, and prevents swelling and lameness." I urged Livy to get on her bicycle; I noticed that the back of her hands were beaded with tiny drops of water. I wanted to look at the ankle, but she hurriedly refused and said she was all right now.

We started out slowly. I rode beside Livy, carefully keeping pace with her. Gradually, as she used her ankle, she gathered speed. She began to talk to me in her usual fluent fashion, but did not look at me directly. I saw that her lips were pale and smooth, and that her face did not regain its earlier color. Dan and Beatrice rode together. They were talking easily, and I heard Dan's amused grunt once or twice at some witty sally of the girl's. She seemed in high good temper, as though she had repaid a bitter thrust. I know now that she hated all of us, even Livy. I knew that nothing we said or did was taken at its face value, by Beatrice, and that under everything her venomous mind was seeking something ulterior, something suspicious and unclean.

The twilight had definitely set in when we reached Livy's house. The church bell was ringing, and Livy regretfully and fearfully said she expected her father was already in church, and what on earth would he think about her?

"Let him think. It'll do him good for once," said Beatrice consolingly. "Come on, Livy, I'll take you in, and we'll bathe that ankle and rest it. Young doctors," she added with a merrily malicious glance at me, "may have new theories, but they don't know exactly everything."

Dan was silent; he had dismounted, and was leaning negligently against the gate. Beatrice shot him a fanged look, though she smiled. "Well, now, Dan, you can run along home, and think about your 'fruitful Grape,'" she said. I was astonished to see Dan jerk upright at this, and to see his tranquil face turn a dull scarlet. His mouth twitched. "Your 'grape,' " said Bee, "is hanging too long on the vine, I'm afraid. It's about time you picked it and ate it."

"Better to let it get ripe than to eat it green," I retorted, without a blessed idea of what I was saying. Beatrice was the only one who guessed that there was only confusion behind my ambiguity, and even in the gathering dimness I saw the enjoyment in her face.

I ignored her with youthful but unconvincing dignity, and turned to Livy. She was wan and beaten, and glanced at us in turn with an aimless smile. I instructed her somewhat pompously as to what to do for her ankle, and she kept on nodding. I noticed, with some irritation, that all the time I talked she looked at Dan.

The girls went into the house together, and Dan and I wheeled away side by side. He seemed disinclined for conversation.

"That Bee," I burst out as we rolled along through the quiet and dimly peaceful streets, "ought to be shot. One of these days someone's going to murder her. I'd like to be that someone. And maybe I will. Maybe when I've got my degree, and I'm practicing around here, I can slip a little cyanide into her coffee without being detected."

He was silent so long that I had begun to think he had not been listening. Then he said mildly:

"Oh, I don't know. Bee says a lot of mean things, but she couldn't be her mother's daughter and be really vicious."

I was sickened at this. Could it be that he was "sweet" on her? I wanted to warn him, I wanted to shout out to him his danger. But I could say nothing. There was something about his silence that repudiated me, that held me warningly at a distance, in spite of our friendship.

Chapter

cccccccccccccccccccccccccccccccccc *Eight*

Mortimer Rugby had written a vast amount of poetry in his life, and all of it was pretty bad. But in the poor, synthetic glass gems of his poetry there glittered one clear crystal jewel, pure as water, simple as love, and lovely as a pool under moonlight.

> How tranquil were the evenings of my youth!
> So fair, so clear, so radiantly pure.

Remembering his poor life, harried from without and from within, bewildered and shabby and broken, it seems to me that that poem was the saddest and most pathetic he ever wrote. Only those two lines he had written, and then had stopped abruptly, either because he could not and dared not go on, or because even he had seen that there was nothing more to write than that. They were complete.

I remembered them that summer. I had read them several years ago, and I think I was the only one who remembered them. But I repeated them to myself several times from June to September of that year. They seemed to me to be filled with everything I thought, with almost every emotion I had. Everything had taken upon itself a clarity and purity, like crystal forms pulsing with some inward color, drawing this color from radiant air and running it through itself, in the manner of the new signs they have nowadays: hollow glass tubes in which flow bright-colored gases. It seemed to me that I hardly met an unfriendly face, and that there was little ugliness in anything. I felt that the future was imminently exciting and tremendous, full of approaching tumult and splendor. Things were in the coming such as had never before been on earth. I suppose that was just youth. I have talked to many young people in my lifetime, and at first I was surprised and sadly amused that they all thought so, that they alone were singled out from life for some magnificent destiny. It seemed horrible to me at first that they later settled down on little farms or in some mean little profession or calling in the small towns, and let the thunderous wheels roll over them, unheeding. Surely such prescience must have reality out there in space; surely no emotion or thought of any man but has its substance in a deeper reality. Why, then, do the dreams of youth dry up like springs in a desert, and the sands of miserable details absorb the bright and living drops? That, it seems, is the saddest thing of all in a very sad world.

Life quickened for me that summer. I enjoyed everything. Nothing, during the first two months, caused me any distress. I liked my friends and my town; both seemed to me to be the very finest in the world.

I even felt sorry for Beatrice Faire. I thought there was something gallant in her assumed pleasure in Amelia Burnett's marriage to Jack Rugby. She attended the wedding, all white muslin and primrose ribbons and radiant hair, and though she had few partners she danced exquisitely with those who asked for a dance. She danced with me, also. It seemed to me that I did not have a flesh-and-blood woman in my arms as we moved over the platform under the dark trees, and the music wailed and swayed as the paper lanterns swayed in the night wind. I almost liked her.

Most completely happy in my memory are the days I spent with Livy Bingham. We wheeled over the rutty country roads, the sun warm on our heads and shoulders; we dismounted to lean against fences and look at the rich fields of wheat and corn and rye. We climbed hills for the view, and then sat in silence, weaving grass between our fingers. It was an enchanted country into which I had wandered, and I wondered vaguely how it was that I had never been there before. I had a feeling that this country was suspended magically in space somewhere, and that earnest seeking could find it at any time. I amused myself by making mental notes of it, noticing familiar landmarks, so that I would surely find it at any time in a future that might be dark or uncertain.

One day I tried to tell Livy something about it, with a certain half-ashamed assumption of amusement. She looked at me gravely and straightly as I fumbled with words, but I knew that she understood. It seemed strange to me that she sighed after I had done speaking, and she looked dimly off to the hills across the valley. On a frightened impulse I took her hand; it lay in mine quiet yet without vitality. My fright increased at this.

"Livy," I said, "before I came home this summer I thought, I'll ask Livy. I'll ask her to wait for me. Livy, will you wait for me?"

To my consternation she did not speak to me for a moment, nor turn her head to me. It appeared to me for a moment that everything splintered into dark fragments, like opaque glass, and that if she did not answer me as I wanted to be answered there would never be anything else in the world but unbearable pain. Then she turned to me and the sun suddenly broke out dazzlingly.

"We're both young, yet," she said gently, smiling. "I guess we can wait awhile. But, don't ask me about it again, Jim, dear, until next year?"

She still smiled. There was something determinedly fixed about her smile, but I was partially content. Of course, I said, I understood about her father. I was about to add that he was an old man, however, and could not be expected to live much longer, but fortunately I caught myself in time. She must have guessed what I had just luckily suppressed, for she laughed heartily. She was never one to have false sentimentalities.

I tried to be content, to feel that everything was all right as we went home. I talked about the future, our future, with confidence and hope. She listened, and nodded. I tried to make myself believe that she was interested, and then was irritated at an abstraction she could not conceal. When I pressed her for more enthusiasm, she suddenly exclaimed: "Jim, please, let's not talk about it just now! You may have forgotten me by next year. Let us wait and see." She did not look at me directly, but I saw that the corners of her eyes were wet. I was instantly contrite; I knew she had a hard life with her father and his everlasting grim platitudes. So I merely reached over and pressed her hand. I had to be satisfied, and in the manner of youth I read into her every word and gesture what I wished to read.

I was hysterically happy during the next week or two. My parents guessed what had happened, and they were indulgently pleased. But I did not talk to them. I was not a boy such as the novelists write of: subtle and obscure and darkly unhappy and misunderstood by grosser parents. I thought my parents rather fine, above the ordinary, and I was content with their ways of life and most of their ideas. However, there had never been any particular meeting place where I could talk to them. I suppose this is the way with most parents and their children. Still, none of us were conscious of any loss of warmth.

And so it was that I at first felt only annoyance when Dan Hendricks broke into the clear placidity and sunniness of life with a loud explosion. I had come, in a measure, to accept Dan's ostracism from our snobbish little group. I was never one to question very vigorously decisions of this group, and though some of its staid pettinesses sometimes annoyed me and some of its prim little conventions irked me, I had a calm acceptance of most of its rules and regulations and ways of living. They say most young men are socialists—or worse—at some time in their lives, but I never felt any burning desire to reorganize a society that seemed to me well enough, and though I had felt all my life that something was very wrong in our group's treatment of Dan Hendricks I had come to accept that treatment as something natural and not to be protested against too much. A Dan Hendricks accepted into our tight little society would have seemed incongruous to me, and a little unnatural and unappropriate. Too, I derived a sort of guilty pleasure in my association with him in the face of my friends' disapproval. It was my one fling, my one kicking up of the heels, my one flaunting before an institution I in my heart of hearts believed right and correct.

The explosion occurred in this way. There lived, on one of the more wretched and poverty-stricken farms in the township a certain farmer, Wally Lewis. The whole family of this man was shiftless, dirty, idle, and impudent. However, they had one virtue: they were not spongers like others of their kind. They had a kind of insolent and hardy independence, a swaggering contempt for the niceties of South Kenton. Wally Lewis was reputed to be an atheist and anarchist, and his shocking sayings and acts furnished delightful conversation. At one time Wally, a middle-aged, gaunt individual, dirty and unkempt and with tobacco-stained whiskers, had stood in filthy overalls before the church on Sunday, shouting and reviling the worshippers therein. It was the Sabbath day, and so hotheaded young men were forcibly restrained by sympathetic parents and brothers from leaving the church and horsewhipping the blasphemer.

Wally farmed desultorily. He never sold any of his

crops, for he raised just sufficient to keep his family alive. How he paid his taxes no one seemed to know exactly, though it was rumored that he made and sold illegal liquor, for which purchasers were not lacking among the young bloods of South Kenton. Ed Ford, proprietor of the American House and Bar, was his bitterest enemy, for Wally cut into his profits. Wally and his family of slatternly wife and three sluttish daughters lived in a ramshackle old farmhouse in the midst of unbelievable squalor. I only saw the man and his family a few times, but they seemed content and self-sufficient. This content and self-sufficiency provoked South Kenton more than did their shiftlessness and poverty.

The three daughters would not have been bad-looking if they had ever taken baths or combed their hair. The youngest, Connie, was even quite pretty. She had a mass of light brown hair, closely curled and shining, and bright brown eyes full of curiosity and smiles. She was a little creature, but beautifully formed, quick, and alert. Occasionally we would see her driving into town in the broken-down family buckboard hitched to a half-starved horse. She would sit on the open seat, coquettishly eying all young men, a ribbon perkily tied in the masses of her hair, a broad smile on her dark and not-too-clean face. The other two girls were sullen and sodden, and rarely came to town. Connie Lewis was her father's favorite; he would often stop in Dan's store to buy her a ribbon or a pair of white cotton stockings or a few yards of gingham. He never bought anything for his wife, whom it was rumored he beat unmercifully, nor did he ever seem to notice his other daughters.

It came as no surprise to South Kenton when it was learned that Connie was "in trouble." There was much ribald conversation as to who was responsible. We would hilariously accuse each other of nocturnal rendezvous with the unwashed Connie, and uproariously bear witness against each other. But the older folk were not so amused. Within a short time the town was up in arms. There was talk of driving the whole family out of the country, but as they had always paid their taxes, and the land was their own, nothing could be done. The girl was "bad," no doubt, but she was not a criminal. Protest meetings were held, but nothing was done about it. Young girls were forbidden to mention the Lewises.

Had Wally Lewis been the ordinary shiftless farmer we would have known nothing about it, or cared less. Since he was not in the public eye, he would have passed unnoticed in his trouble. But he had been such an agitator and a cinder in the eye of South Kenton that the affair became tremendously important and affronting. Nothing he could do could ever pass without comment.

Connie's condition was not known until about three weeks before her child was born. She had kept discreetly away from South Kenton, but someone had seen her in her father's cabbage patch while driving by, and by nightfall everyone in town knew about it. Two days later, a committee composed of my father, Mayor Burnett, Tom Williams and Bill Crawford called on Wally Lewis and suggested that Connie be sent away, as she was a disgrace to the township. Wally, I heard, came rushing from his decayed house bearing a shotgun of ancient pattern, and had threatened to "blow 'em all to hell!" They had left more quickly than they had come, and called an indignant meeting in the town hall.

Soon it was whispered that Wally himself was the father of Connie's child. Nothing was too low to be imputed to him. Anyone with Wally's flagrant ideas and guilty of his lawless and insulting acts was likely to do anything. I had not seen him for several years, myself, but I remembered his face, lean and sunburned and fiery and insolent. I remembered his eyes, too, burning and full of an odd intelligence and ferocity. I did not believe him guilty of any such shameful thing, but I kept silent when I heard the accusations. I had no wish to align myself with anyone so reprehensible.

The younger folk set out to do something, more out of herd deviltry, I think, than any shocked sensibilities.

Looking over past experiences, I am sure that most mob violences and hysterias and brutalities are not due to outraged virtue or true anger, but are merely a release of fundamental human traits: cruelty, bestiality and animal lust. These releases take place, I have observed, when mobs are pretty sure that the law is deliberately looking the other way, and that there is a certain sanction in public opinion, however furtive. But mobs are the most hypocritical masses in the world; they like to believe, and do believe, that they are activated by only the most virtuous motives and indignations.

At any event, Connie had hardly emerged from childbirth when Wally's farmhouse mysteriously burst into flame one midnight. Though all the young fellows loudly proclaimed innocence and lack of all knowledge, it was reliably reported, ("someone said") that Lew himself carried his sick daughter and her child into the barn and made her as comfortable as possible. The other two girls had fled in their nightwear to the barn, but Mrs. Lewis, who had been bedridden for the past month due to the last beating received from her husband, was not able to escape and was burned to death in her bed. It was said, reluctantly, that Wally had tried to save her, though there was dissenting opinion. I do not see how he could have saved her as the house, being weather-dried and a mass of falling timber, had gone up like a match box.

For a day or two even South Kenton's most rabid Lewis-haters were shocked and disturbed, and there was a half-hearted attempt to find out the arsonists. But it was finally announced that no one could have been to blame, the house being what it was, and the family being what it was. However, no help was offered Wally Lewis, no assistance for the young mother and her three-day-old child. Some said it was good for her, that she was only a piece of cattle anyways, and would not mind the straw and filth of the barn, and the broken roof. Public opinion again became indignant. It got over its nervousness when Mr. Bingham angrily reported that he had been driven away by

Wally Lewis when he had gone out to the farm with an offer to officiate at the burial of Mrs. Lewis' charred remains.

A week after the fire Wally Lewis came to town. He walked down Main Street on a Saturday afternoon when the town was crowded with farmers and loungers and shoppers. I happened to be going to Dan's store, but was halted at the corner by a curious phenomenon. The street was full of noise, and the movement of horses and buggies. But when Wally appeared, the whole street became deathly silent. The wave of silence ran before Wally. His path was like the devastating path of a cyclone, leaving stillness and ominous calm behind and around it. Everyone fell immobile, seeing the attitude Wally had at that precise moment. The street was full of eyes and breath and terrible silence.

But Wally looked straight ahead. He walked without haste or hesitation. His overalls hung on his lank figure; his shaggy hair stuck out under his broken old hat. His face had a frozen calm in it, for all its redness. His expression was rigid. He might have been a dead man walking except for his terrible eyes, fixed and flaming and distended. His mouth, under the yellow-stained reddish mustache, was like a slash in his face. He did not seem to see anyone. I wish I could forget that face and that expression, but I cannot. I can see him yet, the sunlight falling hotly upon him, and then shadow, as he emerged from under trees and awnings, and then went under them.

He walked up the wooden stairs of Dan's store, and so complete was the silence that the whole street heard the dull thud of his muddy boots on those stairs. He disappeared within. Instantly, at least twenty men tiptoed to the doorway and peered within, I among them. I wanted to enter, but could not, though I cursed myself. The sidewalk behind those twenty men became thick with congested traffic; everyone waited.

There was only one customer in the store, though the other stores were swarming with customers. And that customer was Sarah Faire, shirtwaisted and cool and gentle as always, though there were whitish streaks in her bright hair and her figure had thickened. She had been purchasing supplies, evidently, for she was putting parcels in the basket on her arm. The store was dim, but her startled expression and suddenly pale face seemed to become very vivid as she looked at Wally Lewis.

Dan waited in silence. Everyone waited in silence. Wally cleared his throat; the sound was clearly audible out in the street. He spat; he spoke, but his voice was so hoarse that at first he could not make himself understood.

"Dan," he said, "I can't pay you—yet. I don't know when I can pay you. But Connie's sick, and needs some things. Will you trust me?"

We all waited breathlessly for the reply. Of course, Dan would refuse. Several of the men shouldered forward to protect Dan, and uphold him in whatever he would say. Then Dan spoke softly.

"Yes, Wally. Anything. Take whatever you want. And pay me when you can. And if you can't, forget it." He did not look towards the doorway, dark with bodies and threatening faces. But at his words a deep growl spread from the men in the doorway to others in the street, and the air about them seemed to become hot and choked.

Wally tried to speak again, but could not. He made queer sounds in his throat. He bent his head, and I saw his raw fists clench on the counter as though he were making a superhuman effort to control himself. Then, to our vast amazement Sarah spoke, gently, steadily, clearly, and laid her hand on the man's arm.

"Is Connie sick, Wally? I was a nurse once. Have you your buckboard with you? No? Then, I'll walk out to your place with you. I've had a child, and I know what to do for them."

We were dumbfounded at this, but even when Sarah continued to speak softly and consolingly to the stricken man there was no sound. As for Dan, he quickly laid on the counter butter, eggs, a slab of bacon, medicines, gingham, blankets, potatoes, and other things, until there was a huge pile between him and Wally Lewis. He found a burlap sack, and pushed the mass into it with speed and dexterity. The three of them seemed utterly unconscious of the mob at the door.

The tension broke. No one entered the store, but there were ominous rumbles from the crowd. "Break his neck! He'd better watch out, that damned atheist, or he'll find his store burning around him, too. Drag 'em both out and hang 'em! No place in this town for such folks. Sarah Faire! She don't know what she's doin'. Drag 'em out!"

But no one dragged them out. Wally gathered the ends of the sack together in trembling hands; Sarah held his arm. Wally swung the sack over his shoulder, and the man and woman started toward the door.

"Wait," said Dan softly. He reached behind the counter and removed from the wall a new shotgun. Deliberately he loaded it. He walked behind Sarah and Wally to the door. The crowd, again heavily silent, parted, and Wally and Sarah started down the wooden stairs. Dan stood in the doorway, calm and very white. His mild brown eyes were full of something very terrible, though he smiled a little.

"The first man that moves is never going to move again," he said, very quietly, as though he were making a commonplace remark.

No one moved. In a deathly silence the stony-faced man and sweet-faced woman went on their way down the street as though they were entirely alone on it, walking steadily and unhurriedly. Sarah was quite small, and her plump shoulders were a good six inches under Wally's, but there was something so resolute, so courageous and strong about her whole attitude that everyone gaped after her with more astonishment than anger. But after the two had disappeared around the corner, the fury of the crowd turned on Dan Hendricks. Almost in a body they surged toward him, and I am ashamed to confess that I retreated a little to one side, against the wall. I would like to say that I sprang up the steps and stood beside Dan, but I did not. I am sorry I did not. I would like to have that to remember.

I would like to shut out from my memory the sight of Dan standing on his threshold, dauntless, quietly smiling, the shotgun in his hands, cocked and ready. I have no doubt that he would have used it to good effect if it had been necessary. But when four men had almost reached him, he began to speak, and his voice was like a trumpet suddenly blown. Yet it was very calm, slow and casual, as though he were merely holding a pleasant conversation.

"You know," he said, and his very voice stopped them, "you know, you are a lot of dirty dogs. Yellow dogs, at that. You won't rush this gun; I know you. There isn't a man among you. Men wouldn't be here, now. They would be minding their own business and going their own ways. Men never gather in mobs to do injury to defenseless folks. Men uphold law and order. But mobs are yellow behind and red in front, with teeth to tear women with, and claws to mangle babies. Being a mob, you won't rush this gun. You care too much for your guts. You know that I'd like to plug you, and that I'd do it with the greatest of pleasure. I'm ready, if you are." He marked a spot with the toe of his boot. "That's the line. Cross it, if you dare."

His eyes roved over them, inviting them, scorning them, jeering at them. Those eyes touched me, I know, but he gave no sign of recognition. I shrank back, hot and cold, covered with shame and self-hatred.

The men looked at each other, but no one moved. Shamefaced expressions began to appear on scattered faces. The mob was composed of those beyond the limbo; I was relieved to see no one belonging to our little society. They were all the lesser craftsmen, village folk who lived precariously and meanly, supplying the wants of the élite, and a scattering of farmers who loved a fight, a "shivaree," and excitement for its own sake. They growled contemptuously at Dan, but they backed slowly and reluctantly from the point of his rifle. They called him filthy names, but still they backed away, for all their threats and their upraised fists.

They began to scatter to distant corners, still looking back at the store menacingly. But it was with the menace of a bull that has been defeated, and roar though they might, it would be another day before the mob attacked.

I edged away along the side of the building, then accelerated my speed, hating myself, but putting distance between myself and Dan's store. I dived through a side street, all cool and massive greenness and quiet houses and gardens afire with zinnias, hollyhocks, phlox, and late roses. My face was hot, and the muscles in it felt drawn and tight. I was almost running, and it wasn't until I saw curious glances directed at me from the vine-hung porches that I slowed down.

My confused thoughts became coherent. I was filled for a while with passionate annoyance toward Dan Hendricks, though I now know the cause of it. I had been too cowardly to stand with him, and so I tried to justify my actions. What had made him such a melodramatic fool? I reasoned. Why did he have to go out of his way to antagonize a community that already hated him, and would gladly do him harm? He could have used tact instead of histrionics. He could ostensibly have refused Wally Lewis any assistance, but helped him through the back door. I persuaded myself that there had been something ridiculous in his attitude as he had stood in his doorway with cocked gun, defying ruffled roosters that he must have known would not have really attacked him. He loved, I proclaimed to myself, heroic gestures, even if they were made only before a barnyard. A Don Quixote, with all the absurdity of the original. Schoolboyish, that's what. Silly. Now he had practically ruined himself, prevented himself from ever being accepted in a decent community. The latter might have forgiven him his origin in time, might even forget that he had refused to join the church, that he had laughed in the Reverend Bingham's face, that he had never conformed even in the most trivial of customs. I recalled slight evidence to bolster up my case that the animosity of South Kenton had been abating towards him. Hadn't Jack Rugby invited him to his wedding? Of course, he had not attended, but even that would not have been held against him very long. Hadn't Tom Williams only recently and grudgingly admitted that Dan "had brains, if he only knew how to use them, and didn't stand in his own light"? South Kenton would make few overtures toward the pariah, but if he had shown a decent and humble spirit, an eagerness to understand and to conform, kept a guard on his frank and slow-moving tongue, demonstrated a desire to be accepted and a willingness to be chastened and taught, South Kenton would have held out a stately and dignified hand to him and helped him up. But he had done none of these, and now he had committed the worst crime of all, aligned himself against the whole community and all its prejudices, and stood squarely with an outcast against all decencies and lawfulnesses. He had lost everything, all his chances, for a creature that deserved no help but only a kick in the hindquarters. What folly, what stupidity!

Then I thought, with the effect of light breaking in on my mind: Why, he did not care a snap for all these things so valued by myself and others like me! I had never really realized this; I had thought it a sort of youthful bravado. But now I knew he really did not care, that they were nothing to him, that he wanted not a thing from South Kenton but a meager living, that should South Kenton hold out its hand to him he would turn his back on it. It was not that he had a vital contempt for South Kenton, but only a profound indifference, such as the wind and the sun might feel.

He had been right! Absolutely right. He had stood for compassion and pity and humanity against all the smallnesses and the venoms of the small town. He had had a large eye; Wally Lewis was nothing to him as an individual, but only as a symbol of all that was outcast and helpless and persecuted and suffering. It did not matter to him if the suffering were deserved or not; he saw only the suffering. I knew with a terrible humility that Dan had never been able to bear the sight of pain; I remembered his almost girlish wincing at the spectacle of a pariah dog with a broken leg, and the sheer agony on his face when he had seen a group of schoolmates chasing and tormenting a cornered rat. Oh, he was right! And we were all wrong, all of us, secure and armored cowards hounding and slashing at a poor naked beast.

My self-hatred rose like a sickness in my throat. I hung around the back streets, unable to go home where I would hear denouncing discussions of what Dan had done. I wandered aimlessly, until it got dark, and then I crept back to Dan's store. It was already closed and unlighted, but I saw the lamp through the kitchen window. I crept to that window and peeped in. Dan was cooking his solitary supper over the coal range, and through the opened window I could hear the spluttering of the bacon and the bubbling of the coffee pot. I moved to the door and knocked, calling his name weakly. He opened the door and I stepped in, unable to look at him. He waited in silence.

"Dan," I blurted. He did not speak, and I looked up at him furtively. His face was kind and grave and contained something of the pity it had had when he had looked at Wally Lewis. I broke down, sniffling like a ten-year-old, and fumbled for my handkerchief, all my shame and detestation for myself and misery making a salt taste in my mouth.

He did not move a step nearer to me, but merely studied me gravely.

"Dan," I mumbled, "I'm sorry, Dan."

He moved slightly, and sighed.

"It's all right, Jim," he said in a gentle voice. "It's all right."

I turned and ran out of the room, stumbling over the steps, and out into the cool darkness. I ran all the way home. Once there, I avoided my parents, and went up to my own room. I had the feeling, when the door had closed after me, that in some way I had grown older, that things would never be the same for me.

Chapter Nine

Though the next day was Sunday, South Kenton was in a ferment against Dan Hendricks. What impudence to threaten a righteously-outraged community like that! Well, that was a piece with the rest of his behavior, the scum! He had gone too far, yes, he had gone too far! Something must be done about it.

My father said that, too, at the stuffily rich and hot dinner after church. He looked at me threateningly as he said it, though my mother tried by lifted eyebrows and pressed lips to keep his attention off me, and to warn him to leave me alone. I ate in silence; thousands of bitter and violent words surged behind my silence, but I kept quiet until coffee and pie were served. Then I looked at my father directly.

"Something must be done, Dad? Yes, but it wasn't. The

sheriff came from Ripley after old Mrs. Lewis had been burned to death. Everyone knew the house had been fired deliberately by skunks from South Kenton. But, nothing was done about it. The sheriff stood around and hummed and hawed, and then made a report that no one was guilty, that it happened by itself, and went away. Why wasn't a decent and honorable attempt made to find out the criminals who had done it?"

My father stared at me. Gradually his face took on a purplish tinge. He waved his knife at me like a weapon.

"I might have known that you would stand up for that—that so-and-so! There's something perverted in you! But now I warn you: if you continue to associate with him, you'll do yourself harm. Harm, young man. You expect to take my place here, you expect to continue to have friends here. Well, you'll find yourself on the other side of the fence with your precious damned friend one of these days, and you'll get no help from me! The dirty atheist!"

"Why atheist?" I asked softly in the face of his mounting voice. "Because he doesn't go to church? Is that the sign of an atheist? You go to church, Dad, but you've got mighty little religion about you. Didn't you say to me only a few days ago that most people needed less God and more soap, and that religion was only an excuse for shiftlessness and stupidity?"

Rage and a sharp fear made my father's eyes suddenly molten. He glanced quickly over his shoulder. Then he stared at me fixedly, and even with a little hatred.

"So, you'll go blabbing what I said to you in confidence as justification for your fine friend Dan, will you? So that's the kind of son I have!"

"I'm sure Jim didn't mean anything like that," interposed my mother quickly, but with a fierce glance at me. "Did you, Jim?"

I stood up and hurled my napkin from me. "You needn't be afraid I'll repeat it to the mealy-mouthed fools here," I said. I went upstairs to my room, seething with rage. I tramped up and down for a long time. Outside it was all clear and golden, with a transparent light over the trees

and in the sky. I could not stand it any longer; I would go
for a walk. I couldn't even bear to see Livy today, for it
would mean going to her house. I wanted to strangle her
father, who had given a sermon that morning about the
stiff-necked who harbored sinners against the people and
upheld unrighteousness and unholiness. I went downstairs.
In the parlor my parents were talking to Beatrice Faire.
She sat facing the doorway to the hall and saw me. She
greeted me with a light laugh and a lift of her hand. I went
in.

She sat there on the big and ugly horsehair sofa opposite
my mother. She looked demure and sad in a plain organdy
frock which swept to her feet and rose about her throat.
On her head was some sort of floppy hat with pale pink
roses on it. Against the cool and honey-colored smoothness
of her cheeks curled tendrils of bright and vital hair. She
had evidently just come, and as she talked to my mother
in a soft and regretful voice, she played with the handle
of her parasol with white-gloved fingers.

"I'm so glad to hear you say that, dear Mrs. Marcy," she
almost whispered, and delicately touched her eyes with a
tiny white handkerchief. After her first greeting to me she
ignored me, as did my parents, and I stood awkwardly
in the doorway. "I said to myself this morning: 'I'll go to
see Mama's dear friends, and try to explain things. After
all, they all love Mama. They know that what she did was
not a kind of defiance to them, but only because she is so
kind and sweet, and can't bear to hear of anyone being
sick, or suffering. They'll know that she did it without
thinking, for Mama always has hated anything nasty or
mean.' Perhaps, I said to myself, they'll forgive her for
being impulsive, and—and, you'll forgive me, dear Mrs.
Marcy?—and foolish. I'm sure Mama already is sorry
and ashamed. But it's because of her kind heart that she
did it. And I thought: 'I'm sure her dear friends, who've
always loved her, won't punish her too severely, but give
her a chance to be sorry, and forgive her for what was
only her too softness of feeling.' "

"I only hope that Sarah realizes what she has done,"

said my mother severely, but her eyes were melting. She beamed on Beatrice with foolish fondness. "Though I felt really cold towards Sarah when I heard about it, I'm sure all of us are Christians and will try to understand. But, dear me," shaking her head with dolorous bewilderment, "I can't see why she did it. It isn't like Sarah."

Beatrice frankly covered her face with her handkerchief, and her shoulders shook gently. My father cleared his throat, and blinked. My mother rose quickly and put her arms about Beatrice, and sniffed audibly.

"You are such a dear child, my dear," she said. "And for your sake, and even for poor Sarah's sake, we'll forgive her. We won't even mention it to her. But I hope, in the future, that she won't cause us such distress again. We're all so fond of her. And of you, dear."

Beatrice allowed my mother to dry her eyes. I watched everything with passionate loathing. I hated my father for the gruff affection he displayed for this young woman. My mother went on to say cheerfully that she would call on her friends this afternoon and persuade them to hold no hard feelings against Sarah. Then as Beatrice arose, my mother glanced at me, and suggested that I see Beatrice home. I was revolted, but there was nothing I could do. Beatrice and I, after she had bid my parents a tearful and grateful goodbye, went out into the warm summer day which now seemed unclean to me because of the girl's presence.

Beatrice kept her head down and remained silent until we had left the important streets behind. Then when I glanced at her sideways I saw that she was smiling a little to herself. I wanted to hit her in the face.

"You aren't deceiving me any!" I burst out violently. "You can only deceive old fools like my mother! You made a filthy display of yourself in order to protect your precious standing in this small town!"

I will give Beatrice credit. She was never hypocritical with her contemporaries, from whom she expected nothing. She merely smiled at me broadly.

"Well, we have to live, don't we?" she demanded

frankly. "Mama and I have to work for a living, or we'd starve. What would become of us if your mother and her friends didn't come to us for their dresses and petticoats? If Mama was fool enough to put us in danger of starving, it was up to me to save her from herself, and myself, also."

Even I could see logic in this, but my bitterness against her did not decrease.

"I bet your mother doesn't know about this!" I exclaimed.

She shrugged. "Mama's down there with that Lewis girl. But I hope you'll have enough regard for her, seeing that you've always hung around the house and eaten her cakes and pies, not to say anything about this to anyone. Don't be a silly, Jim. Be practical for once in your life. When it comes to ideals against bread and butter, only a zany would choose the ideals. I'd rather be comfortable than be right."

"Oh, so you think your mother and Dan were right, eh? Well, that's funny, coming from you!"

"Don't be silly," she repeated in a weary voice, as though she were arguing with a stupid child. "Of course I don't think they were right. One has to live, doesn't one? It's only suicide to poison your own bread. There's no question of right and wrong; there's only a question of money in the bank and food on the table. Animals are much more simple and honest than we. They haven't any ideals, which are only hypocrisy anyway."

I looked at her with horror, not for what she had said, but because an ugly suspicion was aroused in me that she was right. But if she was right, then all beauty and honor and compassion and nobility were wrong. Perhaps, I thought confusedly, all the "fine things" were only hypocrisies, an attempt to glue self-preservation and security and blandnesses and safeties on the wild and terrible face of reality. Behind the pretty cardboard of virtues, frail and painted, howled the raw and frightful truth; perhaps we tried to drown out its howlings with sweet music and soft conversation. My thoughts were so confused and so devastating that I could not reply to Beatrice.

She touched my arm lightly. "You aren't a fool, Jim," she said. "You see what I mean."

"Yes, I see," I said bitterly. "I see. You think a full stomach is better than honor. Hell, perhaps you're right. But, I don't want you to be right. If you were, there'd be no use in anything. All the arts would be foolishness, all attempts at civilization would only be absurd. We—we couldn't go on living. We'd all live in barricaded houses and kill at sight."

She nodded humorously. Then she said, "Let's not talk about it. It's a lovely day."

I felt like a silly and gawkish child who had been dismissed from intelligent discussion. I fumed and hated her as we walked along. She talked gaily and casually, but I did not answer. I could feel her amusement and self-satisfaction, and when I looked sideways at her and saw that she was smiling to herself, I knew that she was laughing at my silly mother and all her silly friends. And I knew I could do nothing. I could not put into words what I felt about her, and anything I said would only hurt poor Sarah.

Then an ugly and sharp realization came upon me with regard to Beatrice. Since Jack Rugby's marriage to Amelia Burnett she had been all sweetness and humor and gaiety towards me. She had tried to keep from antagonizing me too much, and had appeared at our house unusually often on one pretext or another. Horror again struck me, and I moved away from her abruptly. She saw the involuntary gesture, and sighed a little, peeping at me furtively. She must have understood, for a few moments later she said: "Have you and Dan and Livy gone on any more bicycle rides lately? And why haven't you asked me, too?"

"We haven't gone," I muttered.

"Is Livy's foot still bothering her?" she asked with sweet concern. "I didn't think so. It didn't even swell. I wonder why she seemed so upset that day when she turned her ankle? Almost as though she had something on her mind. I wonder," she mused thoughtfully, "if it's because she thinks South Kenton doesn't treat Dan right?"

"Perhaps," I growled, then her words filtering into my

mind with all their significance, I looked at her sharply. "What makes you think that? I can't see the connection between her sprained ankle and her being upset and Dan Hendricks."

"Don't you?" she asked softly. And said nothing else. Her words hung in the bright and quiet air with a sickening significance.

"You've got an evil mind, Bee," I said slowly. "If you're trying to tell me that Livy likes Dan more than ordinary, he being just a friend, you've overshot your mark. What are you trying to say, anyway?"

"I?" She seemed hurt and surprised. "Why, nothing. Livy's my dearest friend, and I love her dearly. I would never say anything about her, even if it were so. I'm sure Livy thinks only of you, Jim."

We had come to her home now, and she exclaimed: "Mama must be home! The door is open."

I wanted to leave her then, but I also wanted to see Sarah. I wanted to ask her some questions. I felt that in talking to her my threatened world would be set aright again. When we walked into the cool brightness of the little parlor we found Sarah rocking agitatedly in her gay little white chair, and sobbing dryly. She looked at us with anguished eyes and did not greet us. She only burst out:

"Jim! Bee! Poor Connie and her poor little baby died this morning! They caught cold during that rainstorm we had last week, and the barn roof leaking and all, and no one to take care of them but Connie's poor father. It was lung fever. Two days ago something might have been done for them. But it was too late, though I did my best, sitting in that awful barn all night, with the mice and the dirt and the manure and the rats, and no light but a lantern, and that poor father crouching there in the hay, wringing his hands and sobbing! Not enough blankets, not enough food; no medicine. Oh, it's a wicked world! And if there's a God He'll punish the wicked people who did this to a poor sick girl and her little baby!" She sobbed again. She looked old and ill, rocking there, overcome with grief. Her eyes were sunken, seemed fixed in their sockets from sleeplessness and pain. "The poor baby, struggling for its breath, and the poor girl trying to nurse it in her fever, and looking at me and begging me to do something for it! Oh, I can't bear it!"

"It's very sad, I'm sure," murmured Bee. She was ill at ease, and a crease of impatience came between her eyes. "But, Mama, you can't do anything about it, now. Perhaps it was for the best."

"Best!" Sarah's gentle face flared with outrage and anger. "You can talk of 'best,' Bee! It's never best, nothing is ever best, if it arrives there by suffering and injustice and cruelty! If you could have seen that poor girl—"

Bee's voice, cool and practical, broke in on the threatened hysterics.

"You're all tired out, Mama. And no wonder. I suppose you haven't eaten anything since yesterday, and sitting up all night in the dampness. Let me help you to bed, and I'll bring you a cup of hot soup and some tea."

I hated her again, but I knew that she was right, and that it was best for Sarah. They seemed to have forgotten me. Beatrice helped her mother into the bedroom. I waited a few moments. I was shocked at what I had heard, but Sarah's words had readjusted my shaken world for me, and I was relieved. I heard her sobs from the bedroom, but Beatrice said nothing. I went home.

South Kenton was ill at ease and unusually silent when the news came out about Connie Lewis's death and the death of her child. Everyone seemed to avoid discussion of the subject. There was even very little denunciation when Dan Hendricks took the distraught Wally Lewis into his own house, and cared for the half-crazy sick man. In fact, to my amazement, a few hang-dog customers actually went into the store, and Dan had a hard time between taking care of them and ministering to Wally Lewis. Even my father, uncalled, went to see the miserable farmer, and prescribed for him. I thought he looked a little softened after his trips. A few more daring spirits actually hinted that Dan had a good heart, and my friend enjoyed a sort of side-door prestige and good feeling. But he seemed as indifferent as ever, both to the reviving of his business and the tentative good will of South Kenton.

Then one night, two days before I returned to medical school, Wally Lewis crept unseen from his bed and disappeared. They found his body in the creek near his old home. In his fever he had walked the five miles there in the loneliness of the night. He had left a scrawled and illiterate note for Dan:

"Thank you for what you done for me, Dan. There ain't nothing more I can say than that. But you know how I feel. I can't lay around on you any more, getting you in bad with the folks. That ain't right to do, and I ain't going to do it. I'm not saying anything about the folks hereabouts, and what they did to Connie. It ain't no use, and someways it don't seem to matter."

The customers swarmed more than ever into Dan's store, but he never answered questions. He was even curt with me, and seemed to wish that I would not come to see him. Livy went to see him, in the face of all the town, but she would tell me nothing. She looked very pale and abstracted, though she was very gentle to me.

I returned to school. I wrote to Dan several times before I received a short and indifferent letter, written with cold formality. Behind the letter I could see his brooding eyes, his bitter thoughts. Then my father wrote irritably that Dan had not taken advantage of the furtively-offered good will of the community and had antagonized it again. I felt only weary impatience, and was glad to forget the whole affair and South Kenton in the pleasures of the city after school hours. Livy wrote to me, also, casual and affectionate letters, but she told me nothing.

Then my father wrote again and told me that the five acres of barren and uncultivated land far out in the country, which had been among the effects Billy Riggs had left to Dan, had yielded up five active gaswells. Dan was now comfortably "fixed," my father wrote with visible annoyance. It had done no particular good with regard to that stiff-necked young fool. He had merely shut up his store, bought a nice little house and ten acres of good land about five miles from town, and had buried himself there. My father said that several people had called on him, had admired the place, and had asked what he was doing on it, but that he had shown no friendliness and had even indicated that return visits would not be welcome.

I wrote to Dan again, congratulating him, but I received no reply. I asked Livy news of him, and she replied shortly and indifferently. No one saw Dan much anymore. When he needed anything he went to Ripley for it, though he came into town quite often to visit Sarah and Beatrice Faire and Mortimer Rugby.

I suffered uneasiness for some time after I had received all this news, but soon the edge was dulled. I felt some resentment against Dan at his apparent desire to terminate our friendship. What had I done, anyway? I would not admit to myself that he was sick of all of us, of our hypocrisies and meannesses and smallnesses and cruelties. But I was indignant that he had included me in his silent indictment against South Kenton.

ᴐᴐᴐᴐᴐᴐᴐᴐᴐᴐᴐᴐᴐᴐᴐᴐᴐᴐᴐᴐᴐᴐᴐᴐᴐᴐᴐᴐᴐᴐ

It was two years before I returned home again, though my parents visited me on the two Christmases, and we all went to New York for the opera and the theaters. I took extra courses in bacteriology in the summers. For a time I had an idea of practicing in Pittsburgh or New York, but I knew inside that I was fitted only to carry on my father's work and take his place. I still had what Bee had called "romantic ideals."

I did not realize until I saw my parents that I was homesick for South Kenton, small and snobbish and narrow though it was, sleeping under its old trees and squabbling agitatedly, and living slowly and peacefully under the surface upsets. Small-town boy that I was, I had never stopped being bewildered and disorganized at city noise and city confusion. Life moved too quickly in the cities, too superficially, as though everyone was a mere shadow, going little shadowy ways through caverns of concrete and stone, and hurrying futilely from place to place. I longed for the static quality of South Kenton, where everyone was fixed and rooted, like the old trees about their shabby old houses.

I was eager for news from home, which seemed to meet my mother's approval. Jack Rugby and Amelia had a baby girl; Mortimer had had pneumonia last winter and seemed a little queer since then. He was shabbier than ever, avoided people, had developed a fierce eye, and was always tramping the five miles to see Dan Hendricks. Dan drove him back to town but never entered the town proper. Sarah Faire had become very quiet these days; she was still the town seamstress and stylist, but did not come often to church and had refused, for the first time in many years, to take part in last winter's church suppers and sociables. She had pleaded bad health, and my father admitted that she was very nervous and somewhat morbid; it was "her age," of course. I had a few disloyal thoughts toward him; I did not like such glib diagnoses. I wondered what was the real trouble with Sarah. Willie Williams had joined his father Tom in the law business, and was making a great deal of money, being a smart young fellow. Ezra Hughes had had the quinsy; Mary Knowles had just sold a parcel of land to someone from Ripley for a very good price. Her daughter, Mary, had opened a real-estate office for herself and her mother, and they were rushing feverishly about all the time collecting rents and selling land. Mary, my father said, looked more like a man than ever. She had developed a great fondness for Jane Mundell, who had turned out to be a gentle and very feminine sort of girl with soft eyes and shy manners. It was real pretty, my mother added, to see the devotion between the two girls. I felt a slight qualm of nausea at this, and looked at my father sharply. But he was merely nodding blandly at what my mother had said. I wanted to mention the term for such devotion, but homosexuality was still not discussed in polite society, not even between men and physicians. It

makes me smile now, listening to the young folks discuss
it glibly and knowingly, with apparent modern candor,
and such innocence!

As for Beatrice Faire, she was dearer and sweeter than
ever, my mother said. She did most of the work now, since
Sarah's indisposition. She had bought a little pony, and
because of her mother's old affection for Dan Hendricks,
she went out to his little farm and took him cakes and
things that her mother had prepared for him. He lived
alone, except for an old woman who, it was rumored, kept
house sketchily for him. I detected no hint of disapproval
in my mother's voice when she spoke of Sarah's kindness
to Dan; Sarah was always so good, she commented.

Livy's father had died. I knew that, and for the first time
in almost a year I felt a quickening with regard to Livy.
There had been other girls, and my thoughts of Livy had
not been so frequent. Now Livy was teaching the district
school since old Mortimer's illness, and she was very
satisfactory, though grown very quiet and quite thin. I remembered with a sudden pain that I had not heard from
Livy for over a year, and I felt an urgency to see her. The
children liked Livy, for she was honest and just and
tolerant, not like other women teachers, my father added.
Her father's place had been taken by a young bachelor
minister from Cartersville, and he was quite a catch, having
an income of his own, which made it easier for South
Kenton during the annual scraping up of his salary. He
seemed to prefer Livy and Beatrice to the other girls in
town, and Beatrice was quite frank in her pursuit of him,
but Livy seemed indifferent.

"I suppose," sighed my mother regretfully, looking sideways out of her eyes at me, "that Livy is one of those born
old maids."

I went home the next June, a full-fledged young doctor,
seething with plans. Livy loomed largest in them. I had
bought a full kit two years ago, but now I had the authority
of a handsome diploma to use it. It was not quite so shiny
as it had been, but I did not quarrel with it for that reason.

Even though South Kenton looked smaller and tighter to me than ever, I was delighted with it. I was further delighted when I arrived home. My father, as a surprise, had built an addition to the house, two small rooms fresh with paint and plaster and a nice rug and two desks on which stood bowls of flowers. Here we would practice our profession. I could not get over it, and my father beamed at my enthusiasm. I hung my diploma proudly over my desk, and stood off and looked at it with tears in my eyes.

There were several parties for me. I enjoyed the friendship and affection of my old friends, and went about busily before settling down to business. I saw Livy the first day I was home. Yes, she was paler than I had remembered, and thinner, and she had an almost permanently abstracted manner. But when she spoke she spoke in her old round manner, looking at me directly with honest and intelligent eyes, as though we were man and man together. There was no illusion in her eyes, but no disillusion, either, and that is quite a difference.

I was not home three days when I urged her to marry me at once. Why not, I said. She did not refuse me, but she evaded me for the first time. "Sometime," she replied. She was busy now, and I was not yet settled. She smiled at me so kindly that I was cheered. She would not enter into a binding engagement, but I felt that things had been arranged between us. After that she would not talk intimately with me, but only of casual things. She and Beatrice had drifted apart somewhat, and did not meet very often. Beatrice, she added smilingly, was too busy trying to marry young Mr. Samuel Pringle.

"It seems to me that Bee is always trying to marry someone," I said. "What's this about her always going out to see Dan, with her mother's cakes?" I spoke amusedly, but I was surprised at the sudden sharpening of Livy's features, and her murmured evasion.

This was the first time I had given undivided thought to Dan, and I asked about him. Livy evaded me, and did not seem to wish to talk about him. He was all right, she said indifferently. No one saw much of him. She didn't blame him much. He kept his money in the First National in Ripley, which made old Ezra Hughes pretty resentful. He did not seem to want anything to do with anyone in South Kenton.

"That's nonsense," I said sharply. I was already becoming as smug as the rest of my friends, and felt resentment against Dan. "He can take his place here as well as anyone, with all the money he is getting. It isn't right to bury himself that way. He owes——"

"What?" Livy's voice was quiet, but there was something in it that disturbed me. "What does he owe to anyone? Nothing. This town has treated him worse than shabbily; if it hadn't been for the money he is getting from the wells he would have starved here. No one would deal with him, except old Mortimer and me and Sarah. Oh, Jim, I know what you'll say, that his ways and everything cut him off from other people. He had no right to be different, you'll say." She looked at me thoughtfully, and with an expression of pain in her clear eyes. "You didn't always think that, Jim."

I started to walk about the room restlessly. Livy boarded with the Kings. Old Endicott had died nearly two years ago, but despite his large leavings to his wife and son, Mrs. King was avaricious and had welcomed Livy's little board money. The parlor was shabby and dark, with frayed carpet and heavy old furniture. I hated it, could not bear to think of Livy in such a house.

"I was young when I thought differently," I said. Livy smiled quickly, then became grave again. "Young men have radical ideas, Livy. But I know the world now. It isn't right to antagonize other human beings when your livelihood depends on their favor. Even if it doesn't, you are bound to be human and friendly. Dan has always been antisocial. There's a medical term for that. It isn't normal."

"Normal," repeated Livy thoughtfully. "What is normal? Smugness, narrowness, cruelty, herd-loyalty? Or is it abnormal to have a large eye, and understanding, and a desire to retain your own identity?"

"Oh, Livy, you don't know what you're talking about!" I said impatiently. I walked about again, and bit my lip.

Livy was silent for some time, then she said: "Have you been out to see Dan, Jim?"

I felt ashamed. "No, I haven't had time yet," I answered. "What on earth made him buy a place so far out like that?" I added irritably.

"Perhaps he wanted to get away from us," she answered. "Jim, you were the only boy he was ever friendly with. Do you remember that? He always liked you so much."

"Oh, I'll go out to see him!" I exclaimed with increasing impatience. I went home, feeling that somehow I had done some great wrong, and that Livy and I were very far apart.

But I did not go out to see him. Two months went by, three months, four. Before I knew it my mother was becoming excited about Christmas, and the first snow was falling. I was very busy. My father did not go out on country calls now, and I made them myself. We had a telephone, and a few of the farmers did, also. It seemed to me that sickness was more rife in the country since the telephone had come in. I made several midnight calls to deliver babies and prescribe for charley horse and lumbago and broken legs. The work was arduous, but I enjoyed it. One day I went down the Cartersville road to some distant farmhouse, and to the right, toward the hills, I saw Dan's house. It was a cold November day and the trees were stripped, but near the house was a line of pines, blackly green against the clear and colorless sky. I could see a low smudge of smoke over the house, and a dog barked distantly at me. The house was long and rambling, but looked well kept, freshly painted white with green shutters. It looked lonely and secret to me. I reined in my horse, and considered. I could drive in for a minute. But some reluctance held me back. I hated to renew an old friendship, for unexplained reasons. Some other day, I thought; I was tired, and I disliked questions back and forth. I was not up to it. Nevertheless, when I arrived home, I was full of depression and uneasiness.

Two days after Christmas a blizzard set in, accompanied by a howling wind and bitter cold. It was almost impossible to see three feet ahead, and the snow was piling up in great ridges like the sands of a desert. My father and I sat and read and smoked before a mighty parlor fire, my mother knitting close by. It was very snug and secure here, and I prayed that there would be no calls tonight. I was just beginning to doze beautifully, listening to the snapping of the logs and the rustle of my father's paper and the clicking of my mother's needle, when there came a sharp knock at our door. Father dropped his paper, lifted a quizzical eyebrow at me. We waited until we heard the girl answer the door. There came quick steps in the hall, and Sarah Faire, her bonnet and coat white with snow, burst into the warmness of our room. Mother rose with an exclamation, the knitting tumbling from her black bombazine lap, and my father dropped his papers and stared.

"Whatever!" cried my mother, going forward and attempting to remove Sarah's coat. "On such a night, Sarah! Are you sick? Is dear Bee sick?"

"No," said Sarah. I had seen her only once since I had returned, and I noticed that the gray had thickened in her hair, which had become duller. She was thinner than before, and there were lines in her gentle face. "I won't take off my coat." The color whipped in her cheeks by the wind and the snow faded, and I saw that she was ghastly pale. "No one's sick."

Then suddenly she began to cry, weakly, wailingly, and wrung her hands together. She put her hands over her face, and her body almost doubled over, like one in great pain. My father took her arm, while my mother stood by, bewildered and nonplussed.

"Sarah," said my father commandingly. "What is it? Here, sit down. No, never mind worrying about the chair, if you're too stubborn to take off your coat." His sharp words had an effect on her; she allowed my mother to remove her coat. She had apparently come out without gloves, and her hands were swollen and red with cold.

Mother called for something hot for her to drink, and the hired girl, who had been staring in the doorway, scuttled toward the kitchen. Sarah sat down in the red plush chair before the fire, allowed my mother to rub her numb hands. She did not cry aloud now, but tears flowed down her face. I knew that such tears meant either terrible physical or mental pain, and I, always the alert young physician, came forward. But I waited until she drank a cup of hot milk. She drank mechanically, as though her thoughts were concerned with something at a distance, tragic and desperate. My mother was questioning her gently, at which she shook her head slightly as if disturbed by sounds that withdrew her from her contemplation. Then her fixed eye moved a little and fell on me. Instantly a feverish animation brightened her pinched features.

"Jim!" she cried. "You've got to do something! He'll listen to you. You always had some influence on him. He won't listen to me, I know, in spite of everything. But, you can do something. Jim!" She caught my hand; her eyes, bloodshot and agonized, glared at me. "You'll talk to him, Jim?"

"Talk to whom?" I asked soothingly. "Sure, I'll talk to anyone, Mrs. Faire. If you'll just tell me what it is all about."

She continued to glare at me; she became silent. Her bloodless lips moved without a sound. My mother and father exchanged bewildered looks. Then it were as though the poor woman collapsed internally, for she shrank in her chair and began to rock violently, moaning under her breath.

"You've got to talk to him, Jim," she repeated after a few moments. "You've got to tell him he can't marry Bee. It can't happen; anything so cruel can't happen." Her voice rose on a great cry.

"Who wants to marry Bee?" exclaimed my mother and father together. But I said nothing. I felt sick, for I knew. "I'm sure," said my mother when Sarah did not reply, "that Mr. Pringle is a very nice young man, and though I know you hate the thought of losing dear little Bee, you must resign yourself to it. After all, she can't be an old maid, she being so pretty and sweet. I know your heart is breaking at the thought of separation from her, but things will be all right. You must just resign yourself to it, Sarah, dear. Well," she added, straightening up and smiling at us brightly. "This is very good news. Bee deserves such a nice young man. I'm sure we are very happy to hear it." She smiled at Sarah indulgently, and my father laughed.

But Sarah was not looking at them; she was staring at me desperately, with wild eyes. She knew I knew. I cleared my throat awkwardly.

"Wait a minute, Mother. Maybe it's not Mr. Pringle that Bee's going to marry."

My parents turned to me, surprised.

"Maybe," I added dully, "it's Dan Hendricks."

"Dan Hendricks!" cried my mother, while my father gaped. "Sarah! It's not Dan Hendricks? Dan Hendricks!"

Sarah nodded. Her face had become dull and lifeless.

"Of all the damned impudence!" shouted my father. "Why, damn his hide—"

"James," said my mother, but mechanically. She laid her hand on Sarah's shoulder. "Why, you poor thing! No wonder you feel so badly. No wonder! I can't believe it; Bee, of all people. And I always thought she had such good sense, always so proper, always knowing what was just right. Bee!" My mother looked wounded and aghast, as at a personal injury.

But Sarah continued to stare at me. Only she and I knew what was in her mind. Dan could not, must not, marry Bee Faire. Sarah had begun to wring her hands, slowly, soundlessly, and the sight was infinitely pathetic.

My father stamped up and down the room, fuming, his hands thrust deeply in his pockets, his watch chain glittering on his protruding belly. He glowered, pulled at his short beard, bit his lip. He turned on Sarah explosively.

"Why, damn it, it's an insult to the whole community, for him to look at Bee. But I don't altogether blame Bee, Sarah." He shook his head at her menacingly. "You've got yourself to blame, too. Always having him hanging around, since he was a kid, always doing things for him, and standing up for him, throwing him into association with that poor, misguided girl. You've got yourself to blame. I always said to Matilda here, that you would suffer for it someday." He looked at my mother for corroboration, and she nodded, her lips tight. "Well, now you're suffering. But we are your friends and want to help you. Have you talked to Bee?"

Sarah nodded. "I've talked to her," she said in a monotonous voice, as though she were speaking in a dream. "It didn't do any good. She laughed at me."

"Girls," sighed my mother. "You knew nothing about it before she told you, Sarah?"

Sarah began to cry again, with little tight sobs, as though she dared not become agitated because of the great agony in her heart.

"No! I would never have let him come again if I had known. Bee never liked him. She used to pick on him, and jeer at him, though he never retaliated. I—I almost died when she told me. I begged her on my knees—"

"But a nice, sweet girl like Bee couldn't really care for a man like that," said my mother incredulously, rubbing her palms together distractedly. "Whatever possessed her!"

I had been thinking in a sick misery for the past few minutes. I had been suffering remorse and shame that I had avoided Dan so long. I was appalled at my smugness; it fell from me now like a smothering coat, leaving me free again. What a prig and a fool I had been! Blind, stupid, chained. No wonder Livy had looked at me so strangely lately, as at a stranger wearing the disguise of a friend. My mind had become blanketed in thick, soft garment of narrowness and convention. I had surrendered without an effort, left the windy places where a man could be free, and had come into this hot and overcrowded room of the accepted. But, it was not too late, I thought, with a fearful feeling that it was indeed too late. I would see Dan; I would persuade him from this colossal folly and calamity. That was what Sarah wanted. I put my hand on her shoulder.

"I'll talk to Dan," I said gently. "We've always been friends. I think he'll listen to me."

I was surprised at the harsh bitterness that stood suddenly in her eyes as she looked up at me. Her mouth curled with denunciation.

"Friends! And you haven't been near him since you came back, Jim."

"That's so," said my father with satisfaction. "Jim's finally got sense. Now, Sarah, I'll take you home in the sleigh. It's a bad night, and we'll see what can be done to save poor Bee from herself. I suppose she was sorry for the scoundrel."

"Girls," sighed my mother again. "Always trying to save reprobates."

When my father had taken poor Sarah away, I walked up and down the room restlessly, consumed with remorse and fear and shame, while my mother sighed and exclaimed, and chattered endlessly. Something can be done, I insisted to myself. Something must be done. I remembered all the repugnance I had felt for Bee, her secret smile, her cruel tongue, her malice-lighted eyes. No, she must not marry Dan. He did not deserve this. I recalled all the things he had done, and knew he had been right. He had remained free, had been born free and lived free. He had not become entangled by life; now, he was threatened by this entanglement.

Oh! I thought. If one could just murder her quietly! She's always trying to marry someone! I suppose it's because of Dan's money.

But I did not know for a long time the real reason for her marrying Dan Hendricks. I hardly believed it when I knew. It was too appalling, too subtle, too beyond all our little experience.

The next morning the blizzard had subsided. The world was all glittering white waves and deep blue shadows under a sun like a blazing crystal. Sleighbells rang through the shining air, and every tree was heavy with white snow. A clear and peaceful morning, somehow festive and exciting. But burningly cold.

I wrapped myself in the bear rug when I had seated myself in the cutter. My mother had heated hot bricks for my feet, for the drive was long, and I had two calls to make in the vicinity of Dan's farm. I drove away, the breath stinging my nostrils, the harness glittering on the black horse's fat body. My bells jingled gaily; holly wreaths hung in every window in front of stiff lace curtains, and children played with bright red sleds in the snow. Against the lighted and colorless sky, plumes of gray smoke rose from snug chimneys, and when I passed a group of pines a shower of snow fell on me. In spite of premonitions, I felt cheerful and confident.

I came to the end of the street and saw a slim figure in black coat furred with a strip of black fur, bowed over a round little muff. I reined in and called, "Livy!"

She came towards me, smiling with difficulty. Despite the stinging air, her face was without color, and her eyes looked tired. She told me she was calling on Mrs. Hughes, who was sick.

"Get in," I said. "I'll take you there."

She climbed in, and I tucked the robe about her. She was shivering visibly. Livy, shivering, Livy who had always been so joyous and vigorous! I looked at her sharply, and did not like her color. I spoke of it with concern, but she shrugged with a manner that showed annoyance. We drove in silence for a while. I wanted to tell her that I was going to Dan, but wondered how to begin the whole difficult story. Unconsciously, she helped me by asking where I was going, and I told her that I had some calls near Dan's farm. She sighed quickly.

"And, of course, you won't go to see him, Jim."

"Yes," I said quietly, "I will." I could feel her surprised eyes on me, but I applied the whip to the horse without looking at her. "You see, Livy, Dan's going to be married. To Bee Faire."

She gave a sharp cry, and I turned to her. She was trembling so I could feel it through our clothing, and her face had become ghastly.

"No! Jim, it isn't true! Tell me it isn't true. I don't believe it." She began to whimper, catching her under lip with her teeth to stop its shaking.

"It's true," I said gravely. She put her small gloved hand to her face and felt it all over with it as though it had gone numb. "Sarah told us last night. She wanted me to stop it; she asked me to see Dan. That's why I'm going out there."

Her hand fell from her face, the tips of her gloves wet. She blinked rapidly and looked into the distance. We had reached the Hughes's house, and I stopped the horse and waited. She seemed to collect herself with an effort and got out of the cutter slowly. Then she looked up at me tragically.

"Jim, don't let him marry her, will you?"

"I'll do my best," I said, a sense of hopelessness coming over me. "Of course, she's just after his money. I'll make him see that."

I waited until she had gone up the snowy walk and stood by the door, hoping that she would turn around and smile at me. But she did not; she walked like an old woman, stooped and uncertain of step. I went on, frowning.

I began to formulate for the hundredth time what I would say to Dan. What could I say? First of all there was the painful business of apology to be gotten over, and I winced at it. Then, after that? What could I say? I remembered his grave kindliness that, however, invited no intimacies. How to begin? On the surface it seemed absurd, a small-town girl marrying a small-town man. What of it? many would say. They would laugh at my fumbling descriptions of Bee and exclaim with ridicule. She was an intelligent and sharp-tongued girl; what of it? She was not soft and gentle, but, what of it? She was competent and would make a good housekeeper. A good housekeeper. I repeated it to myself. But, I thought desperately, there was something beyond that, subtle and evil and treacherous. Nonsense, exclaimed the hypothetical many. I was melodramatic, full of romanticism. I was making a mountain out of a molehill. I could not explain to the many the expression in Bee's eyes, the aura she had about her of something dangerous and deadly. You are a pack of fools, said the many in my mind.

I was in a bad and nervous state of mind when I reached Dan's house. There it was, near its dark green pines shrouded in snow, low and long and rambling, green-shuttered and quiet, its smoke in a hazy column against the sky. There was no sign of life about it, except for the smoke. Suddenly there was a reddish and agitated blur against the uncleared snow, and a big collie dog rushed towards me,

barking frantically. I stopped my horse, and the dog leapt
about it, then tried to get at me in the cutter. His eyes and
teeth were unfriendly. Dogs always liked me, but this dog
responded to my overtures with growls. Nevertheless, he
allowed me to get out of the cutter when we arrived at
the house, and watched me hitch the horse and blanket
the animal with only a dull rumbling in his throat. The steps
of the porch had been cleared, and I admired the fine
oaken door with its fanlight and brightly gleaming copper
knocker.

It was a long time until there was a response; in the
meantime there was the hissing of the powdered snow as a
slight wind lifted it into the cold bright sunlight, and the
cawing of crows as their black forms rose against the sky.
At length the door opened slowly and an ancient woman
with steel-rimmed glasses and a shawl peered out at me.

"I want to see Dan Hendricks," I said. She continued to
peer at me, working her lips, for several moments.

"He ain't home," she croaked at last, with an unfriendly
stare into my eyes.

I looked down the unbroken expanse of snow that
stretched from the house.

"That's a lie," I said loudly. "He's here. Tell him Jim
Marcy wants to see him."

She muttered something, then slammed the door in my
face. Was that final, or had she gone to tell Dan? I beat
my numbed heels together while I waited. I had just determined to pound the knocker again, with great force,
when the door opened once more. The old woman stood
there, and looking more unfriendly than ever, she beckoned
me to enter.

I stood in a darkly paneled hall with polished floor. It
was cold in there, yet gleamed with cleanliness. I almost
slipped on a small carpet in the center of the hall. I followed the old crone to a door, and opened it before she
could. I stood on the threshold of a remarkable and beautiful room.

It was very long and narrow, almost like a great corridor. The ceilings and walls were paneled in dark wood,

dimly shining. Five windows along the side, low, squat windows with beaded glass, let in the brilliant sunlight like dazzling mirrors. High bookcases, filled with books, covered one wall from end to end. The furniture was heavy mahogany, comfortable and low, cushioned in rich, dark colors. On heavy tables stood half a dozen oil lamps with round, painted shades. At the far end glowed the flickering redness of a great log fire. Before that fire sat Dan Hendricks, reading. He looked up as I appeared, and removed the pipe from his mouth in silence.

I went along the thick carpet towards him, smiling foolishly, while he waited and watched. It seemed an endless journey. When I stood five feet from him, he said gravely: "Hello, Jim."

"Hello, Dan," I said awkwardly. He gestured towards an opposite chair with his pipestem. He did not ask me to remove my coat, but I did so. I peeped at him furtively as he watched me. It was over two years since I had seen him. He looked older than his twenty-five years, and heavily grave. He was as shabby as ever, and thinner. There were deep clefts about his big mouth, and a permanent furrow on his forehead. My old affection came back with a rush for him, but he seemed so remote that I could not speak until I sat down opposite him. The dog had entered the room with me, and now lay down on the rug before the fire near Dan. Dan played with the animal's ears, but the dog did not remove his unfriendly and suspicious eyes from me, and once or twice he growled.

"He doesn't seem to like me," I said, desperately breaking the silence.

Dan smiled slightly, patted the dog's head.

I leaned towards him earnestly. "Dan, I've been pretty much of a skunk, not coming to see you. I won't mutter something about being busy or anything. I could have come. I was wrong. I wonder if you know why I didn't come?"

"Why did you come now?" he asked quietly. He was looking at the dog, and smiled at him. I felt my face burn. I laughed forcedly.

"Because I wanted to see you. I've—been in a sort of fog. Gotten smug. Listened to—things. But last night I woke up. Go on, call me anything you want to. I deserve it. But last night I knew I had to come, I woke up, as I said. I've never forgotten you, Dan," I added, wincing as I remembered how thoroughly I had forgotten him.

For a long moment he did not speak, then he looked at me with opaque eyes.

"You're cold, aren't you? Bad weather to be out in." He raised his voice and called: "Martha!" The old woman appeared at the distant door. "Bring in some whiskey and hot water and sugar and some cake."

He looked at me remotely. "You're fatter," he said, without particular expression.

"You haven't forgiven me, have you, Dan?"

He smiled again, and smoked placidly.

"Forgive? It was your business if you wanted to come or not. I'm not asking any questions."

I fished for my pipe and filled it. The dog growled at intervals, and the logs dropped with a rush of sparks. The sunlight poured in the windows. I was in despair. At this rate I would never dare to say anything.

"You're pretty hard on me, Dan. I've apologized. I know what I've been. It isn't like you to hold grudges." I glanced at him expectantly. He did not reply. He stared at the fire and smoked. It was some minutes before he spoke again, and then not until he had mixed me a drink. Then he said,

"Hold grudges? What for? I don't hold grudges. But time passes. It's been a long time, and we've gone different ways. Too far, perhaps, to come together again."

"I had to get news of you from others, and you can't blame me if the news was garbled. Why didn't you write to me?"

He turned to me abruptly, and pulled the pipe from his mouth. His eyes narrowed on me searchingly.

"I wrote," he said sharply. "They were returned. I took letters to your father and asked him to send them to you. I never thought that he wouldn't."

I stared at him blankly, my mind going round. Then a passionate fury rose up in me and I set my glass down on the table with a bang. But before I could speak, Dan lifted his hand and smiled at me. There was the old friendliness in his face again.

"Forget it, Jim. Never mind. It was a mistake. But it's gone, and nothing can be done." I stood up, infuriated.

"Nothing can be done! You always said that, Dan. It's a coward's excuse. I'll find out about it; someone's going to pay for it!"

He eyed me curiously, smiling as though somewhat amused. He shrugged. For some reason the dog stopped growling, and pushed out a tentative muzzle to me.

"Forget it," repeated Dan. I sat down, fuming. He made me feel young and foolish and impotent. After all, what could I do? I picked up the glass and drank the balance of the warming fluid.

"How do you like my place?" asked Dan with sheepish pride.

"Fine, I suppose," I answered morosely. He leaned back in his chair and smoked tranquilly. "I've got five acres. Take care of it myself. Everything I want. I just live here and browse like a starved horse that's gotten into good oats. It's all I want. For awhile. I never knew there would be such peace like this." He closed his eyes. The dog came to me and laid his head on my knee. I rubbed his head, and he closed his eyes blissfully.

"Isn't it lonely, Dan?"

"Lonely? My God! I tell you, I was always lonely until I came here. People make me feel lonely. But since I came here it's as if I have friends. All these books, the farm, the house, the freedom. Freedom. When you are free you are never lonely. It's only when you live among people that you are in prison. You can't be happy in prison, among people."

"Isn't that—a little antisocial?" I asked hesitatingly, and hated myself for the pat word.

"Antisocial?" He smiled at me amusedly. "What's antisocial? Not being able to endure fools gladly? Well then,

I'm antisocial. I must be free, free from eyes and mouths and faces. Faces like prison walls. Now, I'm free of faces. I don't see anyone except old Martha for months on end. And she keeps away from me." He looked about the room passionately. "I love this place, I tell you. Nothing would ever drive me away from it. Not even a fire," he added, and now there was something menacing in his voice. I laughed nervously.

"I don't think there's any danger of that," I remarked foolishly.

He was silent. His tanned face had become a little pale, and I did not like his expression. After a few moments he said, almost under his breath: "Why can't they leave me alone?"

"Are you sorry I came?" I asked, hurt. I expected an instant denial. But to my surprise and increasing hurt he did not say anything for a little while. Then he looked at me straightly as though studying me.

"I don't know," he said slowly and thoughtfully. "I don't know. Dick, here, seems to have accepted you. He only accepted two others, Sarah and Mort Rugby. He hates everyone else."

"Bee, too?" I asked boldly.

He was silent again, but as he looked at me a mask seemed to fall over his face, a rigid and repelling mask.

"So, that's why you came," he stated quietly. I stood up, much agitated.

"Dan, that's part of the reason I came. I woke up when I heard about you and Bee. I would have come anyway, after that. I wanted to see you desperately, even without —that. My God, how can I say it! Anything I say will only make you detest the sight of me. But, I've got to say it!"

"What?" The word was like the touch of an icicle. Dick retreated from me again, looking from me to Dan, and growling.

"Oh, hell, Dan, you know what I mean. Don't make me put it into words. When I heard that, I knew I had to do something to—save you. Damn it, yes, save you. I hardly believed it, at first. You and Bee Faire! I came out—"

"Like a saving angel!" His tone was hard and contemptuous.

"Dan, why are you doing this? She always hated you. Leopards," I added, without originality, "don't change their spots, or their characters. You never liked her, either. Nobody ever liked her, except old fools. Dan, she'll kill you. There—there's something poisonous about her. Look, I can look at you like this and know you don't care about her. You couldn't." He stared at the fire. "Dan, you don't know, but Sarah came to us last night, and begged me to save you, to keep you from marrying Bee. That's why I had to come, if for that reason alone."

He lifted his head and stared at me, his eyes glinting.

"Sarah came to you?"

"Yes." I was delighted that I had moved him at last. "She was afraid for you. She knows what Bee is." He put his pipe back into his mouth, and turned his head aside. I could see the skin on his forehead wrinkling, as though with pain. He began to speak as though to himself.

"I've got to marry her. Sarah's getting old. She can't live forever."

What the devil did he mean? I thought I was enlightened, and I said: "So, you're marrying Bee out of gratitude for her mother's kindness to you! What a damned quixotic notion! But now that you know that Sarah doesn't want you to marry Bee, I'm sure you'll oblige her in this." I smiled. But he neither looked at me nor smiled.

"Bee looks the image of Sarah," he muttered. "It'd be like having—" He put down his pipe abruptly and gazed at me for a long moment. The mask was still on his face.

"I'm marrying Bee in a few days," he said coldly. "After all, it's my business, not yours. I'm sorry Sarah doesn't want me to marry Bee. But I shall, anyway, and she'll get over it. I think you all underestimate Bee."

But I knew, with great clarity, that Dan did not underestimate her, either. I shook my head sadly.

"Always the dramatist, eh, Jim?" He was smiling. "Sorry I can't invite you to the wedding, but it's going to be quiet. In Ripley."

I was affronted. He glanced at my coat.

"You said something about a call around here, didn't you? Better get started. There's a blizzard coming soon, or my barometer's a liar."

I was too miserable to be insulted. I picked up my coat and put it on.

"There ought to be a law against this," I said with childish bitterness.

He picked up his book and deliberately began to read.

"Dan, if I go like this, we can't be friends. Believe me, I came here because I couldn't bear to think of you being unhappy. And you'll be so unhappy that—that you'll want to kill yourself. Or her. Dan, don't do it!"

"You're insolent," he said without looking up from the book. "No, we can't be friends. I don't want to see you. Not for a long time, anyway."

"Dan." I persisted; I felt that something terrible was about to happen to him, and he was too blind to see. "I've known Bee all my life. She's like a poison. I know. There's no heart or kindness in her. Only greed and hate and cunning. She sees only evil. She's always suspecting everyone of the basest motives. There's no good in the world to her. She—"

Dan lifted his head and voice and called, "Martha." The old woman came to the door. "Dr. Marcy is leaving, Martha. Will you show him the door?"

"All right," I said heavily. "I'll go. You needn't throw me out."

I waited a moment; he did not speak again, but read on. I went down the length of the room. I looked back at the doorway; he was still reading. I went out into the cold brightness of the winter day, and Martha slammed the door after me vigorously. The knocker rattled with the impact. Full of wretchedness, I unhitched my horse and drove away.

I hated him furiously for a little while. Then after awhile

I was overwhelmed with a deep and desolating sense of loss. I cursed myself. If I had gone to him six months ago I might have prevented this. And then I knew that I could not have prevented it.

I arrived home later in the deepest despair.

~~~~~~

Three days later, the day before New Year's, Dan Hendricks and Beatrice Faire were quietly married in Ripley. Not even Sarah was there; the witnesses were strangers.

The news exploded in South Kenton like a charge of dynamite. As my father said, there had not been that much excitement since the Civil War. Friends flocked to Sarah Faire with their condolences, and her abject grief and stupefied despair were all that even the most morbid could desire. The death of a dear one could hardly have affected her more deeply, and my mother said that the poor woman could not be alone. So Livy moved into Beatrice's room, and after school hours she filled the house with her resolute common sense and practical kindheartedness. I believe that in all of South Kenton, only Livy, Mortimer and myself understood the true cause of Sarah's anguish.

At first the sentiment of South Kenton was that the man should be horsewhipped, ridden on a rail out of town, even lynched. There were lurid threats made against him. He had seduced and tricked into marriage a sweet and innocent young woman, inveigled her into a secret wedding against her mother's knowledge and desire. There was nothing too bad for him. No wonder poor Sarah was so heartbroken, her lovely young daughter marrying a scoundrel and an outcast and a yellow dog like Dan Hendricks! There were dark speculations as to the sinister and evil pressure he must have brought upon the poor girl to make her commit such a desperate and terrible act. Some of the more romantic asked if he had held a mortgage on Sarah's house; others said he must have threatened her with obscure but dreadful penalties. A few of the young hotbloods suggested that they drag her forcibly from him and thrust him into an outbound cattle car. Three, I believe, actually went out to Dan's farm, but discovered that he and Beatrice had gone on a honeymoon, and old Martha did not know when they would return.

A month later they did return, and bought South Kenton's newest and prettiest house at the foot of Main Street. Old Endicott King had built the house at the request of Jack Rugby and Amelia Burnett, but when it was actually built and paid for Amelia took a dislike to it. Her papa and mama had bought ten acres in the suburbs and had built an immense house upon it, and disliking to be separated from their only child had asked the young couple to live with them. So the house, snug, of white stone and stucco, amazingly simple and beautiful for that era, had remained empty. This was the house that Dan Hendricks bought. Jack Rugby was a shrewd young man, and he saw no reason why he should not turn a handsome profit, even if it meant doing business with Dan.

An ominous silence fell over the town when the bridal couple moved in. With cold and menacing eyes it watched vanloads of beautiful new furniture from Ripley and from distant Warburton carried into the house, furniture which made the ladies sigh with envy. There was even a grand piano of rosewood and mahogany, the like of which South Kenton had never seen before. Beatrice was invisible, as was Dan, but a smart young girl was seen hanging magnificent curtains at the low, bowed windows. Finally two sleek horses appeared in the stable, and a grand new carriage.

South Kenton drew a deep breath, and looked sheepish. It began to argue diffidently. Well, perhaps, it was all for the best. They were moving into town, and setting up housekeeping just like other young folks, but more elaborately. That meant business for the stores and employment for two or three women, at least, for the house had immense gardens, and another smart young girl had joined the first. For a little while South Kenton felt resentment, then curiosity, then an active desire to take the bridal couple to its bosom. Evidently Bee, it argued, was having firm and serious effect on her husband. She would "make something out of him." They were signifying their intention of asking to be forgiven and received. Dan Hendricks' money— Ezra King made articulate the feelings of the whole town when he said: "We're Christians, aren't we? What's bygones is bygones. He's coming to us and asking us to take him in. Why not? It ain't his fault that he had a drunken father and everything when he was a boy. Bee'll make a man of him, show him the right way, civilize him, cure him of a lot of his fool ideas. No good raking up old coals." He spoke virtuously, for Dan had recently transferred his account to South Kenton's First National, and there was self-satisfaction in Ezra's dignified offer of forgiveness.

They moved into their new house quietly. South Kenton did not rush to extend the olive branch, nor did it kill the fatted calf immediately. It held itself woundedly aloof. It saw Beatrice come and go, with humble bent head; it saw her touch her eyes with the finest lace handkerchiefs, heard her soft and pleading voice. It saw Dan, too, but he seemed remote and quiet, minding his own business. South Kenton finally decided that they had been punished enough, and was melted in a rush by Bee's humility and gentleness and tear-filled eyes.

Bee gave a housewarming, sending humble and beseeching little notes to her friends, begging them to come to see her and Dan on the night of Thursday, February 2, 1897, at eight o'clock. Every worthy lady in town pretended to refuse, to shake her head, to demur and sniff, and murmur. They discussed with each other whether they ought to accept or not, but it was a foregone conclusion that they would. The discussion was merely atmosphere. Their husbands were going also. On the night of the party my parents prepared to go, and were astonished when I announced that I would remain at home.

"Why, I thought Dan was a particular friend of yours," said my father.

"Bee has a telephone, and if there are any calls Mabel can call you there, if necessary," objected my mother.

They went away together, unable to understand my continued refusal. When they had gone I dressed hastily and went to Sarah's little house where Livy was boarding. I knew that neither of the two women was going to Bee's party. Sarah's attitude had been the object of great, amazed, and somewhat indignant discussion for several weeks. She had apparently been unable to forgive her daughter, and when her friends urged her to do so, she would merely look at them with a strange white smile without answering. Livy had pleaded tiredness and a cold, and indeed the poor girl had been looking badly of late, and I was much worried about her. Her color was exceptionally bad, and she had become thin to the point of emaciation. She seemed always on the point of bursting into tears; I knew the symptoms of impending nervous breakdown. The children at school were apparently too much for her, just released from the burden of the care of her father and his house. Therefore her absence was not commented upon. As for Sarah, the excited indignation that followed her refusal to attend her only daughter's housewarming almost surpassed the excitement of the town when it had learned of Bee's marriage.

I arrived at the little old house. It stood, its trees weighted down with silent and heavy snow, banks of whiteness rising about it, one or two windows burning with a yellow light that fell softly on the snow, and all wrapped in a wash of dark blue moonlight and spectral shadows. Livy let me in, her slight figure pale and drooping in a dark red shirtwaist and serge skirt, her masses of black hair seeming too heavy for her tired young head. She told me that Mortimer Rugby was there, and that Sarah had been ill and had gone to bed. She did not appear to be particularly glad to see me, or rather, I should say, she seemed overwhelmed with a sort of stupefied lassitude, and her eyes closed frequently as she spoke to me. I tried to express my alarm and give professional advice as we stood in the hallway, Livy waiting for me to remove my coat and hat, but she glanced aside indifferently.

Though a fire burned in the little parlor, it seemed no longer gay and full of joy. A chill gloom had descended upon it; even the lamps looked cold, and the snow that was heaped on the window ledges sent their chill breath into the room. Before the fireplace, crouched in a chair, sat Mortimer Rugby, rubbing his hands. His head was sunken between the shabby folds of his coat, and his hair, white and thin though still long, looked like wisps of dead hair on the head of a skull. He turned his long and sunken face to me as I entered, blinked behind his glasses, and nodded. I could hear the dry whisper of his palms as he kept on rubbing them together. I had not shivered outside in the bitter cold of the February night, but I shivered now. I sat down opposite the old man, and Livy sat down between us. She had been knitting, apparently, and now resumed it. The small coals in the fireplace crackled, but they gave out no warmth, and I started involuntarily when a sudden wind rose and rattled the half-frozen windowpanes.

"Cold night," I said. Livy's needles clicked and she did not answer, but Mortimer nodded again. I remembered the room vividly as it had been in my childhood, bright and sunny and warm, with pots of geraniums burning red and bravely against the snow, and Sarah's happy voice. It was like a nightmare to me now. There was a faint odor of decay over everything, and I saw that the white paint on the gay little table was peeling off, showing patches of dull gray under it. I stood up, restlessly.

"You didn't go to Bee's party, I see, Mr. Rugby," I said. He shook his head without looking at me, then said dryly: "I don't like funerals, even if the corpse is set out pretty and natural and there are lots of flowers."

"I don't understand it," I said gloomily. "I don't know why Dan moved into town. He liked his farm out there; he seemed happy, for once. I thought nothing in the world would tear him away from it."

"Bee didn't like the farm, I suppose," said Livy quietly, without looking at me.

"Oh, it's impossible!" I burst out violently. "It's—it's like an Alice in Wonderland thing. Grotesque. I can't believe it's really Dan. I know him; he's not changed underneath. What has she done to him?" No one answered this; it was as if I had not spoken, and I went on dully, "She's poisonous. She's a—a sort of upas tree!"

Mortimer glanced across at me with a sudden wrinkling of his face into a smile. There was something wryly humorous in his voice as he remarked casually: "Upas tree. That's strong language. We three here don't like Bee. But I wouldn't make her so dramatic, if I were you, Jim. Too dramatic. I've done with drama; it only makes you ridiculous. Life isn't dramatic. It's just long, dull misery. No, I never liked Bee. You make her out to be some sort of a bloodsucker, sort of heroic or something, splendid, like Lucifer. She isn't. She's just a nasty, mean girl, selfish, sly, suspicious and cruel. But nothing so magnificent as a upas tree, which I hear bears very lovely flowers. There's nothing lovely about Bee." He paused. "I used to think Bee was a very bright girl, but it's only the brightness of cunning and self-seeking and greed. Like a weasel. Yes, there's something very much like a weasel about her," he added thoughtfully.

"And Dan's the poor rabbit," I exclaimed bitterly.

I expected him to smile again, but he merely looked at me oddly. "I don't know," he said slowly. "I don't know. I'm afraid not."

His remarked puzzled me then, but a long time later I remembered it, and marvelled at his penetration and the fear that seemed to hang on his words.

"I still don't understand it," I fumed. "It's beyond me. I can't see Dan being the perfect young husband around South Kenton, with a girl like Bee. It's like a bad dream. At any rate, I'm not going near their damn house."

Neither answered me. I looked restlessly from Livy, pale and silent in her chair, and Mortimer leaning toward the fire. Mortimer's legs were like mere sticks in his trousers, which fell over them in greenish folds. I thought involuntarily of the thickness of my father's thighs, straining against the cloth, held apart to give comfortable room to his great round belly. Mortimer was drawing his thin and trembling hand, knotted and corded, over his face, and I thought of my father's glistening white teeth which he picked daintily with a gold toothpick. The involuntary thought occurred to me that my father represented lusty and bellicose life, splendid at the table, loud and hearty of laugh, shrewd of mind though not very intelligent. And here was Mortimer who had thought much and suffered much, who had bruised his poor knees on the rough slopes of Parnassus without arriving at the summit, and now lay exhausted at the foot, defeated but understanding. My father had never seen the distant, incandescent peak of that mountain, and life in its littleness and meanness had satisfied him. He squeezed the last drop of milk from its udders. Nevertheless, I thought that he was the happier of the two. It was very puzzling to a young idealist. Must understanding of life bring decay and death and chill hopelessness? Is the only happiness in gusty animal enjoyments, in sitting back on fat haunches and tearing at red fragments with a strong teeth?

I wanted to go up to see Sarah, but Livy, with some agitation, asked me not to. Sarah was not really ill, she explained, but very tired. She did not add "queer," but I knew that was what she was holding back. We all sank into a cold depression. At last Mortimer rose and said he must go. I wondered with some resentment what he had been saying before I came, and why he did not say it to me. Livy asked him to remain for some hot coffee, but he refused. She helped him on with his galoshes with an almost daughterly tenderness. Just before leaving he put his hand on her shoulder, and pressed it, looking down into her eyes sorrowfully and understandingly. She averted her head quickly, and I saw that there were tears in her eyes. Grudgingly, I offered to drive him home, though I was annoyed at leaving Livy. But she asked me eagerly to return after taking Mortimer home, and I was mollified.

The parlor seemed even more gloomy and dim when I returned than before. Livy had put a small black shawl over her shoulders, and I was alarmed at her pallor. She looked tired and stricken as she gave me a wan smile. I sat down near her and took her hand.

"Livy, you look sick," I said. "Think of me as a doctor and not a friend. What is wrong?"

She smiled at me suddenly with such an utterly amused smile that I felt foolish and pompous and young. She did not withdraw her hand.

"Oh, don't, Jim," she said, and her voice was full of her old cheeriness. "There's nothing wrong. Don't be prosy like your father. I'm just tired, I expect, dragging out every morning in the snow, and everything. And I don't believe I like children very much," she added frankly. "In fact sometimes I hate them. I don't see how their parents bear them. I said something like that to Mrs. King once, and she was very indignant, and asked me significantly if I had ever said that to anyone else. She seemed to imply that it wouldn't be good for my job. She also added that I was a born old maid; old maids, it appears, always hate children, and long to murder them in secret." She laughed lightly.

I looked at her with grave longing, and chaffed her hand between mine. The fingertips were cold and tremulous. I noticed that she did not look at me, but at the fire, and that the smile on her face was a little fixed.

"Livy, why don't you marry me soon, now?" I asked gently.

I expected her to remove her hand. I expected evasion, again. But to my joyful amazement, she turned her face to me. It had become quiet and a little frightened; her eyes were slightly distended, and there was a wrinkling of pain in the clear brows above them.

"Are you sure, Jim?" she whispered. I was so surprised and overjoyed that I could not speak, but I must have looked very eloquent, for she smiled, and put her free hand to her cheek. I knelt beside her, drew her tired head down to my shoulder, and held her tightly. It seemed all at once to me that my depression and all my puzzling thoughts of problems retreated to a dreamy distance as I held her. I felt her slow tears against my neck, and I kissed them away. They continued to roll down her cheeks, but under them she was smiling with a heartbroken quietness.

"Just all worn out," I thought sympathetically. "My poor little Livy."

I forgot everything as I sat beside her, planning eagerly for our future together. She listened, nodding, her eyes fixed intently on my face as though she was trying to make it real. When I kissed her goodnight at last, her lips were cold but very gentle.

South Kenton's exclusive little circle was all agog over the housewarming of Bee and Dan Hendricks. Extravagant praise was expressed about their house, with its black marble fireplaces, thick rugs, rich red draperies and rosewood and mahogany furniture, glistening silver, fine linens, new lamps and beautiful grand piano. A dozen times or more I heard about the high ceilings, the circular staircase with its heavy carpeting, its paneled dining room and fine library. It was only after insistence that I heard much of Dan and Bee.

Bee? Oh, yes, she had been very dear, very gentle and submissive, and girlishly pleased at her guests' praises. She had worn, said my mother, a beautiful black velvet dress with old lace, and had looked exceptionally pretty. She was a perfect hostess, and did credit to her mother. Everyone had been enormously delighted with her and had petted her lavishly. It was just a little harsh of Sarah that she had not been there. No one could understand her.

Dan? This question always brought a blank though puzzled expression to their faces. Oh, Dan had been all right. Very quiet, but gentlemanly, and a little too aloof. He had been caught several times in the background, smiling to himself. No one seemed to like that smile. But he would "do." There was an improvement in him already. In time, she would make a man of him. He was not antagonistic at all, though, had not said one outrageous thing. He had seemed just a little too silent for general pleasure, however. The gentlemen had made dignified overtures to him, with a little something in their manner that suggested they were willing to be convinced and conciliated, but he had responded only courteously. He had been somewhat dense.

There had been a marvelous supper, extravagantly served. People smacked their lips happily, remembering it. In short, the whole thing had been a success, and South Kenton received the young couple to its matronly bosom.

When we heard that Sarah had refused admission to Bee and Dan a few days later when they had called upon her, public opinion became very sharp against her. After all, this was carrying the thing too far. Haven't we forgiven, South Kenton asked with virtuous surprise? What is the matter with Sarah? But Sarah shut herself into her house in silence, and would say nothing.

I did not see Dan, but I saw Beatrice at a distance, elegantly attired and elegantly mannered. I did not speak to her; I avoided her pointedly. When she and Dan called upon my parents, I made my escape before they arrived. My parents could not understand me. My father jeered at me for being a Pharisee and recalled my boyhood friendship with Dan. I remained stubbornly silent. I could not explain.

And Sarah remained silent. On the few times I saw her, when I called on Livy, she spoke to me listlessly, though with her old affection. She seemed to have aged very much. She never spoke of Dan and Beatrice.

Then my curiosity about Dan was swallowed up in my

great anxiety over Livy. Towards the end of March she
became ill, having caught cold in a sleet storm. It developed
into pneumonia, and for a time life became a hot nightmare,
dim and hideous, while my father and myself fought for her
survival. Sarah nursed her with passionate absorption, relieved for short intervals by my mother and other elderly
ladies. Finally the poor girl won through, and the fever
subsided leaving her beaten and haggard, with all her bones
painfully visible.

I breathed easier. Livy would live. For the first time I
was conscious of total exhaustion. I had devoted all my
time to Livy, and my father looked tired, also. When Livy
was stronger, we decided that we would be married about
June fifth. She seemed content. I had the impression that
she had been to a far and dreadful place and was now resigned. I could not shake off this impression, and it depressed me.

Chapter

Fifteen

My parents were outraged and aghast when Livy and I pleaded for a quiet wedding. Their only son, to be married furtively, like a farm boy and a farm girl! They would not hear of it for some time, and my mother actually made preparations for a big wedding. At the last moment, however, Livy had a sort of relapse, a sinking back into a sick lethargy which alarmed both me and my father. This alarm convinced my mother that any excitement would be bad for the girl, of whom she was sincerely fond.

My father said to me quietly, and with some hesitation: "You don't think, son, that Livy's a sickly girl, do you? Her parents weren't what you call husky. A man might as well cut his throat as marry an unhealthy woman. She'll make his life hell, fill up all his days with pills and whinings and self-pity, and won't show up with any disposition to warm his bed." He grinned at me sheepishly. "And there'll always be bills unpaid, and the house run by hired help, and no children that'll be worth having."

"You know Livy," I said angrily. "She doesn't seem sickly to you, does she? Well, then. Anyway, she suits me."

My father spent a week apologizing to his friends, and my mother to hers. So on June fifth Livy and I were married by the Reverend Mr. Pringle in the parlor of our new home. My uncle and aunt from Warburton were there, as were Livy's two sisters, stout, contented young matrons who talked constantly of how bad Livy looked, and gave her copious advice. There seemed little of the old Livy in the pale, quiet girl in dove-gray who stood beside me, except for the straight and resolute look in her eyes and somewhat pugnaciously lifted chin. After the ceremony and the rich dinner, we went away on our honeymoon to New York.

When we returned in July, Livy had gained weight, and there was a slight color in her cheeks. She liked New York; once she said that she wished we did not have to return to South Kenton, which astounded and hurt me. But she seemed delighted with our new apartment, in my parents' house, and directed our hired girl feverishly. We were soon settling down to a pleasant routine, for Livy was a good wife.

The usual course of events in those days was that a bride returned home already pregnant from her honeymoon. But Livy was not pregnant, and I was still satisfied, for I was very happy and wanted her to myself for a while.

We had not yet seen Bee and Dan Hendricks since our return as we sat out in the garden one hot August afternoon, the locusts shrilling in the trees and the yellow sunlight burning in the open places, making the eyes hurt with the dazzle of colors in the flowerbeds and around the white picket fence. There was a breathless and shining silence over the town, and Livy sat in her chair in a thin muslin dress, fanning herself, and occasionally pushing back her dark hair from her forehead. She was rapidly recovering her health, and there was quite a glow in her cheeks.

The garden gate clicked sharply in the hot stillness, and we looked up to see Dan and Bee approaching us smilingly across the grass. Livy sat upright, rigidly, her face paling; she stared at them without expression. I stood up, embarrassed, my own face becoming warm.

Bee lifted her gloved hand to us gaily, and tipped her ruffled parasol in greeting. Dan lumbered at her side, grinning. I shook hands with him awkwardly, and then dragged two chairs forward, making a circle. Bee had begun to talk to Livy in a sprightly fashion, her pretty face beaming, her hair a tangled mass of red gold under her rose-trimmed hat. I remember distinctly that she wore white lace with a pink sash, and all at once Livy looked drained and dowdy beside her. All the life seemed to have gone out of the poor girl.

We all sat down, chattering uneasily, except for Dan. He sat in silence, his long legs crossed. I had to admit that he looked more civilized than I had ever seen him, well shaven, his hair trimmed neatly, his high collar immaculate, his clothes tailored and neat. I kept glancing at him as I talked nervously about nothing in particular. I began to wonder if it was my imagination, or whether he did indeed look grim and tense under his faint grin, and if his eyes were indeed sultry and bitter. But his voice was careless enough when he began to speak; he told me of the new roses he had imported, the improvements he was putting in his house. About him was his old reserve, repulsing intimacy and curiosity. When he fell silent again at intervals, his face settled into heavy and sullen lines, and he stared stubbornly at his polished boots. He had developed a habit of flexing and unflexing his long brown fingers, and I soon found myself unwillingly unable to take my stare from them. Once he glanced at his wife while she was laughing and talking gaily to Livy, and an odd expression fixed itself for a moment on his face. When he found me looking at him, he stared at me coldly, beating down my eyes. I felt that I did not know him at all. I wished he had never come.

Bee seemed agreeable enough. She expressed much solicitude for Livy, rallying her on her pale face, her thin throat and arms. She glanced quickly from me and then more slowly from Dan to Livy and back again. Her rather narrow eyes danced with malicious mirth, for all her sympathetic voice.

"She looks as though she's got a secret sorrow, doesn't she, Jim?"

I felt irritated. She always had the ability to irritate me, to goad me. I felt that under her most casual words was an unclean meaning, a double innuendo.

"I don't think so," I said surlily. "She's had pneumonia, of course, and was all worn out."

Bee looked at Livy musingly. Livy's face was tranquil, and for some reason I felt that she had shut a door and was hidden behind it, even from me. Despite her forthrightness, Livy had never had a defense against Bee's sweet viciousness.

"She looks resigned," went on Bee with a light laugh. "Resigned to marriage, Livy dear? Ah, never be resigned. There's always hope, you know," and she laughed trillingly. She reached over and patted Livy's hand; though she touched it, I knew it was cold as though I myself had touched it, and I was vaguely frightened.

"You talk nonsense," I said roughly.

Bee widened her russet eyes at me innocently. "Dear me, aren't we brusque! I'm only teasing Livy a little. You never did have much sense of humor, Jim." I myself had always suspected this uneasily. She could always find the chink in the armor. But my anger was devoured in my astonishment at the sight of Dan's face. It was a dull and infuriated red.

I knew there were undercurrents here I did not understand, and my anger rose. For a long moment there was a distinctly heavy silence.

During all this time we had not mentioned our long absence from each other. We had not spoken of Dan's marriage; we had talked like casual strangers, warily avoiding all dangerous pits of conversation. But I felt that we were all watching each other, each with a different reaction.

Bee now indicated Dan with an airy wave of her white-gloved hand.

"Haven't I improved him, civilized him?" she demanded playfully. "Come, now, Livy, would you have recognized him?"

Livy looked at Dan straightly, and he looked at her. In his gaze was something sad and understanding beyond my comprehension, but there was no pity. It were as though he knew he could not insult her with pity. Again I was conscious of undercurrents, and I moved restively in my chair.

"Dan looks very nice," said Livy tranquilly, and she smiled with gentleness. "No, I would hardly have recognized him." And now she turned her quiet eyes upon Beatrice, who, to my increasing bewilderment, colored. Her lips tightened shrewishly, and she breathed quickly as though she were restraining herself.

"Yes, I've improved him," she said carelessly, and when she smiled at her husband her eyes sparkled humorously. He returned her look, and then I saw something in his face that horrified me. It was hate, not a hot and furious hate, but a calm and unashamed hate, steady and unmoved. "He looks almost as if he's forgotten his 'fruitful grape,' doesn't he?" Bee went on, twirling her shut parasol under her hand. She glanced at us archly. "Surely you haven't forgotten Dan's 'fruitful grape'? Don't you remember how he quoted it to us a long time ago, when we rode out on our bicycles to the hills?"

"What are you talking about?" asked Dan in a low voice. "Don't you know you are boring them?"

"Boring them?" Beatrice lifted hurt and astonished eyebrows, and glanced pleadingly from Livy to me. "Am I boring you, dears?"

Livy murmured deprecatingly, but she looked a little sick, and I was alarmed.

"I'm sure I wouldn't bore anyone for the world," said Bee animatedly. "Dan is always so careful about conversation. He doesn't like nonsense." She smiled at us girlishly.

"But I like nonsense. It's such an airy, pretty thing, like shuttlecocks dancing in the sunlight."

"There are hard blows under the shuttlecocks," said Livy. Her voice was soft, but it seemed to have a bell-like ring like a warning.

Bee shrugged. "You are all so difficult. I'm afraid there's not a drop of humor in any of you. Well. I wanted you both to see Dan again. Of course, I know with your wedding, and Livy's illness, and everything, you have been very busy. I must admit that I wanted to show Dan off. I'm so proud of him," and she smiled humorously at her husband. "And he does everything to please me. He even gave up his horrid little farm, with that old witch Martha, for me, and let me persuade him to move into town."

Dan's face was without expression. I made a valiant attempt to wrest the conversation from the woman.

"Well," I said cheerily, "everything's going fine, I see. And we're coming to the twentieth century. Think of that! Sometimes I can—I can almost hear it, like great wheels rumbling. I'd like to bet anything that we'll see mighty changes in the twentieth century. Peace and glory and wonders and marvels such as the world has never seen before. Think of it! Our children will have something to live for in that century, I can tell you!"

Bee gazed at me blandly. "Peace? I think not. A bigger world, more hate and bigger wars. It wouldn't surprise me to see us wipe each other out. Glory? You can't put glory into dark minds, and human nature never changes. Wonders and marvels? For what purpose? To be swallowed up in wars and hate and stupidity?"

"I don't agree with you," I said angrily. "We'll have security we never had before. Our children will be secure."

"Secure?" Dan's quiet voice broke into the conversation. "Yes, perhaps it's our duty to make the world secure for our children."

"Secure?" asked Livy clearly. "No, I would not want my children to live secure lives. I think security is something like dying; wasn't it Homer who said that the arts die in peace? If I have children, I want them to live splendidly. You can't live splendidly in security; it chokes you."

I was irritated. During the past year Livy had seemed to forget her old "notions" which had occasionally annoyed the older people in South Kenton. But my irritation grew less as I saw how her eyes were sparkling with their old resolution and courage, and how her lips had suddenly become warm and rich again. She was not speaking to me; she was speaking to Dan Hendricks, and as he studied her gravely a warmth came into his face also, a slow and kindled animation that I had not seen for a long time. But he said nothing.

Beatrice laughed lightly. "Dear me, what a radical! I thought you had become such a sedate puss this last year or two, Livy." She touched her lips with her handkerchief and looked over it at us merrily. But the glow left Livy's face as Beatrice spoke, and she looked down at her clasped hands. What hideous enchantment did this woman have, that her lightest words seemed to cast a shell of stone over everything that was moving and living? A certain rigidity passed over Dan, also. I stared from one to the other, increasingly annoyed and puzzled. Beatrice turned to me. She spoke casually, but in the clear brown of her small eyes there lingered and danced the old malice and cruelty.

"I hear marvelous reports about you, Jim. You seem to have settled down comfortably in your papa's shoes. Well, they are well-lined and very warm, I have no doubt. Fortunate young man! You, at least, prefer security to danger, don't you? The fireside, while the battle goes on outside. Locked shutters, while the mob passes. High walls shutting out the war. I think you are very wise. Politicians seem alarmed at the trend from the farms and the farm towns to the cities of ambitious young men and women. I think they would be pleased to see you settling down so snugly, without any desire for Livy's fine danger, and getting gray and stout like your papa, and rich, taking care of all of us."

She regarded me with hypocritical admiration. I found it suddenly difficult to swallow. As though she had been an evil witch, she conjured before me with consummate and diabolical skill all the dreams I had had when I had been a boy at school—all the beautiful and opulent dreams that were ending here in this quiet little town and dying of inertia. She must have remembered the few juvenile things I had said. She never forgot. I was conscious of overwhelming misery and pale despair. While I floundered about in the welter of my painful thoughts she continued to regard me with smiling admiration, but in her smile was that wicked glee she always had when she had hurt someone bitterly. A sodden silence seemed to fall upon all of us except Beatrice, who, after waiting for my reply which did not come, glanced at Livy and Dan with the utmost good humor. In that silence the leaves of the trees began to lift and shiver like sharp dark shadows against the intense and shining blue of the sky, and a dimness fell over the bright garden.

I cleared my throat. I had an odd notion that if I did not speak, did not stir her other victims to life again, we would sit there forever, petrified by a sinister enchantment. I turned to Dan.

"Are you selling your farm, Dan?"

He stirred with visible effort and glanced at me almost listlessly.

"No. I'm renting it to old Martha's grandson and his wife. She's living with them out there." He fixed his eyes on mine, and we both remembered the time I had been there, and my ignominious dismissal. I felt myself coloring. But in his expression was not apology nor expression of any kind. I wondered vaguely if he thought we were enemies; there was something inimical in the set line of his lips. I looked from him at last to Beatrice, so graceful and gay, and watching, always watching. It seemed to me like a dream, without explanation and full of torment.

Beatrice laughed a little, and said to Livy: "Dan and I went to see Mama two weeks ago. Dear, silly old thing, to make such a fuss about our wedding! Well, she came to the door, and tried to close it again when she saw us, but Dan held it open with his hand, and said: 'I want to come in, Sarah.' And would you believe it?" Her roving eye flicked each of us like a red-hot lash. "She let us in! And cried, poor old darling, looking so broken and old and faded! But Dan always did have a way with Mama. Sometimes, jealous little goose that I am, I thought they were both fonder of each other than they were of me! Well, Mama wouldn't let me kiss her for awhile, and kept staring at us both so mournfully, that I thought I would break down myself. And then she said to me: 'Bee, you'll be good to Dan, won't you?' I was so surprised! And after that, she and I just cried together like silly babies, and I knew I was forgiven. She has been to see us several times since then, and we are to have Sunday dinner with her. I asked her to live with us, but she won't. Likes her silly little old house too well, I suspect, but Mama always did have queer tastes. She never liked grand furniture and plenty of big fires and damask drapes. Sometimes I wonder if she really had much taste. I always felt pained at home."

"Your mother had more than good taste," said Livy quietly. "She is a good woman. She would never hurt anything or anyone." She looked directly at Bee, who laughed again, her light and affected laugh.

"Sometimes I think the desire not to hurt anything is just cowardice," she said smilingly. "Life is harsh and raw; you eat or be eaten. I think it is much nicer to eat."

"Even at another's expense," I said hoarsely.

Bee nodded delightedly. "Why not? Life for the eater is very interesting. I would rather be a lion than a rabbit. I would rather hunt than be hunted. You have only those two choices." She stared at me with her light-filled eyes, and I had the eerie sensation that behind those eyes was nothing but a devouring hunger and lust and hate, an elemental power that flowed directly from elemental Nature, who has no conscience and no compassions. That is why I think, even now, that Beatrice was more alive and vital than any of us; she was atavastic, and we were attenuated by the consciences and the ideals of an artificial civilization. A host of platitudes blew about in my mind like scraps of silly paper in a high wind, but I dared not speak them for fear of her ridicule. I knew she was wrong, that natures like hers are the deadly foes of all nobilities and human grandeurs, but they are alive, more vital than those nobilities and grandeurs. And she gleefully watched me suffer, seeming to know everything that went on in my mind, knowing she had defeated me.

"Why so glum, Jim?" she purred. "Have I hurt your feelings? I hope not. I'm just teasing you. I used to tease you a long time ago, and you used to get glum, just the way you are doing now. Don't be glum; it's the first sign of fatness, and dear me! aren't you getting a little stout already? Oh," she continued animatedly. "I heard about that free little hospital you are trying to interest us all in, where children can get treatment and care, and others who can't pay won't have to die because they are afraid they can't pay their bills. I think that is just splendid. So Christian and noble—and everything. You must let us contribute too. We would feel hurt if we were left out."

The little hospital-clinic had been my dearest hope and dream for the past few months, inspired by Livy. I can say honestly, even now, that I had no "noble" motive, or ulterior object, in planning for and speaking of it to my friends, but suddenly it seemed to me that Beatrice had stirred up all sorts of base motives in my mind, was making me feel small and mean and crafty, a petty philanthropist making a bid for virtuous applause and approval. My heart began to pound.

"You can contribute a thousand dollars," I said, staring at her. I was pleased at the startled expression in her narrowed eyes. "Everyone else is giving. Of course, it isn't settled yet, not even the site decided on. We're going to have a meeting next Monday. I hope both of you will be there."

I was so intent in my effort to beat her down, that when Dan spoke, though very quietly, I was startled.

"If you want, you can have the land Billy's old store stands on. The store is empty; there is an acre behind it. I think that would be a good location, right in the center of town."

"But Dan," said Beatrice quickly, with a sharp flush on her cheeks, "Mr. Ezra King told you that William Goodrich from Ripley would give you a good price for that store and the land." Her mouth worked with tense anger and greed, though her voice was ever so soft. Dan did not look at her; he continued to regard me quietly.

"The land's yours whenever you want it," he repeated. "For nothing."

I thanked him confusedly. Beatrice had fallen silent, but her eyes glittered. Before any of us could speak again, the garden gate clicked, and old Mortimer's lank and blowing figure, like that of an ancient scarecrow, came across the grass to us. He carried his hat in his hand, and the summer wind tossed the silvery wisps of his hair about his pale skull. The sun was in his eyes and he did not see us distinctly until he was almost up to us. Then he started visibly. He looked slowly around our little circle, and deep lines fell about his mouth. I pulled a chair forward for him. Beatrice seemed to forget her rage; she began to fan herself gently with her perfumed handkerchief, and regarded Mortimer with a smile, the old malice lighting up her face again. She shook her finger archly at him.

"Ah, you bad old thing! You haven't been to see us at all. Are you a hermit these days?"

Mortimer glanced heavily at Dan, who was again regarding his feet, then glanced back at Beatrice.

"Yes, I'm a hermit, except for my friends," he said in his dry and rustling voice.

"Then, you mustn't be a hermit with us," exclaimed Beatrice. "Dan often speaks of you. You hurt us badly. Only last night I said to him: 'I wonder why our dear old poet never comes to see us?' Why, I can remember whole lines of your 'Man—Crucified.' I really think that was one of the most wonderful poems in the world. So beautiful and sublime. You ought to be world-famous now, a sort of poet laureate. The world is so unappreciative."

I writhed internally. Dan's face had become a dull red, and Livy had turned her head aside. Mortimer said nothing;

he merely regarded Beatrice intently, his withered hands swinging between his knees. Beatrice beamed on him fondly, turning her knife in the poor old wretch whom none of us could rescue without betraying to her that we recognized her viciousness.

"The world is so unappreciative of real worth," she went on. "It gives fame and fortune to everything trashy, and never remembers the truly great until after their death. It's poor consolation for you, however, isn't it, Mr. Rugby?"

The poor, defeated starer at the brilliant peak of Parnassus still said nothing. He continued to regard Beatrice without expression. Once he drew his hand slowly over his face. Dan stood up abruptly. He glanced at his heavy gold watch.

"It's time to go," he said rudely. Beatrice rose, and I stood up. But old Mortimer did not stir. He looked stricken.

"Now, you must all come to see us soon, all of you. We haven't measles, you know," said Beatrice, glancing brightly at all of us. She pulled on her gloves. "Livy, you mustn't be a hermit, too. Remember, you are my dearest friend. And Jim, here, and Dan, always used to be together. Marriage doesn't change anything at all."

Dan did not even say goodbye; he and Beatrice went away together across the sun-bright grass, she swaying gracefully. We could hear her light hum. There was a slight stoop to Dan's shoulders. They went out the gate, and at that moment my father and mother drove up after a day's shopping. My mother leaned out of the carriage to kiss Beatrice warmly, and shake her head at Dan. They were too far away for us to hear what they said, but we heard Bee's gay laugh, and my father's lusty rumble.

As for us, it seemed that something unclean had left us, but left us with a sick odor in our nostrils. Mortimer was the first to speak.

"You know, of course, Jim, that Dan loves Sarah Faire, don't you?"

When I looked at Livy I saw by her expression that this

was no news to her. I stood up, fuming, and thrust my hands in my pockets.

"Why, that's disgusting!" I exclaimed. Mortimer shrugged.

"Why? I don't think so. It answers all the questions you ever asked about Dan's marriage, I think. It happens to be true, too."

The forgiving ardor South Kenton had extended to Dan Hendricks began to cool, for though he continued to be courteous and properly silent on forbidden topics, he never allowed anyone to approach him. South Kenton resented this hard reserve. Dan was showing no real appreciation of South Kenton's magnanimity. He did not seem to remember that he had once been an outcast. He had no becoming humility and gratitude. He went wherever Beatrice went, but no one could remember afterwards what he had said. He did nothing outrageous, but public opinion turned against him. Openly expressed pity for Bee was frequent. The older people loved her more than ever.

Even her contemporaries became affectionate towards her. As they grew older their perspicacity lost its keenness and clarity. Bee was so sweet, the younger matrons said, blissfully forgetting how they had avoided her during school-days. Such a perfect wife and housekeeper and hostess. Always so gently grateful for all patronizing favors. Livy and I were forced dozens of times to listen to eulogies about her, to be silent before lifted brows and acid comments when Dan was mentioned. I was even compelled to keep still when it was learned of the free gift of land for the little hospital. Opinion was unanimous that Bee was behind it, and South Kenton wrapped her enthusiastically in its arms. She did not deny the affectionate accusation, but merely smiled deprecatingly.

Livy and I avoided as much as possible any contact with the Hendrickses. This was difficult, for our circle was small. We were obliged to call on them and to receive them. On the surface everything was pleasant and amiable. But Dan and I never approached friendship and familiarity. He held me off with unseen arms. Often I could not believe that we had ever been friends. Bee was always dropping in to see Livy, and it enraged me that after these visits the poor girl looked beaten and drained, though so far as I could tell Bee had been her most affable self.

In the fall Beatrice was taken ill with quinsy. I made an excuse to keep from tending her, leaving that to my father. But I hoped feverishly that she would die, and on one hideous occasion I regretted that my father had taken her case and not I. A little neglect, a little carelessness—I shivered for days after, remembering that one blazing moment when I had thought of it. I was still the idealist, the devoted worshipper of Hippocrates. When my father announced that she was recovering I felt an hysterical relief, as though I had been delivered from committing a crime.

Life moved on heavily and placidly in our little town. We were mildly excited by lectures, and the majority of us were delirious when that noble Don Quixote, William Jennings Bryan, passed through South Kenton and deigned to illuminate our bucolic minds with a few kind words. For several weeks afterwards no one spoke of much else besides free silver. Because of him our aristocrats looked graciously and pityingly at our proleteriat and farmers, and Willie

Williams affected a Bryanese haircut for a long time and spoke of devoting his legal talents to heroic causes.

Then we were filled with horrified thrills when Jane Mundell quietly committed suicide, smothering herself with gas from her mother's new kitchen range. The girl was a pale and ultra-feminine creature, with a slight figure and a pretty face of such little expression that one hardly recalled her features afterwards. She had very little to say, was very religious, possessed a nervous and uncertain smile and voice and little deprecating, timid gestures. She had had one or two suitors, the most ardent of whom had been Willie Williams, who had developed a profound and inarticulate hatred for Mary Knowles, Jane's "dearest friend," masculine and arrogant and excessively definite.

I had heard casual rumors that Mary had quarreled with the pathetic little creature, who always seemed to be looking for someone to vent her devotion upon. Mary had called her "a complete fool," and when the two met, the gentlemanly Mary had been aggressively rude to the poor girl, who had wilted visibly. South Kenton was too innocent to realize or see the undercurrents here; they thought it was really very hard of Mary Knowles to refuse to see poor little Janie when the latter came to see her. They saw no connection between the tragic suicide and Mary Knowles; I am sure they would have torn her to pieces had they known. Neither did they see the slimy thread that had begun to grow stronger between Mary and Susan Crawford, a prim, old-maidish girl who had taken Livy's place at the school. They merely commented that Susan had never seemed to care for young men, that she was a born old maid, with her priggish manners, oversensitiveness, and air of continually looking for slights. They did not trace the sinister connections between Jane's death, Mary Knowles, and Susan Crawford.

But besides myself, there were two, I am sure, who suspected the truth. My father seemed abstracted for some time after Jane's death, and finally he told me guardedly that he had gone to Susan's father, a beefy and noisy man with whom my father had little in common. I understand that

Mr. Crawford had palmed off an inferior horse on my father, who fatuously believed he knew something of horse-flesh. What my father had said I do not know, but Susan was suddenly shipped off to relatives in Pittsburgh, "for her health." It was the first time that I had heard that city recommended as a health resort, but I kept my thoughts to myself. Six months later Susan married one of her second cousins.

The other one who knew was Beatrice Faire. Trust her to know everything evil and obscene! One night some dozen of us young married couples were sitting together at a church sociable, Bee exquisite in dark blue wool and silver. Mary Knowles sat there in her excessively mannish suit, her arm over the back of her chair and her legs crossed in a most gentlemanly manner. She was talking indulgently and affectionately to Matilda Hughes, who had just recently married Bob Cunningham, and her free hand touching, very delicately the girl's round and rosy face. Then Bee's voice, clear and sharp as a rapier, rose above the casual chatter about us. She spoke to all of us apparently, but her dancing eye roamed to Mary Knowles.

"They do say poor Mr. Withers has taken to drink since poor little Janie's death," she said, sighing. "Wasn't it awful? I'll never forget it. I'm sure it was an awful shock to you, Mary, wasn't it, you two being such dear friends?"

Mary's horsy face thickened with dark blood. She and Beatrice stared at each other with naked hate. Then Mary shrugged; her voice was a little hoarse when she said:

"We weren't 'dear friends' for a long time, Bee darling. Jane become quite impossible. No intellect. Really very tiresome. Of course, I'm sorry she's dead. But she never seemed to have anything to live for."

"I'm sure life must be very interesting for you," said Beatrice with an air of soft meditation and envy. Mary was silent; she sat glowering, her sharp bold eyes betraying, to me at least, sudden fear.

Beatrice murmured. The others glanced questioningly at each other; they felt undercurrents of tension, but were too ignorant to understand them. I understood them, and for the first time I felt glee myself and silently applauded Beatrice. I watched, gloatingly.

"Life is always interesting, except for fools," said Mary at last; above her collar I saw the straining cords in her neck. She knew that Beatrice knew, and Beatrice knew that Mary knew this and Bee daintily moistened her lips.

"I suppose so," she said regretfully. "I have always been so sorry that I am not so intellectual as you, Mary. It must be quite—exciting, to have such—intellect. So, sort of strange, isn't it? Something quite out of our humdrum experience. I've sometimes thought that you were one of these New Women we hear so much about, but I'm sure now that I'm mistaken. I don't think even the New Woman is so—so intellectual, after all.

Mary stood up abruptly, tall in her tweeds, her shoulders unusually broad and straight.

"I don't find your conversation intellectual, Bee," she said insultingly. But again I saw fear in her eyes. She glanced about her uncertainly at the surprised faces of our innocent friends, and drew a sharp breath. She looked at Bee again, who was gently and musingly smiling, as though at angelic thoughts.

"You're—you're pretty much of a skunk, Bee Hendricks," she said shortly, and stalked away from us. Stupefied silence followed this apparently unprovoked insult, and after a moment everyone but myself and Livy made indignant comments and sympathized with Bee, who sighed regretfully.

"Mary is so touchy," she murmured. "She always was. She doesn't look very well, either; she hasn't looked well since poor Janie's death. She ought to go away for her health."

Mary apparently thought so, too, for a few weeks later she and her mother went away for a long trip.

ぞぞぞぞぞぞぞぞぞぞぞぞぞぞぞぞぞぞぞぞぞぞぞぞぞぞ

One night in early spring I returned at ten o'clock at night from a country visit. It had been a long, hard confinement case, and I was worn out. I passed the brightly lit American House Bar, and hesitated. It was pretty late, and I was tired, but the sight of several of my friends standing at the bar persuaded me to enter. It was a Wednesday night, when a few farmers came to town, and the thought of a cold glass of beer and a little chaff was attractive. I might even have a game or two of checkers, or a few rounds of poker. I entered, and was greeted vociferously. I was surprised to see Dan Hendricks smoking quietly at a table in a blue haze of smoke, a glass of beer before him. He did not often go there at night. He returned my nod curtly, and I stood at the bar and ordered whiskey. The bartender was a smart young man from Ripley, with deft elbows and a flashing grin. Ed Ford often came in for a word with us, a broad and ruddy man with curled mustache and shirtsleeves and heavy gold chain. I did not see him tonight. He usually spent his evenings playing cribbage with his stout and placid wife in the ornate red plush parlor behind the saloon.

Though my back was to Dan I was acutely conscious of him. I had the idea that he was watching me, but that if I turned to him he would repulse me as usual with his cold gravity and impersonal remarks. We all laughed, and joked, and ribbed each other for a time.

The door opened, and we glanced at it expectantly, hoping for another reveller. But the man entering was one we all knew only slightly. He was a poor miserable farmer of the Wally Lewis type, shambling, emaciated, with weak pale eyes, and a frightened air. He lived on a stony plot of land near Big Creek, and though he worked hard he seemed to have the perpetually hard luck of a lot of dirt farmers. He was about fifty years old, with sunburned, wrinkled face, and broken hands. His name was Abe Witherbee. I knew him better than the others, for I had recently attended his wife for goiter. I nodded to him in my father's best casual manner, and went on talking to my friends.

The man glanced about him timidly, almost imploringly, rubbing his hands together. He wore a rough buttonless coat over his clean and faded overalls, and his high boots were caked with mud. He seemed to hesitate, begging for notice. At length the bartender looked at him with his tiny sharp eyes, and grinned impatiently.

"Well, what'll you have, Abe? Come on up to the bar." He grinned at us with a foxlike smile. "Whiskey? Beer? Gin?"

The farmer still hesitated, but did not approach the bar. He glanced at all of us imploringly, as though seeking a friend.

"You know I'm a teetotaler, Barney," he whined diffidently. "You know I don't hold with liquor. Signed the pledge when I was a boy. But that ain't what I come to tell you." He swallowed convulsively. My friends leaned idle elbows on the bar and waited; there was an air of resolute fright, which amused them, about the man.

"Well, speak up!" said Barney, shaking up a Tom Collins for Willie Williams. "I can't wait all night. Get it off your chest."

The farmer gulped. "Well, sir, I jest wanted to ask you not to sell my boy Charlie any more liquor. He ain't a bad boy, Charlie, but he's got a taste for the drink. Spends all his money, and all he can git or take from me, on sech. All the last spring he came home, jest a reelin', and takin' on so his maw's scared to death. Almost got killed yistiddy mornin' runnin' the plow. All on account of his drinkin'. He ain't a bad boy when he don't drink. Good's a boy you'd find anywheres. But it's killin' his maw slow. He's the only boy we got, and we was always right proud of him. Wanted to send him away to school. He ain't but eighteen even now, and when he ain't drinkin' he's got all sorts of idees. Might amount to somethin'. I got five hundred saved, and I want to send him to Ripley. Once he had the idea of bein' a doctor." And now the poor wretch glanced at me timidly with watering and terrified eyes. I stirred uncomfortably.

Barney laughed shortly. "If he don't get it here, he'll get it some other place, Paw," he sneered. "Besides, we ain't in the church business, and ain't aimin' to save no souls. Long's your Charlie's got the cash, we'll serve him liquor. When he ain't, out he goes," and he made a flippant motion with his hands towards the door.

"No!" said the farmer eagerly. "If he don't get it here, he can't get it nowheres. Other folks promised not to sell him anythin' they made theirselves. And Ripley's too far. By the time he got there he'd have his sense back. Charlie's a good boy—"

"If he's that damn good, you can keep him at home," snorted Barney. "If that's all you got to say, git. I'm busy. This saloon ain't run for love. We're in the business." He pointed at the door.

Abe wrung his hands together desperately, and anguish stood in his pale eyes.

"Please listen to me jest a minute," he begged. But at that moment Ed Ford, who had an uncanny ear for altercations even of the mildest in his saloon, entered, scowling. He had no desire to embroil himself with the virtuous ladies of South Kenton, and always notified us that if we weren't gentlemen we could get the hell out of his place, and stay out.

"What's all this?" he growled, his red face barren of its usual affability.

"Oh, this here hick's raisin' Cain 'bout us sellin' his good boy Charlie liquor," shrugged Barney. "I just told him we'll sell it to him long's he's got the money."

Abe turned passionately to Ed Ford, who had advanced threateningly, one big fist clenched.

"Mr. Ford, you'll listen to me, won't you? Charlie's a good boy. It's jest that he drinks too much, and I been askin' this boy here not to sell him liquor. I been sayin'——."

"Out!" roared Ed, like a maddened bull. "I'm not listenin'. Out!" He seized the hapless devil by the scruff of his neck and started to drag him towards the door. Then suddenly Dan was beside him, his hand was invisibly removed from Abe's neck, and Dan, quiet and grave, was between the two men.

"No, you don't," he said calmly. "You'll listen to what he has to say, Ed Ford. When you listen, you can decide what you have to do. And perhaps you'll decide to do it."

My friends stared at each other with consternation and outrage.

Ed Ford swelled with fury; his vast cheeks turned purple. He raised his fist, but looking at Dan's quiet face, he let the fist fall slowly to his side. He twisted his loose mouth into a smile, and put his hands jauntily on his huge hips, rocking back on his heels.

"So, Mister Dan Hendricks, you'll tell me how to run my business, will you? You'll tell me who to sell liquor to, and who not to, eh? You'll stick your ugly face into my affairs, will you?" His smile faded suddenly, and he thrust Dan furiously in the chest. "Why, you so-and-so, who the hell do you think you are?"

Things moved so fast then that I could barely follow them, but the next instant Ed Ford hit the floor with a crash, and Dan stood over him, rubbing his knuckles. Everyone at the bar was stupefied, and merely stared. Abe Witherbee cringed backwards, rubbing his hands uneasily over his hips.

"You wouldn't listen to Abe. But you'll listen to me," said Dan in his slow voice. "And now, listen. You won't sell his Charlie any more drink. You'll kick him out if he shows his face in here. If you don't," and he rubbed his fist meditatively, "there's more where that came from."

He took Abe firmly by the arm and led him out of the saloon.

Uproar broke out. Several helped Ed Ford to his feet, and everyone talked at once. What Dan had done was unpardonable; comment upon him came fast and furious. Everyone threatened to cut him off from that moment on. Why, the dirty, sneaking, cowardly so-and-so! Taken in by good society, and the first chance he gets he commits assault and battery on a decent citizen! Well, that went to show you that a yellow dog was a yellow dog, even if he got himself a golden collar! All the stored and unexpressed resentment and hate they had all felt for him since Dan had acquired his money a few years back foamed to the surface. Tension was relieved; everyone expressed himself freely. There was a sort of exhilaration in the townspeople, now that they could speak their minds. They crowded outside, filling the cool spring night with their indignant voices.

I went home alone. The only thing that seemed important to me was that Dan's eye had touched me during his altercation. All I could think of was the old affair about Wally Lewis. And somehow I knew that Dan had remembered, also, and was also remembering that now, as then, I had only stood by. I went home, hating both myself and him.

∾∾∾∾∾∾∾∾∾∾∾∾∾∾∾∾∾∾∾∾∾∾∾∾∾∾∾∾

Eighteen

By early morning the whole town knew about the affair, and the reaction of South Kenton was identical with that of the young men who had witnessed it. There was a sort of sadistic pleasure in everyone's face; everyone could express openly what he had been constrained from saying recently about Dan Hendricks. It were as if a tight constraint had been loosened, and all breathed freely and delightedly. They again had an excuse to lacerate the stranger they had always hated.

I was eating breakfast the next morning when my father stamped upstairs, smiling unpleasantly.

"They tell me you were around when that precious friend of yours beat up poor old Ed Ford," he said, nodding at Livy, who was pouring my coffee.

"Yes. I was." I told my father what had taken place. He growled.

"No sense to it, at all. You'd think he'd mind his own business, and step careful, now that we've taken him in. But no, he's got to make a damn fool of himself. Well, let him take care that this ain't the end for him. We've stood him on account of Bee——"

"You've stood him on account of his money," I broke in, throwing my napkin from me. "Just his money! He was right; he's always right. But none of you have the guts and the decency to see it. What's Ed Ford to you? Nothing. But you've all just been looking for an excuse to knife Dan. Why not be honest about it? Bee! Why, by God, if he strangles her some day, it'll be what she deserves! He's too damn good for this town, for all you——" Fury choked me, and my father and I glared at each other. He was petrified, and I stamped out of the room.

I drove madly over to Dan's house. I had always detested its pretty elegance, it artificial daintiness. It reeked of Bee. But I burst in, calling for Dan. He was sitting alone eating his breakfast. He did not seem surprised to see me, but neither did he say anything. He merely waited.

Suddenly I felt foolish. We were all, in small-town manner, making a mountain out of a molehill. Dan's expression seemed questioning, as though he were wondering indifferently why I had come.

"Dan," I mumbled. "I want to tell you that, as usual, you were right."

A silence fell. I had had the feeling, before arriving here, that the past years had vanished from between Dan and me, that we were where we had been before. But, as I stood before him now, the years crowded up between us like a glacier, and I felt a complete fool.

Dan smiled slightly. He indicated a chair.

"Sit down and have some coffee," he said. I listened eagerly for the old friendliness, but it was not there. There was only faint amusement. I sat down awkwardly, cursing myself for coming.

I drank the coffee, almost choking over it. Dan ate calmly. Then he said with indifference:

"About last night? What's all the excitement about? You act as though I had been accused of murder, and you were rushing over to tell me you were going to stand by me." He shrugged. "That isn't the first time Ed Ford's been knocked down, after all."

I started to get up. I could feel intense heat in my face. I was about to make a sarcastic comment and leave, when the dining room door opened and Bee came in. In the early morning light she looked strained and pinched, her eyes hard and vicious. All the burnished color, which made her such a startling replica of her mother had gone. Here was just a pale and shrewish woman, venomous and full of hate. She stopped when she saw me, and then put her handkerchief to her eyes and burst into tears. Dan waited indifferently, idly stirring his coffee.

"Oh, Jim!" she sobbed. "I'm so glad you came! It shows me that my friends haven't deserted me after all! Even after what he did! Making such a fool of himself, alienating everybody, after all the work and effort it took me to make people look at him and treat him like a decent human being! Trying to make everybody forget what he was, coaxing and wheedling everybody to accept him—" She became hysterical.

"Stop making a fool of yourself," said Dan quietly. "Sit down and eat your breakfast."

She dashed the handkerchief from her face. Her features were contorted.

"'Eat your breakfast!' Just like that, as if you didn't know or care! After all I've done, crawling to idiots, licking their feet, kissing their hands, to make them take you in! All the humiliations, smiling when I wanted to kill them!" She had lost all reason, all restraint, and utterly forgot me in her rage and malignance. "I dragged you up from the gutter, tried to make something of you. Tried to make a gentleman out of you. Hah!" Her voice rose to a shrill scream; she bent over him with clenched fists. "A gentleman! You'll never be that! You couldn't be, being what you were! All the money in the world wouldn't make you human. It can't change a swine into a man. Look at me, Jim," she cried, turning to me dramatically. "I haven't slept a wink since last night when he told me. I sobbed all night. All these months of work, and he throws it all down! Oh, I can't bear it," and she went off into hysterics again.

Through all this tirade Dan had eaten his breakfast, as though she had merely been the wind blowing. Now he looked up at her, and his face was white and strained. But he still spoke calmly.

"Well, if you have no shame before him, neither have I. Dragged me up from the gutter, eh? Made a gentleman of me, eh? Well, let me tell you this: I liked my gutter. I'm going back to it. I'm no 'gentleman.' No, I've got some sense of justice and real decency. Not the kind you talk about. What you've done, you've done for yourself, wanting to make a place for yourself in this goddamn stinking hole. I've been watching for months. It kind of made me laugh, watching them taking me in, because I've got some money now. It was better than a show, watching them. Don't know when I've enjoyed myself more. And you! Pretending to be the nice sweet little wife! I've watched you too, and had my laughs. You see, Bee, I've always known what you were. You never fooled me the way you fooled these half-wits here. And recently I've had an idea you knew why I married you."

While he had been speaking, her face had become that of a fury, blotched, hideous. Her hair flew out from its coils about her face, as though a terrible wind had blown it; her features sharpened, became livid, her mouth curling back from her teeth. She laughed wildly.

"Yes, I know! That's why I married you, too! To make you suffer for it! But since I married you, I thought I would let it go, I would try to forget it. I would make something out of you, give you a place in this town! And now, there's nothing left, nothing at all, but being married to the town outcast, chained to a fool and an idiot! I tell you, I can't stand it!" She screamed again. Dimly, in my confusion and sweating urgency to leave, I could see the avid face of the servant appearing and disappearing at the door.

She turned to me with a gust. I recoiled slightly. She stretched out her taut and clutching hands to me. She tried to assume an expression of broken pleading, helpless despair.

"Jim!" she sobbed. "You'll help me, won't you? You'll try to hush this down, won't you? You'll help me? You'll tell your dear mother that we are both sorry, that Dan's sorry? You'll tell everyone, beg everyone to forget it, and that Dan just lost his temper for a minute, and that he's willing to apologize, or anything?"

I could see that she was already terrified at what she had said before me, and giving no one any credit for reticence or kindness, having none herself, she was afraid that I would go out immediately and repeat everything. She even tried to smile cajolingly, touched her hair with her hands, tried to compose herself. She reached out her hand to touch me softly.

I retreated from her. My gorge rose in me; I wanted to strike her in the face.

"All I can say is this," I said in a thick voice, strange to my own ears. "If you were my wife, I'd choke you. Choke you to death."

And I fled out of the horrible house without another look.

Chapter Nineteen

I felt sick and trembling for hours afterwards. I had never seen a woman like this, so unrestrained, so beastlike, so monstrous. Even my worst thoughts of Beatrice Faire had been mild in the face of what she really was. I can never forget that morning, that mad mouth, those insane eyes. It was as though a dark door had opened and I had seen into Dan's life with her. I remembered what Mortimer had said. It was terrible to me, like some ghastly dream. I could hardly believe it. I longed passionately for everything to be swallowed up, for all our lives to be as serene as they had been on the surface, for everything to be forgotten. I could not speak of this even to Livy, but she seemed to know.

I had always had a love for the established and the simple and uncomplicated. It was a shock to me to discover that life was not like that, and that under its daily air of calmness frightful things were about. I felt robbed and sore and cheated. I never wanted to see either Dan or Beatrice again. I was overcome with shame. I knew, of course, from reading and from other impersonal things which I had seen in hospitals, that life could be horrible and loathsome. But I was outraged when the impersonal became the personal, when actualities actually lifted their heads and grinned at me obscenely. It shattered my whole belief in the orderliness of the average life, in the decency and regularity of things.

Indignation ran high against Dan Hendricks. Bee, with her usual shrewdness, did not appear at all, waiting for the story to become old. I knew her; I knew that she would not relinquish what she had gained. And sometimes with sickness, I wondered what sort of a life Dan was having these days.

Everyone virtuously avoided the Hendricks house. No one saw Sarah either. When women called upon her, the door remained silently closed.

But eventually South Kenton became bored with its indignation, and by slight signs indicated its willingness to forgive. Bee, who had an uncanny nose for intangibles, reappeared, pale, subdued, eyes always ready to be filled with tears. She conciliated everyone, but she did not come near Livy and me. When she had betrayed herself, she made no effort to conciliate the one who knew everything. A general could have learned a lot in strategy from her.

But Dan did not seem to know that he could be forgiven. He did not accept invitations, though God knows what he must have gone through with Bee when he refused. (I was told that Dan was seen in the early mornings riding on his new horse and furiously galloping down the country roads.) When Livy suggested that I go to see him, I shivered. I was sure he hated me for having been a witness to his degradation. I begun to have tentative thoughts about him. What had been his private life with his wife before his indiscretion? I found myself thinking erotic thoughts against my will in connection with them. What had they talked about when they had been alone? Dan had said he had seen into her all the time; how had he endured being married to her? How had he made himself marry her, even in the face of a romantic and secret obsession which would hardly have had weight with even a fool in his right mind? I felt that there was something here I did not understand. I did not know then that men live and die for more tenuous things than that, that even gods can be made or unmade in the dark complexities of the human mind.

\~

The storm that had gone before was nothing to the storm which now took place. It started sordidly enough.

Abe Witherbee's boy Charlie continued to visit Ed Ford's saloon, from what I heard. And I suspect from accounts of the boy's condition that Ed took a malicious delight in loading the boy with drink beyond even Charlie's capacity to pay. Ed loudly expressed his desire to meet Dan again, and gave lurid descriptions of what he would do to him if he *did* meet him again.

Two months later the drunken boy had wandered away from the saloon, had lost his way home, and had gone suddenly asleep on the railroad track. When the eastbound thundered into the station, it brought a decapitated body with it.

Because of Dan, the story caused more excitement than

it would have done in an ordinary occasion. For the first time indignation was expressed against Ed Ford, and perversely, uneasy public opinion swayed towards Dan Hendricks. Bee took avid and clever advantage of it. She adroitly changed her story a little; Dan must have known this might happen. She was increasingly humble. She and her friends might have been just a little too hard on Dan, after all. Wasn't it strange that even the best of friends could be just a little blind? South Kenton surged in spirit towards Dan, opened its arms to him. But he did not reappear. Beatrice went about, resolutely smiling, but her face became pinched, and in repose, visibly malignant. Dan was not very well; he was hurt by the treatment his friends had given him; he was so sensitive. She smiled deprecatingly, but with such dovelike eyes that South Kenton almost groveled.

Then two weeks after the tragedy, Abe Witherbee walked simply into Ed's saloon and shot him as he stood laughing and talking with his customers. He shot him with an ancient rifle, rusty and crooked. But he did a good job. Ed fell without a sound and never spoke again. He died before morning.

Abe Witherbee had walked without haste out of the saloon, for no one had either the courage or the strength to seize him. He went, still without haste, to the constable's house, woke that worthy, and delivered himself calmly into his hands.

South Kenton went into a prolonged uproar. The sheriff came from Ripley and took Abe into custody, spiriting him out of town because of the open threats of lynching. Abe was lodged in the Ripley jail, and extra armed guards were put about it, for Ed had been well known and liked in Ripley, and that town of some eighteen thousand souls was in scarcely less rage than South Kenton. I would say it was even more incensed and dangerous, because it knew little of the story behind the crime, and cared less.

I might have been amused at the sudden veer against Dan Hendricks again, but I was too miserable with my own thoughts. I listened indifferently to rumors and wild ac-

cusations that Dan Hendricks had "put Abe up to it," and
that Dan was the real criminal. I don't think anyone really
thought it in his heart, but it was an excuse to turn on Dan
again. However, Dan was still invisible, and for a time
Beatrice was also. That intrepid woman seemed for a time
to give up in despair. And again I wondered what took place
behind closed doors of the new house.

South Kenton was thrown into greater consternation and
fury when it was reported that Dan had appeared in Ripley
and had gone to see Abe Witherbee in jail. The *Ripley
Evening Star* noted that Mr. Daniel Hendricks of South
Kenton, who was interested in the accused, had engaged a
famous criminal lawyer from Warburton to defend him.
Everyone knew the fees of the lawyer. Dan was indifferently
known in Ripley, but he leaped into prominence now. But
strange to say the Ripleyites thought it rather gallant of him,
and comments in the newspaper were almost friendly. This
further infuriated South Kenton. I think bodily damage
might have been done Dan had he remained in town, but
instead of that he took a room at the Ripley Arms during
the trial.

South Kenton seethed. Of course, they all said, Bee
would leave him now. She would go home to her mother.
But Bee did not go. She took to bed. Friends, cold and
denunciatory, visited her. It seemed she was really very ill.
But, she declared, even though everyone abandoned her, she
would not abandon Dan. She was his loyal wife, his only
friend. It was her duty and her place to remain beside him.
Everyone urged her to leave Dan, that it was her duty to
her friends to leave him, but when she refused to do so,
everyone was loud in praises of Bee. South Kenton had
never seen such devotion, such loyalty. Beatrice had not
defended him at all, it was reported; she had only cried over
and over that it was her duty to keep her place beside him.
She was more loved than ever. She was held up as an
example to the occasionally mutinous young matron of what
a wife should be. In a few weeks she was received everywhere with open arms, and made much of. But she never
came near Livy and me. Livy, I knew, passed her with

averted head on the street, and even when they met among friends Livy did not speak. And the result of this was that opinion was sharp with Livy for being so hard to Bee, because Bee would not leave that reprobate husband of hers!

I wonder how Livy knew? But Livy was always intuitive, and though I had told her nothing, I am sure she knew.

The famous lawyer earned his fee, which was reported to be three thousand dollars. Abe escaped the noose, was declared insane, and was committed to the State Asylum. Dan returned home, became invisible again, but Bee went everywhere.

Chapter Twenty-One

Yes, Bee went everywhere, but Dan went nowhere. "He hides himself for shame, probably," said unanimous opinion. "He doesn't dare show his face."

He was seen at a distance. He rode his horse, it was said, out into the country in all kinds of weather. Like some wild horseman he could be heard galloping past lonely farmhouses in wild storms, when the trees were bent double and roared in colossal torment, and the moon went skipping in terror through rushing clouds. He was seen when the snow flew, crouched over his steaming horse. There was something eerie in it to the townsfolk.

I had not thought of it for years, but his favorite old phrase recalled itself to me: "Look—and pass." Somehow, I felt that I had never really known him, not even when we had been children. I found myself wondering with a kind of sickness what sort of life he was leading with Bee, for all he was never there when her friends called, and no one heard his voice or saw his comings or goings. I tried to see him, tried to waylay him, but he was as fluid as water, slipping by when I tried to grasp, and as unseen as the wind.

I heard rumors that Sarah saw him, however, that he often went to her little house. When she was asked, she was silent. She was not very well; there was something wrong with her heart. I visited her with Livy a few times, but the old Sarah, gay and loving and in love with life, had gone. She seemed always waiting for something dreadful; her eyes and mind were fixed on it, and though she talked casually and rationally enough to us, I had that uneasy sense of her waiting for some frightful thing that was inevitable. She would not speak of Dan or Beatrice.

One night in late fall I was jogging wearily along a country road back to South Kenton, after a three-hour battle to save the life of a farmer who had almost cut off his leg while trying to chop down a tree. A livid moon stood heavily in a black sky; by its light I saw the lonely stacks of corn, the colorless countryside, the dark horizon that met the darker heavens. Everything was flooded in a spectral light, so that it glimmered as though unreal, shifting, and drained of life. When the chill wind blew, the leaves ran running before me with a dry and hissing sound; an owl hooted somewhere, and an uneasy dog howled in the distance. I was glad of the companionship of my horse in the ghostly silence, and found myself talking to him.

Then, approaching me, I heard the rapid gallop of a horse. It was still very faint, and when the wind blew in another direction the sound vanished, only to be carried louder to me when the wind shifted again. For one moment I remembered the headless horseman who rode in darkness on lonely roads, and though I laughed I felt uncomfortable. To add to the eeriness, the moon went behind a cloud for awhile, and the battering hoofs sounded almost at my hand. When I could see again, a horseman was rounding the bend, riding furiously. My horse neighed and stopped by himself, and the approaching horse neighed in answer. I breathed easier; it was Dan Hendricks on one of his rides.

He would have gone past me, but I called him, and he reined in beside me. I peered at his face; God knows what I expected to see in it, but I was not prepared for the relaxed and youthful expression on it, the easy smile in his eyes and on his mouth. I suddenly felt absurd. Always the romanticist, I thought.

"Hello, Jim," he said, and I thought there was genuine friendliness in his voice. "Out on a call? They don't give you doctors much rest, do they?"

His horse was a black stallion, a devil of a beast, and much taller than mine, so that Dan towered over me. He sat his horse well, even nobly, with a light touch on the reins. He had an appearance of strength and easiness, of power and assurance which he did not possess when afoot. His horse pranced a little, restlessly.

"Not much rest, that's true," I said ruefully. "Where are you going, yourself? I don't like the roads tonight, and I'd be glad of your company back, Dan."

He hesitated for an instant. I looked into his eyes intently, and he looked back, gravely. I don't know what he read in my eyes, what pleading, but he said jovially: "Fine! I was just going to turn around, myself."

He swung about adroitly, and we rode side by side towards the town. A quick sense of gladness came over me, and an obscure content. We did not talk for awhile. Then I said involuntarily: "Dan, why don't I see you anymore? We were friends, once, you know."

I despised myself for begging for his friendship again, and after he had shown me only too often that he did not want to give it, and I waited for his usual cold evasiveness. But to my surprise, he laughed a little.

"Well, of course we are friends! Don't act so doleful, Jim. But you know I never was a fellow for running around and visiting. Besides, I haven't seen you around my house, lately, even though you know where I live."

"Do you want me to come, Dan?" I asked soberly.

He laughed loudly, and I felt absurd again. But angry, also, that he put me in a light where I appeared a fool. He was always doing that, I said to myself with irritation, always laughing at a situation which everyone thought serious, and becoming grave over something that did not matter at all.

"Certainly I want you to come. How about tomorrow night? You and Livy?"

He made it sound so matter-of-fact; his voice leapt over chasms and events and crises, made them look as absurd as he made me feel.

"We'll be glad to come," I said sedately.

He asked me a few casual questions about Livy and my father. I thought at first that his air of health and good temper and well-being was affected, assumed to mislead me. But even against my reason I was finally convinced that this was not so. He was really at ease, really exhilarated. Everything had been tragic and sordid and impossible during the past few months, and everyone had been oppressed by it. But this inscrutable young man did not appear to find it so, did not appear to consider it in the slightest. This annoyed me; I had to break through the shining glass through which he glanced at me.

"You make it appear as though I've avoided you, Dan, instead of you avoiding me," I said. "That's all nonsense. I never see you. You're invisible during the day, and at night you take these rides alone, galloping along as though the devil were after you."

I expected that my directness would make him retreat again, but he did not. He merely chuckled.

"Maybe he was," he admitted. "I expect everyone tries to outrun his devil." He was silent a moment. "Yes, there's always a devil. Man is so damned lonely. He has a feeling that if he is not very careful, he will disintegrate, become a part of static and meaningless objects. When it oppresses him too badly, he runs to drink, or to women, or to ambition. Always trying to retain his identity, to keep himself from dissolving even while he is still alive. He surrounds himself with other people, and finds himself like a house with all the windows and doors wide open and unprotected, and everyone marching through at his own sweet will. Well, that's why I keep to myself. That's the only way I can retain my identity. I like to ride at night. No one has any hands on me. I've always been afraid of hands," he added, half to himself.

"No one has tried to be anything but friendly, until you showed us all that you didn't want to be friendly," I said with uneasiness. His words had made something cold run down my spine.

"But I don't want friends!" he exclaimed, almost with violence. "The only way I can hold on to myself is to be alone. No one ever understands that. Friends! I haven't any, thank God! A man with friends has no identity; he is just a pleasant eating place for a flock of fools, just an open house. Friends steal away your time, your thoughts, yourself. That's why I don't want friends."

I knew he had no intention of affronting me, and so I merely shrugged.

"How do you know that you are worth keeping to 'yourself'?" I asked. "Perhaps, though, you consider yourself very valuable? But I'm a doctor, and I don't find anyone or anything very valuable anymore. We're just a mass of protoplasm, chemical reactions, and automatic movements."

He shrugged also. "Well, whether I'm valuable or not isn't the question," he said. "I don't want hands on me, that's all," he added. "I'm happy now. I'm alone. I've always wanted to be alone. Damn it! why can't fools realize that? Why do they find it incomprehensible that another man doesn't want them? Oh, call it antisocial, if you want to; what of it? That's the way I'm made, and I can't have any peace unless I am rid of the sight of eyes and mouths and faces."

"If you feel that way—" I began with dignity. He reached across to me and punched me lightly, laughing.

"There are always exceptions, Jim. I'll expect you and Livy tomorrow night. Bee will be glad to see you."

Bee will be glad to see you!

As though nothing had happened, as though he were

merely an ordinarily married young man, placid and content, as though nothing had passed between him and his wife, and the whole world was his friend! I was dumbfounded.

We parted as we reached the town, and I went on alone, feeling somehow that I had been made a fool of, and outraged that I could not put my finger on the time when this had occurred. I told Livy about it when I reached home, but she merely listened without comment. She consented, however, to go with me tomorrow night. Staring at her quiet face, as she sewed under a lamp, I again had an unreal sensation. Was I again up to my old tricks of making mountains out of molehills? Why couldn't I accept things at their face value? And then I was filled with fury; Dan knew the truth, but he had deliberately put me into a position where, if I spoke the truth, and showed that I knew it, he would make me look silly. That was his way of keeping me at a distance, I thought bitterly.

When we arrived at Dan's house, Livy and I, it was brightly lighted. It looked warm and hospitable. The smart young girl led us into the lofty parlor with a fire roaring under the black marble mantel and all the lamps lit. Bee and Dan were waiting for us in deep upholstered chairs near the fire, just as any young and contented married couple would wait for their guests. Dan was bland and utterly at ease. If he were hiding anything, pretending anything, it was not visible. He shook hands affectionately with Livy, and greeted me with the closest approach to effusion he had ever shown. Bee greeted us sweetly and warmly. She was considerably thinner, and the mauve satin she wore seemed to give her face an unhealthly tinge. She looked as though she had been very ill; even her hair was less bright. When she stopped smiling for a moment, her face had a wizened and intense look, and her eyes pointed. As on that day so long ago in the August garden, nothing was said by any of us of anything that had happened, or of the fact that we had not seen each other for a long time. It was as though we had seen each other only yesterday.

Livy conducted herself with kind dignity; she had become plumper and rosier, and beside the too-thin Bee, with her restless, hungry and avid air, she was the very picture of a wholesome young matron. She had acquired an aura of serenity and poise, which I felt nothing very much would shake.

Dan served us all small glasses of wine as we sat around the fire. I glanced about the beautifully furnished room, at the polished walnut, the blazing lamps, the roaring fire, the dark red curtains. And then I had a strange sensation; the room suddenly looked too bright yet bitterly cold and empty. There seemed a glare in it, not the warm and inexplicable light that lives in a room where love is, and kindness. It was a stage room. Even the fire was false; it burned and roared, but it did not warm. There was a chilliness in here that had nothing to do with the seasonable chill. Bee, in that mauve satin, looked like a stage property also, a little rigid, a little too hectic, with her eyes like copper. She was talking to Livy of small matters and laughing somewhat too often. Dan sat opposite, smiling, swinging the foot of his crossed leg and leaning easily back in his chair. Livy's quiet voice rambled on, unmoved, and I could hear nothing in it.

When people in small towns do not talk of their acquaintances and friends, and the small events that happen daily, there is nothing much to talk about. I tried to interest Dan in the threat of a Spanish-American War, but he was obviously not interested. "Wait a few years, and you'll see a real war," he said indifferently.

Bee did mention her mother, regretfully, speaking of Sarah's apparent physical decay, but that was all. No one mentioned anyone in the town. With a sense of panic, I told Dan of a few of my cases, of the complications I had encountered during a certain confinement, and of the gangrene that had set in in the arm of a boy who had infected his finger. He listened politely. I found myself talking alone in that glaring void of a big room; Livy and Bee were watching me absorbedly as I talked.

I could not get close to Dan, for all his bodily nearness. I could not approach him. I found myself hating to look at Bee; it was like looking at a corpse which yet had acquired a supernatural life, sinister and horrible. The palms of my hands sweated; I felt a terrific urge to run out of that house, dragging Livy with me. What was the matter with me? Why could I not accept things that were given me to accept? Why was I always looking for the something that crawled and writhed under the surface?

The girl brought in a beautiful silver tray of coffee and cake and small sandwiches. I was desperately grateful for the interlude. While cups clinked and sugar wriggled from tongs, and the plates were passed, I could regain possession of myself. Things became almost normal. And then I had the ill luck to glance at Beatrice's hand as she poured the coffee. It was very thin, almost gaunt, and the diamond on it glittered. But that was not what attracted my attention; the hand was trembling continually, and the knuckles were white. The cake in my mouth became dry and choking. I was conscious of an unreasonable terror. I glanced at Dan; he was eating with apparent good appetite and placid well-being.

Something must happen, I thought desperately. It did, and almost immediately, and innocently enough. I turned to Dan.

"Where's that dog of yours?" I asked. "Haven't seen him around lately. Did you send him back to the farm?"

There was a short pause, then Dan said casually as he scrutinized another piece of cake: "No, I didn't send him back. I should have done it, though. He was a funny dog, poor devil. He took violent likes and dislikes, and if he really disliked you he would attack like hell, trying to tear your throat out." He paused. "He attacked Bee one day; might have killed her. So I had to get rid of him."

Unwillingly, I looked at Bee, and was startled. Her eyes

were glittering. She was still smiling, but the smile had become a grin, almost fiendish. The cords were rising in her throat, and her complexion had become the tint of her dress.

"Yes, it was too bad," she said gently. "But Dan was so soft about the nasty thing. I knew he couldn't bear to do anything about it, so one day when he was out I had it poisoned."

There was an awful silence. Then Livy said "Oh!" very softly. Her face had paled, and her mouth fell open. My eyes dragged themselves to Dan. He was very white, but between his smiling lips his teeth glinted. I did not like his expression. But Bee had shattered the careful glass he had raised to protect himself; husband and wife stared at each for a long while, both smiling intently with hate leaping between them. I stood up involuntarily.

"Yes," said Dan, without removing his eyes from his wife, "Bee had him poisoned. He had nothing but his teeth to defend himself with. He was helpless. Then, besides, he loved me."

Livy stood up also; I saw that she grasped the back of her chair, and that she was unbearably shaken. But neither Dan nor Bee noticed us, standing there in terror. They were too intent on each other.

"Loved you?" meditated Bee gently. "Perhaps that's so. Nothing but a dog could love you. That's why lots of people prefer beasts; they don't see into one. Feed them, shelter them, and they'll accept anything."

Livy turned to me imploringly. "I think we'd best go, don't you think, Jim? It's getting late."

"Yes," I said huskily. I turned to go towards the door, but Bee sprang to her feet. She stood rigid, her hands clenched at her sides, her face shining with such evil that I fell back from it.

"So, you got what you came for, didn't you? That's what you came for, wasn't it, to see what was going on here, to gloat over it with your filthy curiosity? Yes! You wanted to see what I was doing with my poor, innocent husband, what I was making him suffer! Yes!" Her voice was shrill, almost impossible to endure. Dan still sat; his face was turned to the fire. She advanced on us with fury; I recoiled from her, but Livy stood her ground, looking at Bee quietly and intensely, as one would look at a wild beast, waiting for the moment of attack. "You wanted to see! Well, see! This is how we live, under the surface. You've always been probing under surfaces, haven't you, Jim? Nothing smooth on top ever contented you. Well, look! Probe! This is how we are, tormenting each other. No!" She exhaled fiercely, "He doesn't torment me. He hasn't the brains! He endures, and endures, and keeps his vile silence, torturing me. Do you know why? Because I know everything about him! That's why! I know what a fool he is, what a rascal—"

"Don't say that about Dan!" exclaimed Livy softly, as though in great pain. "Bee, you don't mean it, but even if you don't I can't bear to hear you say it."

The whole concentrated fury of the woman turned from me, like a pillar of fire, and roared upon Livy. She stuck out a pointing hand at my poor wife, threw back her head, and laughed madly.

"You would say that!" she almost screamed. "You've always been whining after him! You thought no one knew, except me, but now that fool of a husband of yours shall know now! He'll know now why you wouldn't marry him until I got Dan away from you; he'll know why you had your sicknesses and your sickly faces, why you couldn't stand coming here, why you avoided me, and shivered so delicately all the time! It's time he knew how he's been made a fool of, having his wife whimpering around after a man that wouldn't look at her!"

A red haze dimmed my eyes; I felt myself preparing to spring on this monster, but the sight of Livy's face, ghastly pale, her eyes half-closed as though she were about to faint, stopped me. I put my arm about her. Dan was standing also, now, but at a little distance, with a strange, impersonal attitude. Bee turned upon me savagely; there was an exultation in her crazy eyes, a beastlike joy in her ability to rend and tear.

"That's why he avoided you, you fool! Because he knew your wife was in love with him! But he didn't love her! You see, he was, and is, in love with my silly mother!"

I saw Dan leap at her then, and strike her full in the face with his clenched fist. It was like a dream, without reality and without substance. Bee fell without sound, headlong, her hair almost touching the gleaming andirons. Stupidly, I noticed the coppery waves of it, unrolling, spreading over the white-tiled hearth. Her body writhed in its sheathe of lavender satin, and then was still. I felt a heavy weight on my arm; Livy had fainted.

Dan turned to me. The jaw bones were rigid under his livid skin, but he was very quiet. I could feel myself trembling, but when he would have helped me with Livy I gestured him off in horror. I was not thinking coherently; I was sweating as though in some horrible nightmare. I don't know how I pulled Livy's cloak over her limp arms, how I got into my coat. But I remember than Dan opened the door for me, and that the cold night wind rushed in on us into the hall as I carried Livy out. He stood by the open door, silent and tall and motionless in his black suit, and as I passed him he looked at me with a removed pity and compassion, a very strange look.

Livy regained consciousness just as I was putting her into the buggy. She assured me faintly that she was well. We drove away into the night. I felt something dissolving in myself, something so full of agony that I could scarcely endure it. We did not speak; I dared not speak.

We were almost home when Livy timidly touched my arm. I did not turn.

"Jim?" she whispered.

"Please, Livy, don't let's talk about it," I said huskily.

She began to cry, and then clutched my arm desperately. "Jim, you've got to listen. It's true, I—I did care for Dan. All my life. Perhaps if you hadn't gone away to school, and forgotten to write me after awhile, it wouldn't have been so bad. But Dan was the only one in town who knew what I was talking about; we seemed to know just what either of us was thinking. Perhaps it was because everyone was so down on him, and all. Oh, I don't know. I always saw deeper into Dan than anybody did, even you. I'm not going to be a hypocrite and say that the way I cared for him was different from the way I cared for you, and yet I always loved you, too. You were so funny, and so earnest, and so careful and good— Jim, it's all over now. If it hadn't been over, I wouldn't have married you."

"You mean, Livy," I said lifelessly, "that it's hopeless, don't you? Look, Livy, I think I must have known all the time. Deep down, I knew. I wouldn't let myself believe it. I always wanted you; there was never anyone else, and I expect we always believe what we want to believe."

She pressed her face convulsively to my sleeve. "Jim, we've got to forget it. I love you, my dear. I'll always love you. Please believe me." She cried very bitterly, and I could feel the vibration of her sobs. I put my arm about her, stopped the buggy, and held her close. I was filled with compassion and love and sadness. There were always compromises with life; I would have to compromise, now, knowing everything. But it was almost too much, this hopeless compromise. Livy loved me, I knew. She would always do that. But Dan had taken something from her that I did not have, and I felt grovelling shame that he had not cared about it, had not wanted it. He, too, had his obsession, and was resigned to the knowing he could not have it.

"That woman!" I said, with a return of the horror. "I wish someone would kill her!"

Chapter

It was a long while before we came in contact with Beatrice and Dan Hendricks again. Bee avoided us as assiduously as we avoided her. I happened to hear that she had given no real explanation of refusing to attend any affair where we were expected, but opinion seemed rather stately towards us. I raged at this, but Livy merely smiled. Of course, Dan was not invited anywhere.

I suppose to follow out tradition I should have hated Dan Hendricks. But I did not. I felt merely sad; I felt that fate had warped all our lives in some incomprehensible fashion, and that as victims we ought to sympathize with each other. What if Dan had not come to Sarah Faire's house that spring day, and if she had not taken any interest in him? And those violin lessons, given to an impressionable and lonely boy? In the natural course of events, meeting with sympathy and kindness and complete, voiceless understanding from Livy, he would surely have loved her, as who did not? Her honesty would have answered his honesty; her amusement at illusions and delusions would have replied to his. And I? I would not have had this sick heaviness in me all the time. It would have taken a long time to get over Livy, but I would have done it eventually. Not that I even now doubted Livy's love for me. I knew she loved me. She was devoted to everything that concerned me. No one could have had a finer wife. But I had always known of a little reserve in her; her ideas often conflicted with mine, and so eventually she did not argue with me on anything important to her. But that quiet, reserved room would have been flung wide open for Dan; he would have been at home there, familiar with everything in it.

No, I did not hate him. Strange to say, what I knew only made my love for him stronger. I pitied him, and this pity prohibited any hate or jealousy I might have felt otherwise.

Months telescoped into months, and a year passed. And another. We had no children, and my mother, who felt deprived, seemed to feel that Livy might have had a child if she had wanted it. At any rate, when she mentioned our childlessness she would glance at Livy reproachfully. I did not care particularly, and as we grew older, I cared less.

Livy did not mention Dan or Bee to me. I did not speak of them, either. But one day something brought Beatrice irresistibly to my mind, and I cursed her to Livy. To my surprise, she shook her head slowly.

"No, you ought to pity her, Jim," she said sadly. "You see, Dan is the one at fault. He did her a great wrong. He married her, not caring for her; he knew all about her. He had some vague obsession in his mind, and made her a victim of it. I saw Bee a few times before she married him. Of course, his new money was the most important thing in her mind, and I think she despised him for what she believed he felt for her mother. But I think in a way she came to care about him as much as she could care about anyone before they were married. He—he could be very nice when he wanted to be. And then when she married him, she must have seen anything wholesome or decent would never happen. If he had liked her at all, he might have saved her from herself, or himself. But he didn't. So she tried something else. I don't know why, but a standing in this little town was important to her. She tried to substitute what she would call social position for what Dan had cheated her out of. But he would not help her. I'm not blaming him, Jim. It seemed so trivial to him that he hardly thought of it. But he could have helped her, even out of kindness. That's all she had, her poor little ambitions. But, he would not help her." She took a few careful stitches, without looking at me. "And that's why she really hates him, though I don't suppose she knows why. He had no right to marry her, knowing that he could not, and would not, try to make her at all happy. He just didn't consider Bee as a human being at all. She was just a symbol to him. He bought her just like he would have bought a picture that reminded him of something precious, without a single personal regard for the picture at all."

I was astounded at this compassion and mercy. So I could say nothing. I knew that Livy had hit upon part of the truth, anyway. But not all of the truth, I am sure.

Sarah was sick again that winter, and I cared for her. I looked into her soft and bewildered eyes, the skin wrinkled about them like old silk. Her red hair was almost white, and her fingers trembled continually. I remembered what Livy had said, and I could not help wondering what Bee might have been if her mother, during Bee's childhood, had recognized the inherent evil in her daughter and had met that evil nobly and courageously, marching towards it, full of love and understanding, breaking it down, raising up what good there was in the girl, and resolutely and honestly cultivating it. But she had been shrinkingly silent before that evil; she had turned from it, and so it had flourished. Perhaps that was because Sarah was not intelligent, and Bee was very intelligent. Intelligence of any kind seems to loathe cowardice, and Sarah, in her gentleness and retiring timidity, had been a coward. Bee, as much as Dan, stood alone.

I found myself pitying her, and angrily tried to whip up resentment again. She was an adult now, no longer very young, and, as I have said, exceptionally intelligent. She must have seen that there was something besides baseness in other human beings, that occasionally an altruistic act is done for other than ulterior motives. She must have known that our new little free hospital gave profits to no one, and that my father and I worked in it without recompense, and that the salaries of the nurses and other attendants came out of private pockets, many of which felt the pinch. She must have known that there was beauty in the world besides greed, honor besides dishonor, unselfishness as well as avarice. But she would not see. If she had been a fool, this might have been forgiven her.

The Spanish-American War threw us into wild excitement. I went, of course, very smart if I must admit it, in my officer's uniform. I was assigned to Army hospitals, and was never in any danger at all, even what there was of it in that comic-opera war. I met Theodore Roosevelt, and was not particularly impressed either by his sincerity, oratory, or teeth. I thought the Big Stick idea very silly, personally. He lacked dignity, and I have always been a stickler for dignity and smoothness.

Practically every young man in South Kenton enlisted or tried to enlist. All of them, except Dan Hendricks. He was as remote from this war as he was from South Kenton. I doubt if any calamity would ever have brought him very close to living as we knew it, not even the World War that occurred so many years after his death. For the first time I resented his remoteness; I thought it unhuman, almost insolent. No human being, I thought, has the right to show by every gesture and glance, that he considered himself not one with the rest of humanity. Then I had to admit, with bewilderment, that I knew very little about him after all. No one had ever known much about him.

Except, perhaps, Mortimer Rugby. Mortimer was growing old. He had retreated into himself like an old tree, turning his roots away from the tangle of roots of his fellows. When I returned on a furlough, I asked him somewhat sarcastically if Dan had enlisted yet. He smiled at me dryly, and shook his head.

"Dan doesn't think much of war," he said, eying me humorously. "He doesn't disapprove of it, either. Thinks it's a healthy, natural instinct. Only last night he talked to me about it. Said we had transformed the sexual instinct into literature, sculpture, music, and brotherly love. But we hadn't transformed the natural, primitive instinct of war into anything valuable. We can't have war in civilized society, he said, not if that society is to exist. But, we haven't turned its great force into anything valuable. All we've done is to substitute monotony for it; we teach monotony in our schools, we preach it, calling it law and order and regularity and peace. We get deadly people to teach it, mediocre people without strength or integrity. No, Dan said, the deadly people are not the criminals and the war-makers. They are not the exploiters or the thieves. They are the people who teach conformity, mediocre wretches without imagination. Remember what Napoleon said, Jim, when advisors told him that he wouldn't be able to get war-tired men to follow him again? And he said: 'Yes, they will. You see, I am rescuing them from button factories.'

"And that's the cause of war, Jim: button factories. Squeezing out of the adventurous human animal every drop of color and adventure and excitement and glamour. People go mad in monotony, Jim. Monotony is death, living death. And, as Dan says, they'll escape from this death in life, this organized and colorless living, into the grand and healthy and natural explosion of War. To prevent war, you must direct its glory and power into an exciting, valuable and adventurous peace."

"Sounds crazy to me," I said. "How would you, or Dan, do it?"

He shrugged. "I don't know. Dan says the first thing you must do is to get rid of mediocrity of any kind, any formula, whatever its name. Mediocrity, he says, is always dead. It never lives. It is static and motionless. Part of 'deadliness.' It's like a corpse's hand on a living heart. You've got to get rid of it."

I did not see Dan during that visit. If possible, public hatred was stronger against him than ever. War is a great knitter of all sorts of souls, but he had not been touched. As far as he was concerned, there was no war.

When I came home after peace was declared (wondering what it had all been about, anyway), Livy told me that Dan had left Beatrice. Oh, nothing final and public, of course. He had merely gone back to his farm. Beatrice had explained that the separation was only temporary, and that she had to stay in town because of her mother's chronic illness. But, she said—and I found it to be true—she visited Dan at his farm, and often stayed two or three days. Sarah had refused to live with Bee, much to public indignation, but Bee gently and affectionately explained that Sarah was deeply attached to her own dear little house. Wasn't Dan queer, liking to live out there in that old farmhouse, without conveniences and everything? However, when Mama was better, she would, as a dutiful wife, leave town and live with him on his farm, if he did not finally decide to return "home."

I felt that Dan and I would never meet as friends again. I often passed his farm, and glanced at it from a distance, wistfully. At night there would be a light in one of the windows, and the garden was full of color in summer. But somehow it seemed as remote as Dan, in another dimension, where one could not go.

I remember most vividly passing there late one night. It was early spring, a still night full of sharply exploding stars and breathing earth. Everything was very still. I stopped my horse and waited. I had no intention of turning in, but looking at the house I had a sense of remoteness, of otherworldliness, of great peace, foreign to my experience. I felt the old sadness, the old puzzled longing for Dan, a desire that did not seem connected with any human emotion or affection.

I could see the yellow light pouring out onto the earth through the leaded windows. It was not a light that invited or beckoned; its very warmth warned one away. Then, of a sudden, Dan began to play his violin, and the distance muffled the usual strong blurring with which he played. The notes entered the silence of the night, pure and lonely, as lofty as unearthly thought, full of unhuman pain and longing. They were like the clear, faint light of the stars, untouchable, unwarming, unknowable. I recognized the melody as being that of the *Meditation from Thaïs*, but into it Dan had infused his own meditation, so that it seemed like a strange voice singing a familiar song, giving to it alien meaning and unknown emotion. I felt somehow that if I could only understand it, I would understand Dan, but though the notes reached my ear they told me nothing, and only made me unbearably depressed, filling me with a sort of vague and spiritual suffering. I could stand it no longer and rode on; I had the odd feeling that I was leaving a friend forever behind because I could not understand him.

Late that fall there was an unusually violent outbreak of influenza in South Kenton, and my father and I were kept very busy. My father finally took sick and the whole burden fell upon me. We moved patients from the farms and slums into the little free hospital, and sent to Ripley for nurses. Dr. Winslow came to South Kenton to help me, but as he was a genial tea-drinker, and better at holding feminine hands than at making a correct diagnosis, he was not of much assistance.

Livy's sister, Lucille, was ill in Ripley, and Livy went there to be with her, and to help in the crowded household of little children and two servants. I ate my meals with my mother, who was tired from nursing my father.

The farm folk, as usual, seemed to be hardest hit of any, and I rode in a weary daze over the country roads, half asleep in my saddle, and arrived home in a state of total exhaustion. Even when asleep, I shuddered at the ringing of the telephone, for it meant a weary crawl out of warm sheets into the cold and bitter air of November nights.

But eventually the accumulating fatigue-poisons in my systems served to intoxicate me so that I felt a high nervous tension, and could not sleep even when I finally got to bed. I was painfully awake, every nerve twitching, "worms crawling in my bones," as my father used to express it. For the first time in a long while I was conscious of a feverish desire for excitement, for color and vivacity. My life suddenly seemed drab and tedious, when it wasn't aching with weariness. I hated to return home at night, even when I was so exhausted that every step was an ache. To return, to close the door after me, to go to bed, was revoltingly final, as though I had shut life out.

I came back from a country trip one night about eight o'clock. The town looked unbearably shut and shabby by the few street lamps. Not a friendly light anywhere, not a gay voice or an invitation to relaxing merriment and cheer. I knew that I could not return home just then; I had to see a healthly face, hear a healthy, serene voice.

I passed Mortimer Rugby's house, gaunt, grim, unclothed under the cold November sky. Every window was shut and dark, except one. This one was called Mortimer's "study," and was on the first floor. It was his retreat from a life that harassed and tore him even now. It had a separate entrance with a little porch hidden from the street, so that in the summer the thick vines gave him privacy. In the large window of the study shone a friendly lamplight. Mortimer was poor company, if one was seeking lightness and gaiety, but he was better than nothing. I could smoke a pipe with him, look at his books, and warm myself at his fire. I remembered that he had a few bottles of old wine which he occasionally brought out for me when I visited him. I decided to go in, and went round the side of the house to the separate entrance.

Looking back, now, I wonder what would have happened if I had not gone there that night, if I had ridden by? I did not know, then, that on this innocent act a man's life hung. Sometimes, remembering, I wonder if I would have gone in, knowing in my heart of hearts what a coward I really am, how I have always felt a passion for ease, for lack of complications.

I knocked on the door of Mortimer's study. I thought I heard the murmur of voices in there, and I was pleased. I knew it was not his wife, for he did not let her in there often, and besides, I had passed her only fifteen minutes ago on the way to see a sick friend.

The door opened, and Mortimer blinked at me. For a long moment he hesitated, then he said so heartily that I suspected he spoke for the benefit of his other, invisible visitor: "Jim! By my soul! Come in, boy, come in!"

I went in. It was warm in there, shabby and a little gaunt, but comfortable. Sitting by the fire, placidly smoking, sat Dan Hendricks. He looked up idly as I stood awkwardly in the middle of the room, and nodded, smiled, as though he had seen me only yesterday.

"Hello," he said in a friendly voice. "Cold out?"

"Yes," I answered. I could feel my face burn, and even my ears. My heart thumped dizzily; if I could have run out without shame I would have done it. Mortimer pulled off my coat, and pushed me towards the fire. I stood before it, rubbing my hands in an agony. The last time I had seen Dan rushed up, obliterating time, making it only yesterday. And in the meantime he looked at me with his bland and unreadable eyes, smiling affectionately, his legs crossed as he slouched in his chair, his pipe gripped between his teeth. He looked much older than his thirty years, but it did not seem the physical age of wrinkles or even of the small gray patches that had begun prematurely to bleach his temples. No, it was an age that had nothing to do with the flesh. He was a great deal thinner than when I had last seen him, and shabbier. Yet I had an impression of unusual force and power in him, a compactness and ease.

Again, there was no mention of the years that had passed silently between us. He merely asked me, with casual solicitude if I hadn't had my hands full lately. Fools, he said, blamed the unusually cold weather, but wise men were look-ing for a virus. There was always a virus in every illness, he said, looking at me with the clear eyes of a child. But somehow of all the casual and hatefully indifferent things we said that night, that is the only thing I remember very clearly.

He did not ask me about my parents, of Livy, or anything that had occurred to me. He forced me back, invisibly. He never gave me a chance to cross that silent bridge. I saw you yesterday, he seemed to say. Deny that, if you dare, either to yourself or to me.

So we all talked of the weather, the late crops. Dan men-tioned with a smile that, because of the flooded fields that year, he had the only decent crop of potatoes. He told us a humorous anecdote of a neighboring farmer, and we laughed. Mortimer sat between us, facing the fire, his dry, veined hands between his knees, the firelight in the wrinkles on his nutlike face, his bright and bitter eyes wandering from Dan to me and then back again. I knew I was an in-truder, but not an unwelcome one, at least to Mortimer. What Dan thought of my coming I did not know. But I found myself staring at him earnestly, almost imploringly. Come back, Dan, I begged inwardly. He suddenly glanced at me as I said that in my heart, and his eyes rested on me with a grave, startled expression, as though he had heard. I felt my eyes grow tight and arid. He glanced away after a moment, and stared at the fire. His face fell into lines of grim dignity and removed weariness. My throat was dry and taut; it was as if he had openly repudiated me, warned me off, and I could taste a heavy sickness in my mouth.

"I heard you playing your violin one night recently," I said.

He looked at me again, raising his eyebrows in a friendly manner. "Did you? On the farm? Why didn't you come in?"

I stared at him somberly, trying to touch him. But his bland and questioning face, his smile, challenged me, warned me not to speak.

"Oh, I was tired," I answered lamely.

"Tired," said Mortimer. "As we grow older we get tired.

It isn't age. It's because we know too much. Even our thoughts are too familiar. We are tired of them. They are like clothes we have worn too long, and they have become shabby. They hold no newness for us. We know every seam. It's a chronic tiredness. Only death can cure it."

He got up and went to a little cupboard, and brought out a decanter and three small red glasses. He filled them carefully. He lifted one glass and held it upright.

"Here's the cure for knowing too much," he said wryly. "Not a permanent cure, sad to say. Jim, why don't you doctors discover a cure for mind-weariness? You fellows are always puttering around with bellies. Why don't you try probing into souls? You'll find all the ills of the world, the flesh, and the devil there."

"Well," I said, "you hear a lot nowadays about psychology. Perhaps it will be your answer when more is known about it. But, somehow, I feel it's sort of indecent to probe and pry into souls, to turn over intimate details with blunt fingers. I think more injury can be done than good. What's hidden in a man should not be touched by another man."

"I agree with you," Dan said quietly, and he looked at me squarely. Again I felt my face grow hot and angry. Damn you, I thought, I won't touch you!

The clock ticked loudly in a sudden silence. I glanced at it with a sense of escape. It was nine o'clock. I was just about to stand up and announce my departure when Dan rose, yawning and stretching.

"Guess I'll go for a ride," he said. He looked kindly from me to Mortimer, and, taking the pipe from his mouth, he laid it carefully on the tray on the table and picked up his coat. "Too early to go home, yet. Bee's been down on the farm with me for a couple of days, Jim," he added, looking at me with the open eyes that told me nothing. "Drop in the next time you are around."

The coat hung on him carelessly, and he put on his hat. Trying to remember, now, I can say with all truthfulness that there was nothing then in his expression, his eyes, his smile, that gave a clue to any frightfulness. He bid us both goodnight with the utmost geniality, and went out.

Mortimer and I sat in silence for a long time after he went. Then Mortimer shook his head slowly, as though trying to free it from a heavy weight.

"There's a lot there I don't understand," he muttered. "I expect none of us will ever understand. Behind any facile explanation is the dark continent of the human mind, hidden in fogs, sinister and unknown."

"I suppose so," I said listlessly.

Mortimer glanced about the room. "Dan's left his pipe," he said. He picked it up gingerly. "Hell's bells! It's hot, and heated right through the tray onto the table! Alice will raise the devil when she sees that." He put the pipe down, and poured some more wine for me.

I had no desire to go home. I was warm, relaxed by heat and wine. Mortimer and I talked desultorily. I smoked, and almost forgot my companion. Then I mentioned that I had seen his wife. He chuckled.

"Yes, Alice stopped by the door on the way out. She wouldn't come in. She knew Dan was here, and she hates his guts. She glared in the door at him for a moment, and didn't speak to him. Then she slammed the door and went out the front way. Women are queer."

I must have dozed, for when I started awake it was after eleven, and Mortimer was dozing also. The fire had died down. I threw a scuttle of coal in on it, and the fuel spluttered and roared and threw out sparks. Mortimer sat up, blinking.

"Eh? What time is it? Eleven? Ain't Alice come back yet? Guess not; she would have stopped in. Hates to see me sit up late." He ambled wearily to the door that led into the body of the house, and shouted into the dark hall. There was no reply. He shut the door again, yawning.

"Expect old Mrs. Burnett must be pretty sick," he commented. "Maybe Alice will stay all night, or Jack will bring her home. Beats all how much she thinks of the boy, almost as much as though he were her own son. Have another glass of wine, Jim, before you go. And smoke another pipe. You don't come around often enough."

It was half past eleven before I reluctantly thought about going. There was nothing to return home to, nothing but the tedious company of my father, if he were still awake. He had an insatiable curiosity about my cases, and I had to relate all details to him. Mortimer was yawning again, and I waited for him to cease, and then said I must go. But he exclaimed eagerly and hurriedly that it wasn't often that he could stay up late without his wife nagging him and coming into the study and bullying him into going to bed and taking his medicine.

We heard the outside door open, the sound of goodbyes, and steps approached the study floor.

"Alice," groaned Mortimer softly, and I stood up. He kept the study door locked. He said that it gave him a feeling of privacy, that no one could lacerate his nerves by sudden, uninvited entries, and in this pathetic way I knew he had retained his identity. Now he glanced at the bolted door with prideful satisfaction. The handle turned, and his wife said crossly: "Mortimer! Are you still having company in there, at this time of night? You ought to be in bed."

Mortimer winked at me and shook his head slightly.

"Yes, I'm still up, Alice. Dan's still here. Want to come in and say hello to him?"

I smiled. "No, I don't!" replied Mrs. Rugby irritably. "Dan oughtn't to keep you up. All decent folks are in bed. I'll expect you upstairs in five minutes, Mortimer," and she went away, muttering. I was sure she was tossing her head.

"Why did you tell her Dan was still here, and not I?" I asked idly.

"Well, I want to talk to you for a couple of minutes more and if she knew you were here, it would be the end. She'd bounce in and annoy you about her symptoms; funny thing, when women haven't much brains and they grow old, symptoms are the only real things in their lives. Men have money to comfort them in their old age, and women have the creakings of their old bodies. Keeps their minds off their souls." He grinned at me, shamelessly.

"Well, anyway, she is right, and you ought to be in bed," I said. I stood up, feeling lame and stiff, but not very tired any longer.

The telephone suddenly trilled upstairs on the landing. Telephone calls are always frightening at midnight, but they were more so in those early days of the twentieth century, when not many had telephones and used them mostly for emergencies. We heard Mrs. Rugby's footsteps upstairs, and heard her alarmed voice answering. Mortimer, in spite of his philosophy and bitterness, still had human curiosity, and he tiptoed to the door, unbolted it, and listened. Mrs. Rugby's voice, loud with alarm, could be heard very clearly in the silence.

"Jack? Is she worse? No? Then what is it?" There was a humming pause. Then Alice cried out, loudly, sharply: "No! Bee murdered? When, where? On the farm? Who did it? Oh! Oh! No, Jack, that's wrong! Why, Dan Hendricks is still here, talking to your father! I just passed the study door and heard him talking, and your father asked me to come in to speak to him! Jack, you've got to go out and tell the folks that, that Dan is still here, and couldn't have murdered poor Bee two hours ago! He couldn't be two places at once! Mortimer!"

I was paralyzed with horror. Through a haze I saw a white glare stand for a moment on Mortimer's profile, and I saw him shut the door swiftly, shoot the bolt into its socket. I don't know what must have passed through his mind with such lightninglike swiftness, but no one can measure the speed of the human thought processes in dire emergencies. I still marvel at it. A whole plan must have leapt into his brain in the space of three seconds.

I stared, stupidly. He stood by the door, turning on me a stern and dreadful face. His eyes glittered. He put his finger imperatively to his lips. His wife was almost at the door now, crying aloud. He leapt on me, seized me by the arm, rushed me to the outside door. He opened it noisily, talking loudly and rapidly about God knows what; I was too confused and overcome to think anything.

"Goodnight, Dan, and come again, soon!" he shouted

loudly and genially. I heard his wife's hand rattling the knob, calling for both him and Dan Hendricks. He thrust me out, slammed the door crashingly after me. I fell down the stairs in my agitation and sprained my ankle. But I hardly felt the pain. A frightful nausea had gripped my stomach. I fumbled for my horse which I had hitched and blanketed, and mechanically, with another side of my brain, I mounted, and so weak and sick was I that I almost slipped off the other side. But that part of my brain which operated coldly and mechanically made me whip my horse, ride off with a great clatter of hoofs. Only when I was galloping down the road could I gather my disordered thoughts together. I slowed down my horse, and closed my eyes against my nausea.

It was nine o'clock when Dan had left. Nine o'clock. It was now midnight. The town hall clock pealed out thinly on the frosty air.

I could see it all now or at least a lot of it. Mortimer was forming an alibi for Dan. I don't know, now and I didn't know then, whether he thought Dan was guilty of a horrible murder or not, but that did not concern him. He knew that I would not speak against Dan. But I felt a sudden surge of wonder and gratitude towards him; he would involve himself in this, but he had delicately refrained from involving me. He could have opened that door and asked me to tell his wife that Dan had just gone, but he had not done that. Any lies that were to be told, he would tell. He would ask no other man to perjure himself. All he asked was my silence, and he knew I would keep it. Thinking back, now, I wonder, with grim amusement, if he doubted my ability to tell lies adequately.

I had to go down Main Street to get home, and when I reached it, it was alive with running men, cursing, half-dressed, and with groups talking and gesticulating in the pale moonlight, full of threats of lynching. The wildest rumors were running along the street like thin fire. The town bell suddenly began to toll with what to my ears was a terrible sound, a bloodthirsty and insane sound. Recognizing me, a group of men seized my reins, and stood about me, panting and waving their arms, their faces ghastly in the moonlight.

"He's done it!" one man shouted. "Doc Jim, he's done it! Dan Hendricks! He's killed his wife. So, that's what it's come to, lettin' him live here! But, we'll get him, and tear the guts out of him before we lynch him!"

I felt such an awful giddiness come over me that for a few moments I could not speak. I did not know what to say, anyway. But after awhile I stammered: "Say, now, you mustn't do anything rash. You don't know he did it. I—he—"

"He did it, all right," said another one, ominously. "He did it. He's skipped, seems like. But the constable phoned the sheriff, and they're on the way here. Bloodhounds to find him, they got. We'll get him this time," he added, gritting his teeth.

I looked down at their faces, glowing with savagery, white with satisfied rage. The Pack. Out at last after the hated fox. They'd run him to earth, they'd— Oh, God, what could I do? Where was Dan? What was it all about?

I finally reached home. Every house along the way was lighted from top to bottom. Women shivered in shawls on the porches; men stood on the walks. From everyone came a hungry, subdued roar. A dozen times I was stopped to hear the news. When I arrived home, I was hysterical from the tolling of the bell that never ceased, from the wild-beast odor that seemed to blow through the town. I found my father sitting by the fire in his dressing robe, my mother, hastily dressed, crying. They both shouted to me as I came in.

"Jim!" bellowed my father. "Where you been? Have you heard the news?"

"Yes," I replied. My tongue felt thick and dry in my mouth. "I don't believe it. I just heard it on the street when I got into town from the Horlicks. I don't believe it."

My father glared at me, outraged, turning in his chair. "What d'ye mean, believe it? Of course he did it! I knew he'd do something like that, some day, the goddamn so-and-so and so-and-so—"

"Oh, it's terrible!" sobbed my mother. "Poor Bee. Poor girl. This will kill Sarah—"

I could not stay here. "Has anyone told Sarah?" I asked dully. I turned to the door. "I'll tell her."

I found myself riding along the cold and windy street. The bell was still ringing, long and resonant. I put my hands suddenly to my ears. I found myself retching, and my thoughts began to spin in my head like wide rings of fire. When I reached Sarah's house, a little group stood on the road near it. No one, I was informed, had had the courage to tell her. The house was dark. I went up the stairs and lifted the knocker. I had to knock several times until I heard Sarah's sleepy voice in the room above the small porch.

"Mrs. Faire," I said urgently, hoarsely. "It's Jim Marcy. Let me in, Sarah."

I heard her exclaim feebly; I heard her slow steps, and then her descent down the stairs. She opened the door for me, a thick garment over her nightgown, her red-gray hair tumbling over her shoulders. She looked sick and dazed.

"Jim," she faltered, holding the candle she held high. "Come in. What's the matter?" She led me into the cold and dusty little parlor, and set the candle on the table. She stared at me, her face pinched and fallen in the wan light. I wrung my hands together impotently.

"Mrs. Faire," I said imploringly. I glanced at the shut door over my shoulder. "Bee's been hurt. Quite badly. You've got to try to understand—"

I looked at her. A strange and frightful smile stood on her lips. "She's dead," she whispered softly.

Her eyes dilated. When I dropped my lifted hand, she was still smiling. She did not remove her gaze from me. She began to speak, softly still, like a child memorizing a lesson.

"Dan didn't do it." She clutched me suddenly, the smile gone, mad terror twisting her features, making them ghastly. "Jim! They can't hurt him! They can't hurt him! No! He didn't do it! Not Dan! Don't let them hurt him! He's suffered so, he—"

Her voice rose to a scream, and I felt with dreary satisfaction that that would satisfy the morbid listeners outside. Someone was already pounding on the door.

"Listen," I whispered urgently. "Don't say anything. Here, lie down on the sofa. You are heartbroken, but you don't believe Dan did it. You don't know anything, see? You say, over and over to them, that Dan didn't do it, you know he didn't do it! You're not to say anything against Bee, or they won't believe what you say about Dan! Bee was your good daughter, and she had a good husband—"

I threw her on the couch, and pulled her clothing smoothly about her. As I went to the door, I glanced back at her. Here eyes were closed, her face half covered by the heavy lengths of her fallen hair; she looked dead. I flung open the door, and looked down at the avid and sympathizing faces below.

"Here, you, Mrs. Fitz, and you, Mrs. Simmons, both of you come in. Sarah's fainted. You'd better stay with her tonight. I've told her."

I went home.

But when I reached the house door, I could not go in. I went to the barn and unsaddled my horse, and then wandered out to the street again, in spite of my exhaustion and the burning heat which was rising in me. I felt really ill, physically as well as mentally. I ran, and soon arrived on Main Street. It was crowded. Men were carrying lanterns and screaming at the top of their lungs. Lights bobbed all over the square, and many women were out, shivering in shawls and coats. A dry snow had begun to fall, and its light haze made everything look unreal, the dancing lights, the flickering street lamps, the running men, the bare and empty trees.

"They've got him!" a man shouted at me as he recognized me. "He's in the jail! But he won't stay there; we've got a rope and we're going to hang the son of a—"

I fought my way through a congestion down to the side street, where a wilder crowd was gathered, their faces fierce and contorted. The congestion was thickest about our inadequate little jail, which looked frail and helpless with the crowd before it. I pushed my way through the crowd, and gained the steps. The jail was glaring within with gaslights, and the constable, who stood uneasily on guard reinforced by about ten sullen deputies, let me enter.

"Sheriff's here from Ripley, Doc Jim," he muttered. "They're questionin' Dan in there. Old Mr. Rugby's there, too, telling the sheriff that Dan left his house not half an hour or more ago. They got Dan ridin' easy-like towards his farm, and hell's bells! but we had a hard time gettin' him in here without the folks here tearin' him away and lynchin' him."

In the bare and ugly little room, the office, with the gaslights flaring and stinking, were a group of agitated and madly smoking men. They stood about Dan, who was sitting easily and smilingly in a wooden chair. Beside him, his hand on his shoulder, stood Mortimer Rugby, holding in his hand the still-warm pipe that Dan had left behind in the study. Mortimer was not a smoker; what nausea he must have suffered to light up that pipe and smoke it furiously after I had left!

The uproar stopped for a minute when I entered. They all looked at me. I stared for a long moment at Dan; he returned my regard almost indifferently. But Mortimer stopped in the middle of a vociferous sentence, the pipe held in mid-air, and looked at me. His old face was ghastly; his eyes fixed themselves on me. For the first time a flicker of fear agitated his eyelids. I advanced slowly into the room. Could I say anything? Could I help? I asked myself wretchedly. No, said Mortimer's sunken and blazing eyes in reply, you must say nothing. That is the way to help. He turned from me to the burly sheriff. I saw his hand pressing Dan's shoulder fiercely, so that his knuckles became white.

"What was I saying, Sheriff? Oh, yes. Well, you can ask my wife, Alice. She knows Dan was there; she heard us talking, and I invited her in to say goodnight to Dan. But she was tired out, and she went upstairs. Yes, I heard the telephone ring, but didn't mind, thinking it was something about old Mrs. Burnett, Alice just having came from her house. Dan was just going, anyways, and he had been gone only a couple of seconds when Alice ran down to tell me about poor Bee being murdered. Ask her yourself. She heard him ride away. And here's the pipe he left behind."

The sheriff shrugged, spat into a cuspidor, and rubbed the back of his head distractedly. "Well, we'll ask her tomorrow, Mr. Rugby. No use upsettin' her tonight." He turned to Dan and said surlily: "Well, you ain't said nothin' yet, Dan Hendricks. Got anythin' to say? I got to warn you anythin' you might say will be used against you, so you can please yourself."

Dan lifted his hands and let them fall casually on his knees. He smiled. Did you, Dan? I thought passionately. Did you? I don't blame you. But did you? He did not look at me. He was regarding the sheriff and smiling.

"You've heard Mr. Rugby. I haven't much else to add to it. I left Mr. Rugby's house, as he said, about forty-five minutes ago, and started home. I remember looking at the clock. It was about ten minutes to twelve. My farm's six miles out, and takes about half an hour or more to get there, fast riding. Your men picked me up half an hour ago, just halfway to the farm. I was just jogging along. I missed my pipe, and was half decided to go back for it, but thought it was too late. Yes, I heard the telephone ring in the house just when I was going out and saying goodnight to Mr. Rugby. He said something to me about it being a sick call, most likely. Yes, I had seen Mrs. Rugby earlier in the evening, and when she came back Mr. Rugby invited her into his study, but she must have been tired, for she merely said goodnight. No, she didn't say that, I don't think, but she did say something about his going to bed. Well, we heard her calling him; she must have left the telephone, and I went out and rode away."

"That," said Mortimer in a trembling voice, as he turned to the sheriff, "was the news that Bee had been found murdered, dead about two—three hours. Dan never left me a minute, from eight o'clock on, until almost twelve. You can see yourself that he couldn't have done it."

He looked from one to the other of the men imploringly. They were nearly strangers to me, all living in Ripley, big burly men like the sheriff. They stared at the sheriff, discomfited, half convinced, and discouraged. He shook his head.

"Well, seems like we've got to a stone wall. If what you say is true, Mr. Rugby, Dan here couldn't have been murdering his wife at around half past nine or ten, and been with you. Coroner says it was between half past nine or ten when she was murdered, her head half chopped off with a hatchet. Hatchet belongs to the house, too. No one was at home. I thought it looked bad, the old housekeeper being told to go home for the evening, and by Dan here, too. But folks around here think he did it, though they don't know why. I talked to a few of 'em, and they said they never heard anythin' about quarrels or anythin', but you seem to have gotten a reputation in South Kenton, Dan." He smiled at Dan in a friendly way. Dan smiled in return. His face was still bland, his eyes quiet and inscrutable.

I leaned against the ink-scarred table, feeling increasingly ill. Had he done it? Could a man commit such a ferocious murder like that and look so calm, so indifferent, so almost amused?

"You don't seem much concerned over your wife's death, Dan," said the sheriff suddenly, his smile dying. He pushed aside Mortimer, whose arms fell like dead sticks to his side.

"Concerned?" said Dan slowly, as though he were considering. "I can't seem to think much at all." He shuddered a little, and it were as though a thin, opaque skin fell over his eyes. "Beatrice and I had had some trouble lately. She insisted on staying in town with her mother, and came out to visit me only occasionally. We quarreled a lot," and he raised candid eyes to the sheriff with an expression of distress. "It was a long quarrel; I did not want to do the things she did. We didn't see things the same. Quarrels like that, lasting for years—and they did last between us, though no one knew about it—kill most affection between married people. We never saw alike. In the last year, we were almost like strangers. I know I'm not making things better for myself by saying this; you can use it against me, if you want to. But that's not the point. The point is that I couldn't have been with Mr. Rugby and been at home at half past nine, murdering my wife," and he gave a twisted smile. He looked slowly from one to the other, but he did not look at me.

The sheriff seemed impressed by Dan's candor. I saw Mortimer close his eyes for a moment as though he were about to collapse, but when he opened them again they were steady and alert. The sheriff scratched his head aimlessly.

"No prints or marks on the hatchet, either," he mused. "And nothin' was taken from the house."

I cleared my tight throat. "Where was the body found?" I asked. It was the first time I had spoken, and the sheriff turned to me in surprise.

"Eh? Oh, Dr. Marcy. Well, it was found in the settin' room, near the fire. The old woman, the housekeeper, decided to come back to the farm after all. Seems like she had a quarrel with her daughter. She thought she heard the front door shut soft-like when she come in the back door, and thought it was someone comin' in. She called, but no one answered, and she got kind of scared, thinkin' that someone must be home, for it's lonely out here, and no near neighbors, and she'd left Dan and his poor wife there when she went out about seven o'clock. So she came into the settin' room and found Mrs. Hendricks lyin' there dead. That was about fifteen minutes to ten or somethin'. She said she almost fainted, but she got herself together and called the constable here in South Kenton, and he called me, and I took Doc Andrews out there with me; he's kind of our coroner. We got out there about eleven o'clock, fast ridin'; might have been a little after eleven. The constable was waitin' for us.

"Well, there she was, all dressed, and lyin' in blood. So, we started to look for Dan Hendricks here, especially after the old woman got hysterical and said that she, Mrs. Hendricks, got just what she deserved, that she was always raggin' Dan, and naggin' him, and raisin' Cain, and that she, the old woman, was glad he'd done it, and ought to get a medal!" He smiled at us ruefully. "Well, we found Dan ridin' slowly down the road towards his farm, as he says, about forty-five minutes ago. He was more than four miles from it, and we brought him back here."

The constable came into the room. "Say, Sheriff, I ain't easy 'bout that crowd out there. They're plottin' mischief. They're threatenin' to break in and take Dan out and hang him. What'll I do? If they rush the jail we can't hold it."

The sheriff scowled. "They'll take him out over my dead body." He went to the wall and took down the receiver of the telephone, and called his office in Ripley. "Sam? Say, Sam, bring over about fifty of the boys, with shotguns. The folks here think they're goin' to have a little hangin' party, but they ain't. We're bringin' a prisoner back for safekeepin'. Hurry up, now." He hung up and turned to us.

"You're not holding Dan, are you?" cried Mortimer, almost hysterically. "You know he didn't do it. You have no right to hold him."

"Easy now, Mr. Rugby," said the sheriff soothingly. "In the first place, we got to hold him, until we talk to your wife, anyway. If you're all tellin' the truth, he's got nothin' to worry about. He'll be free tomorrow. He can get a lawyer, if he wants to, but don't seem like it's necessary. Then, in the second place, we can't let him go now, if we wanted to. That mob out there would tear him apart. So, we'll take him to Ripley, and then we'll have an inquest, and you and your wife will testify, and then if there's no evidence against him, he'll be released. But, we got to take him to Ripley anyway for his own good, safekeeping, until everyone knows he's not guilty, and believes it."

"I'm willing to go," broke in Dan quietly. He stood up, and, taking Mortimer by the arm, he shook him affectionately. "It's all right, Mr. Rugby. And, thank you."

For the first time the two men stared intently into each other's eyes, and then Mortimer's mouth worked. He put his hands on Dan's shoulders. "Dan," he said deeply, slowly, "I'm your friend. Remember that, I'm your friend."

"Yes, I know," said Dan softly. His face was suddenly very sad. "You are my friend. I'll never forget that."

Mortimer suddenly began to sob. Dan helped him to a chair. The old man shed no tears, but he covered his face with his hands and trembled frightfully. I went to him, and patted his back.

"Brace up, sir," I said in a low voice as I bent over him. "Everything's all right. Everything's all right."

Mortimer removed his hands slowly and looked up at me earnestly, as though he were questioning me, imploring me. And I nodded my head. He sighed with a heartbroken sound.

"You wouldn't know anything about this, would you, Dr. Marcy?" asked the sheriff halfheartedly. My flesh became rigid, and I felt sweat break out over my hands. But I looked at the sheriff calmly.

"No, nothing. Except that I've known Dan Hendricks all my life, and I know he couldn't have done it."

"Well, you've got a character witness, anyway, Dan," said the sheriff, smiling at him.

In all this time Dan and I had not exchanged a word, but now he looked at me directly, and I looked at him. His face was grave and quiet, but his eyes were as inscrutable as ever, as unknowable. They were like shallow water lying over a slab of rock that hid secret things. I could see the rock very distinctly. Behind that, he and everything he thought, were safely hidden.

Oh, my God! I thought desperately. Did you do it, Dan? Can't you let me know? You know my silence is the only thing that will save you. Where were you after nine o'clock? Where did you go?

For a moment I had a vivid picture of Bee Hendricks lying in her pool of blood, her bright hair dabbling it, her head half severed. The vision nauseated me, and I looked again at Dan. It were almost as if he saw my thoughts, and again presented the water-covered rock for my answer.

We had to wait a long time for the arrival of deputies

from Ripley, and in the meantime the mob outside became restive. The sheriff went out to talk to them, to gain time. We heard his booming and bawling voice outside, but did not listen. We were all very still.

They took Dan to Ripley under cover of many rifles, and I finally went home. It was nearly three o'clock in the morning.

Chapter
Twenty-Six

I went to bed, but not to sleep. There was a burning weight in my head, and I shivered with icy cold at intervals. I knew the symptoms, but grimly refused to give way to them. Not now; later, I thought stubbornly. I had to see the end of all this before I succumbed.

One thought rolled in my feverish mind: If Dan had not done this, where had he been between nine o'clock at night and midnight? If he had done it—I refused to let my mind go on, for it went on into horrors. But it was not horror for the murder; it was horror that perhaps something might slip, some fatal little word, and he would be lost. What would Alice Rugby say? With feverish clarity in the darkness, I could see the psychological deceit that Mortimer had practiced on her. Would the deceit be sufficient to delude her so thoroughly so that she would say positively

that she had heard Dan's voice at midnight in the study?
I knew she had heard mine; would she mistake it? Was
mental suggestion in her case sufficient to deceive her as
Mortimer meant it to deceive? The slightest doubt would
resolve itself into conviction.

But if he had done it, what agonies of mind he must
have endured to be whipped up into sufficient frenzy to kill
Bee, evil and monstrous though she was? What must he
have suffered for years, unseen, unknown, to anyone? I
was more horrified at this thought than at the thought of
her bloody murder.

I came downstairs for breakfast, weak and haggard,
dreading to meet my father and to give him a long story of
what I had seen and heard in the jail at night. To my un-
speakable relief, he had already heard the story from an
early visitor. He looked sullen and suspicious, like a beast
deprived of its prey. He kept shaking his head and muttering, wondering aloud if there wasn't something fishy about
it, and if Mortimer was telling the truth. The inquest, he
informed me, was being held in Ripley, the county seat, at
three o'clock that afternoon. Bee would be buried tomorrow
morning. Sarah was very ill, unconscious, and so would be
no use even if it were desired to produce her at the inquest.
My father was going to visit her that morning; as for me, he
said, I'd better rest today, for I looked half-dead.

My mother was really ill over the tragedy. She wept continually about Beatrice, staring at us in horror as she
exclaimed feebly. Poor Bee, poor dear, sweet little Bee, so
dreadfully done to death. And by an ax, too!

"What's so bad about an ax?" grunted my father. "Good,
clean killing. Better than being choked or shot, anyway.
Once the spinal column was severed, and they say it was,
there's no pain or anything. Out, like a lamp."

"You're—you're heartless!" cried my mother. But my
father and I exchanged involuntary smiles.

I tried to lie down while my father went on his calls. But
though I passionately longed for rest, I could not relax. A
thousand frightening thoughts possessed me, even against
my better judgment. What if someone had seen me enter-

ing Mortimer's house, or leaving it? What if someone had seen the same of Dan? Where would I stand, then, keeping silent? I would be an accessory to the act. I had lurid visions of going to prison, and Livy in tears, my life ruined. Dan would be lynched legally or illegally. Because of the hatred in which everyone held him, he would have no defense. He would never be believed. He could never tell about Bee, for their ears would be deafened with their hatred. He would be considered maligning a helpless and well-liked young woman, dead now, unable to defend herself.

I groaned and tossed on the parlor sofa. The door opened and Livy came in, returned from her sister's. She was still in her hat and coat, my mother gesticulating and crying behind her, telling the news.

"I've heard it, Mother," she said gravely. She came to me, very grave and composed. Her eyes were shadowed in deep violet, her lips bloodless. She kissed me gently.

"Jim, dear, you don't look well," she said. "Come upstairs with me and lie down." She took my cold hand and rubbed it. I went upstairs to our own apartment with her, leaving my mother very offended.

Livy made me eat some lunch. She would not let me talk until I had swallowed the hot soup. Then she listened while I told her the story I had heard in the jail, and of Dan's quick removal to Ripley. She got up and went to the door, opened it quickly, shut it, then returned to me. For a long time she studied me thoughtfully.

"Jim," she whispered, "you haven't told me everything. What do you know about it?"

I started, and choked over a piece of bread. She moistened her lips as she waited for me to speak. Her expression was affectionate and sad, but her eyes were intent and full of terror.

I felt an hysterical relief. It would be a blessing to have someone else share my secret. I opened my mouth to speak, but she suddenly put her soft hand over my mouth.

"No!" she whispered. "I knew there was something! But I don't want to hear it! No! You mustn't ever speak of it to anyone, not even to me. No, I won't listen!"

I subsided, and after a moment she removed her hand. She looked utterly exhausted.

"Well," I said hoarsely, "perhaps you are right. I'll never speak of it to anyone. But Livy, I know he is innocent, anyway." I did not know that my voice had risen on a question until she smiled slightly.

She looked off into the distance. "Yes, Jim, whether he did it or not, he is still innocent," she said.

At noon I was burning with fever, but I set out for Ripley, nevertheless. Only a pair of broken legs would have kept me away. Livy was not going, and neither was my father. I took the obscure road that led by Dan's farm, which lengthened the journey by three miles. But I wished to avoid the exodus from South Kenton, which was going to Ripley. And indeed, fully a third of the population of our little town was headed there.

I remember distinctly the pale and brilliant sunlight of the early winter day, the sharp frost that tingled in the air, the brown bare trees, the long gray winding of the country road, the smoky floating of the distant hills. So clear and empty was the atmosphere that I could distinctly hear the clucking of distant chickens about lonely farmhouses, and the noises of barnyard animals. It was a landscape of complete emptiness, drained of all color, drained of life. I seemed to be the only moving thing. An awful depression settled on me, so that I kept glancing over my shoulder in the hope of any comforting sight. There was none. My horse trotted heavily, as though he too was weighed down, not by any visible oppression in the landscape, but by the psychic apathy that emanated from me.

I passed Dan's house, deserted and motionless behind its line of pines, the small fields about it stricken and sterile. No smoke came from its chimneys; it did not seem to brood in the manner of many farmhouses, but looked merely like a painted house, without dimension.

My fever was mounting, and I had begun to cough sorely. I am sure I was a little giddy, also, for I found myself clutching the saddle with cold, damp hands. And I am sure it was because of this that that inexplicable thing happened to me just as I came abreast of Dan's house; in the indeterminate region of the early fever of an illness, almost any delusion might occur to the victim. But at any rate, when things for a moment became unreal to all my senses, and the landscape seemed to float in a sick brilliance not at all real, I distinctly heard Beatrice's sly, sweet voice in my ear, or rather in my inner ear. First there was a soft weird ringing in that ear, like a warning note, (a faint "ping," to be exact), and then I heard her say, idly, amusedly: "You are saving the life of the man your wife loves, Jim."

I am certain that I had not been thinking of her objectively; in reality I had not been really thinking at all, conscious only of mental confusion and rapidly increasing physical distress. She had always seemed somewhat unreal to me, even when alive, a sort of bright, disembodied evil that had for a moment caught with avid fingers at a lump of immobile flesh, and manifested itself for a very short while in alien gestures, grotesque words. (I think I said once before that in the light of newer, more modern knowledge, Beatrice seems to me to be the only natural, fully rounded personality I have ever known, because she rarely troubled to hide her true self from fairly intelligent people, and because she knew absolutely what she wanted. And yet, because of this naturalness, she seemed unreal.)

No, I had not been thinking of Beatrice, and when I heard, or thought I heard, her voice, I involuntarily jerked at the reins. My horse stopped apathetically. I stared around me with affrighted eyes, stared at the farmhouse, at the silent and dazzling landscape. I had always wondered if that phrase, "And his tongue clove to the roof of his mouth" was merely a picturesque figure of speech, but I knew it was not in that moment. My throat contracted, my dry tongue stuck to the roof of my mouth, and an indescribable horror clutched me. Then for some reason my horse moved on, slowly, as though touched by an invisible hand. He began to trot and finally to gallop. I found myself panting and I slowed down the animal. I did not look back until I was sure that I had put some two miles between myself and that dreadful house.

In my dreamlike state induced by fever, a thousand formless and terrifying thoughts passed through my mind. I had never been one to speculate very much on the immortality of the individual, and my medical education had wiped out any faint speculations I might have had. But now I began to wonder. If souls do survive, I found myself thinking in my sickness, then they are not purged and given noble enlightenment immediately. They must, if they survive at all, carry with them into the outer spaces of reality their own identities, personalities, evils, and virtues. If Beatrice survived, then she was just as she had been, and was invisible evil as she had been a visible one, bent on hurt, on malice and cruelty. I confess the idea did nothing to restore my confidence, and I urged my horse into a gallop again, running full into a raw wind as though fleeing from something. Why, she can still hurt Dan! I thought wildly. She can still hate him, and pursue him!

I don't know how I arrived at Ripley, but that whole awful ride was obsessed by the fiendish thought. I could see nothing but Beatrice's face; I could not escape its smile; if ever a man was haunted, I was. But what she had said, or what I had imagined she had said, did not occupy me actively, so she defeated her own purpose.

It was only two o'clock when I arrived, and in accordance with my plans, I went to the jail to see Dan before the inquest. Something obscure was urging me there. The first person I encountered was the sheriff. He looked important and pompous, but grinned amiably when he saw me.

"Hi, Doc," he said, shaking hands. "Say, your little hick town has had more doin' in it the last few years than Warburton itself has had in twenty years. Always someone shootin' someone, or killin' himself, or gettin' murdered. You ought to incorporate; too much doin' in South Kenton for a village. Ought to spread itself out."

I wasn't amused at this joke, and I told him I wanted to see Dan. He led me into the jail proper. I could see that this tragedy did not displease him; he informed me that three reporters from Warburton were waiting for the inquest, and that he shouldn't wonder if New York itself gave a prominent place in its news to the case. He had had his photograph taken that morning, and he told me candidly that the boys had gotten him in a bad pose, he was sure of it. He also told me that old Mortimer had ridden over to Ripley at the crack of dawn that morning, and that he had just left after an interview with Dan. I imagined very clearly what was said in that interview. The sheriff volunteered the information that Dan had suffered no inconvenience during the night, but was occupying the best cell. I did not make any answer to all this, for I felt the ominous waning of my strength and so conserved it as much as possible.

He opened a cell door with a flourish, and Dan, who was sitting on his bed looked up without surprise when I came in.

"When you are through, yell," said the amiable sheriff, and strode humming down the dank corridor.

Dan did not seem to be the worse for his experience. In fact, he looked as though he had had his first good night's rest for a long time. He was neatly dressed, shaved, smiling and calm. We shook hands in silence, but even in that intimate moment I had the old feeling that he stood behind a thick wall of transparent glass, that he could speak to me, gesture to me, but that I could not touch him. For one moment I had the childish thought that this was no way to treat a friend who had your life in his hands. What he was thinking I did not know.

"Sit down, Jim" he said genially. "Smoke? No?" He had offered me a box of cigars. "Jim," he added in a kindly voice, "you look sick. Anyone would think you were the suspect and not I."

I was silent. I could think of nothing to say; my thoughts ran around dully, like stupefied animals. My body was alternately icy cold and burningly hot.

"Can anyone hear us in here?" I asked heavily, after several moments.

"No, not if we sit close together and talk softly," he answered. He raised his eyebrows, as though surprised that I might have something dangerous or too intimate to say.

I moved from the wooden chair to the cot beside him. I stared at him somberly and piercingly. I am sure there was no excuse for the sudden amused twitching of his mouth as he returned my regard, as though a child were subjecting him to scrutiny.

That expression of his broke down all my composure, and I cried, half-hysterically, half-frenziedly: "For God's sake, man, don't pretend now that I am being preternaturally solemn and funny! I'm not, and you know I am not!"

My breath was hoarse and painful, and I think that concerned him more than what I said, for he put his hand over mine gently. It was only when his calm flesh came over my hand that I realized that it was trembling violently.

"Jim," he said, "you are sick. You are flushed, too. You ought not to have come. I'm not laughing at you. What do you want to say to me?"

"You are always so damned untouched, as though nothing really concerned you," I said bitterly. "Always the impersonal spectator."

He said nothing, and looked away from me. That opaque look came over his face again. I edged closer to him, shivering in my thick coat.

"Dan," I whispered, "please tell me. Where did you go after nine o'clock last night?"

He continued to smoke for a moment or two, then turned an unreadable face to me. "Why do you ask that, Jim? Do you think I murdered my wife?"

"No!" I shouted violently. "Of course I don't!" I lowered my voice. "But someone—might have seen you. What will you do if old Mort's alibi falls down?"

He put his hand on my shoulder, smiling. "Suppose you let me take care of that, Jim. Let me do the worrying."

And that was as far as I got. I fumed miserably. I wiped my face with my handkerchief. My irritation against him became frantic. I heard myself talking again, but it was an instant or two after I had begun to speak before I realized what I was saying. Fever, and a mounting sense of unreality, broke down all my reserve.

"I've always been your friend. But these last few years,

you've put me off, as though I was your enemy. I couldn't get close to you. You wouldn't let me. What have I done? I admit I'm a coward; you'll notice I don't say 'was.' I still am. I'll run from anything disagreeable. That's the way I'm made. But discretion still seems the better part of valor to me. But that's no excuse for the way you've put up something between us—"

"Excuse?" he broke in. He was completely serious now. "I've never excused myself to you, Jim, for anything. Look here: when a man is loathsomely sick, or taking a bath, or doing other intimate things, he doesn't make a public display of it, does he? He shuts his doors. It is a private matter, kept apart even from his friends. Friends are damnable! They think they ought to be admitted to your bedroom and your privy. They think they can walk through your house, and demand that every door be wide open for their casual inspection at any hour, on any day. They give you no privacy; you are not a dignified individual to them, with decent doors and reticences; you are a book they can open any time, a table they can sit at and eat whenever they wish, a tramping place for their muddy boots. Jim, you are a fine fellow, but you always wanted to walk through my house uninvited and got all huffed up when I tried to inform you that there were rooms closed even to you. You invaded my privacy."

"Thank you," I said angrily.

He nodded his head gravely. "It's true, Jim, and you know it. Hell, I have no patience with people who let their friends in all the time. It's because they have nothing valuable to hide or have no self-respect. I don't trust a man who has nothing to hide, nothing he considers inviolate or private. You wanted to swarm into my life, touching everything, leaving prints on things I didn't want touched, that were half a secret to me, myself. Beatrice," and he spoke without visible wincing or awkwardness, "Beatrice always said you were a 'prober.' And once I said to her: 'No, he is merely a friend.' "

He looked at me mildly, and in spite of my humiliation I could not keep up my anger.

"You can be sure," I said stiffly, "that I won't go into your bedroom, or your privy, as you say so elegantly, anymore. Keep your damn secrets."

He smiled. "I shall," he promised, and once again I had the feeling that he was warning me off.

"Hell, I only wanted to help you, Dan," I said brokenly and humbly.

"I know it, Jim," he said gently. "But there are things that can't be helped, that only get festered from handling. Old Mort doesn't handle; he touches what I let him touch, and keeps away from the things that I don't want touched. But I know I haven't any better friend than you."

I had wanted to talk about the inquest, but I did not, now. I left him a few moments later, very heavy-hearted.

Ripley had no personal animosity toward Dan, not knowing him. In fact, the crowds gathered about the jail seemed to wear grateful expressions. Dan had brought color and excitement into their monotonous lives. The Ripleyites, being on the scene, occupied all the available seats in the room where the inquest was held, much to the annoyance of arriving visitors from South Kenton. But the Ripleyites placidly refused to be turned from their seats by angry hints and angrier looks. "We are personally interested in this," the visitors seemed to say, "and so we are entitled to your seats."

The inquest jury was composed of sunburned farmers and small tradesmen unknown to me, and for this I was deeply grateful and relieved. Dan would have a fair hearing. He had waived immunity, he had told me, and the famous criminal lawyer was going to be present to protect his interests. That lawyer was a tiny and emaciated Jew, with a clever, ugly face, and a pair of the most brilliant and beautiful eyes I have ever seen in either man or woman. He looked like a midget beside Dan as he accompanied his client into the inquest room. I was not particularly impressed with either the stature or the manner of the lawyer, for he seemed fussy and had a high, piercing voice. Dan sat down, but his lawyer stood up, full of nervous energy, perpetually shifting his position, cracking his knuckles, and talking, talking incessantly to the reporters about the table, to Dan, or to some casual acquaintance. I was disappointed and apprehensive; I had expected some imposing personality, someone who would dominate the proceedings, a man who would charm, hypnotize, awe and intimidate. It was not until the proceedings began that I realized his genius and his power. His name was Sam Walstein.

Disappointed and threatening-faced South Kentonites and Ripleyites who had arrived too late had actually climbed up on the window ledges outside and were pressing their faces whitely against the glass in an effort to see. The heat and odors in the small room were stifling; the jury sat in its box, all round and solemn faces, removed and important. Luckily, for some mysterious reason, I had been able to gain a seat in front. I saw Mortimer at a little distance, haggard and absent of expression, and old Martha, shivering in a shabby coat, her ancient face blotched with tears, her eyelids continually trembling. I tried to catch Mortimer's eyes, but when I did so he remained aloof and blank.

The sheriff entered, swollen with importance, but happily genial. Thank God, I thought, he's not inimical towards Dan, but he's out for a show and will make himself chief actor.

The hum in the room died down into complete silence. The coroner was called, and made a lengthy and prosy report. He might have been talking about a slaughtered hog, for any horror or color that he gave the proceedings. I remarked one or two errors in his report. He did not want to give up his place in the spotlight; poor man, this was probably the only important spot he had ever occupied in his life. He submitted with relish to questioning by the sheriff, and was hurt and annoyed when Sam Walstein said that he had nothing to ask the witness. The coroner left the stand with visible reluctance. But he had definitely established the time of Beatrice's death as between nine-thirty and ten o'clock the previous night.

The next witness was old Martha. She was helped to the stand by the constable, and sat shaking on her chair, sunken in her coat, her jet-strung bonnet twinkling. She gave Dan a wild and pleading glance. He did not move an inch, but he smiled at her encouragingly. She began to cry. The sheriff questioned her.

Yes, Mr. Dan had told her after supper that she could go see her daughter, who was sick, and that she might stay overnight if she wanted to. No, he did not seem to want to get rid of her, exactly. In fact, she replied, with a suddenly hopeful lighting of her old face, he had not told her she might go until she had asked him. She repeated this over and over, until the sheriff irritatedly halted her.

The sheriff cleared his throat.

"What were the family relations between Mr. Hendricks and his wife, I mean, what you could see of them?" he asked.

Again she sent Dan that wild and pleading glance and wrung her hands together before she replied. Well, sir, she was always a-naggin' him and a-naggin' him. She, Martha, didn't know just what about, because she didn't listen— much. (Laughter) Anyways, it was about him ruinin' her life, or somethin', because he didn't like sassiety and was always a-disgracin' of her. There was somethin' about her mother that she said, too, but Martha couldn't understand it, for Mrs. Hendricks didn't say right out what it was, but just sort of hinted about it. It was Martha's opinion that she was a nasty, mean woman, never a kind word to say to anybody or of anybody.

At this Sam Walstein broke in, with a deferential bow towards the sheriff.

"If it may please the sheriff," he said courteously, "this isn't a murder trial, where justification for a murder is being brought out. No one is being accused of the murder, yet. In fact, it hasn't yet been established that there is a murder."

The sheriff glared at him. "You ain't, I mean, you aren't trying to say she might've cut her head off herself with the ax, Mr. Walstein?"

"Not exactly," replied the attorney, still courteous, "but until we have evidence that someone did murder her, we must assume that she did."

"Well, it's irregular," said the sheriff, somewhat nonplussed. He resumed his questioning of old Martha. I felt some respect for him. With surprising adroitness, considering the watchfulness of Sam Walstein, he did bring out that there had been a more serious quarrel that night between Dan and his wife, and though Sam objected to some leading questions, I could see that the jury was impressed. The sheriff was no fool.

The inquest, Sam remarked gently, was to discover if there had been a murder, and if so, to disclose sufficient evidence against anyone to submit to the grand jury. One must always keep in mind that there might have been a half-dozen murderers, and no particular man. His voice, suddenly soft and calm, began to dominate the proceedings; I saw he was deliberately trying to disconcert the sheriff. And yet, neither by gesture nor word nor voice, was this evident. However, he succeeded so well that the sheriff missed several good points that could have been used advantageously against Dan; this was evident even to my inexperienced eyes. The jury did not seem to notice this.

Mortimer was called. He came deliberately to the stand, submitted to routine questions put him by the sheriff. He repeated, calmly and unemotionally, the story he had told the night before. He referred repeatedly to his wife. Sam took him over.

"You are positive it was nearly twelve, or twelve, when Mr. Hendricks left your house, Mr. Rugby?"

"Yes, positive. I remember that I was worried about Mrs. Rugby, and I looked at the clock. I hoped I should not have to go after her, and then remembered that Jack, my son, would probably bring her home. And then she came home."

"There was no earthly reason, if someone other than Mr. Hendricks was in your study, to tell your wife it was he?"

"None at all," was the calm reply. "I invited her in to say goodnight to him."

Sam looked calmly about the room.

"I hope, if anyone else was with Mr. Rugby last night, that he will come forward now."

There was a prolonged silence. Nobody moved. I looked at Mortimer, but he did not look at me.

I had not seen Mrs. Rugby enter the room, but she was called as the next witness. She, too, looked haggard. And somewhat angry and truculent, for all her long, melancholy face and prominent blue eyes. She settled herself fussily; in every gesture was the annoyance of a woman who disliked appearing in defense of someone she detested, but who would nevertheless tell the truth dutifully. The sheriff questioned her. She began a prolonged story full of intimate details of Mrs. Burnett's illness, and it wasn't until the sheriff sarcastically assured her that no one suspected her of visiting anyone else but Mrs. Burnett that she halted. She was slow-witted; outraged color did not mount into her pale face until everyone laughed. Urged by the sheriff, she told her story, with long side remarks. Dan had been there with her husband in the study when she had left, somewhere around half-past seven or so. She had seen him; he was smoking that pipe there, and she pointed to the exhibit on the table. How was she sure that was his pipe? Well, she hated tobacco smoking, and she had stared at the pipe pointedly as she stood in the doorway, but he had refused to take the hint. So, she remembered it. She was sure that was the pipe. She had come home at twelve; she remembered that very clearly, for Mrs. Burnett lived on the other side of town, and it was a good twenty minutes away from home, and she had been startled when she had seen a clock in the Burnett house and saw it was after half past eleven. She had come home and heard voices in the study, and when she reached the door Mortimer had asked her to come in to say goodnight to Dan, and she had refused after telling Mortimer to go to bed. Then she had gone upstairs, and the telephone had rung, and she had heard the news from her son, who had just heard it when he got home. Yes, he could get home in ten minutes. She had run downstairs to tell Mortimer and Dan, and heard her husband just saying goodnight to Dan, and closing the door, and then she heard Dan's horse going away.

"Did you see his horse before you went away?" asked the

sheriff. The question came as a jolt to me, and I sat up, my senses swimming. We had not thought of the horse! It had been hitched to the post, which was in clear view from the street. I looked at Dan; he was listening to this, as he had been listening to all the testimony, with utter impassivity and calm.

Mrs. Rugby wrinkled her forehead, and in the momentary silence, I glanced at Mortimer. He had turned ghastly pale, and was leaning forward slightly in his chair. Yes, said Mrs. Rugby at last, she had seen the horse. She had passed the front of the house in going away, and when she returned, she had seen the horse still standing there, blanketed. Was she sure it was the same horse? Yes, she replied firmly, after a moment, she was sure. And she had been very angry, seeing that Dan had kept her husband up, and Mr. Rugby a sick man. I sat back in my chair, shaken; thank God the night had been dark! The shot that might have killed Dan had saved him.

She went on to say that her husband had run to the door after she had told him the news and had called Dan, and that he had shown her the still-smoking pipe. No, her husband did not smoke. Sam took her over.

"Was she certain that the voices she had heard in the study were those of Mortimer and Dan?" I thought this a dangerous question, but Sam Walstein was a bold man. I am sure, looking back now, that his shrewdness must have suspected something which he would have designated as not being quite kosher, but his whole career was based on such apparently reckless strokes.

And masterfully was it proved the adroitness of the mental suggestion that Mortimer had practiced on his wife. In a loud firm voice she declared that she was positive that it was Dan's voice that she had heard; why, she had known him all his life and couldn't be mistaken!

The sheriff had ruffled her, and Sam's manner was all respect and tenderness. She regarded him with more graciousness. He soothed and flattered her with his eyes.

"I am sure that you are a very intelligent lady, Mrs. Rugby," he said softly. "I am sure that your husband would not have had so low an estimate of your intelligence as to try to deceive you, would he?"

"Indeed not," said the lady with a toss of her head. "Mortimer had never deceived me, no, indeed. He was as innocent as a little sheep, and knew as little about taking care of himself as a sheep."

Then Sam dealt his master stroke, a stroke of pure genius. He leaned towards Mrs. Rugby ingratiatingly, pleadingly.

"My client, Mrs. Rugby, is in a rather difficult position. I understand that he is not very well liked in his own town. Can't you tell us all something in his behalf, something to his advantage, about his character?"

Mrs. Rugby's pleasant expression vanished; she glared down upon the little lawyer, pursed her wide lips, and tossed her head angrily.

"No, I can't! Everything everyone said about him was true. No one liked him. He had done lots of awful things, and no one ever spoke to him. If it hadn't been for his poor young wife, heavens knows what would have happened." No, she had nothing good to say about him, and she only wished that she hadn't been put into a position where she had to tell the truth, that he was with her husband last night. Otherwise, if she hadn't known him to be there, she would have believed, indeed, that he had killed poor little Beatrice.

And thus Sam cleverly removed from the jury's mind any possible doubt that she had lied or been mistaken. Her outright animosity towards Dan, her announced reluctance to appear for him, settled the case. Within a few minutes the jury brought in a verdict of murder "by a person or persons unknown."

The crowded room began to empty. I saw Sam Walstein and Mortimer Rugby beside Dan; Mortimer had his arm around Dan's shoulder, and the little lawyer's face was wrinkling grotesquely, and he waved and gesticulated. He must have been saying something humorous, for Dan suddenly laughed loudly, and Mortimer chuckled. None of them looked in my direction. I felt deserted and depressed. Moreover, my fever was at the stage where the air alternately darkened in front of my eyes and then was full of tiny slivers of dazzling light. My sense of illness was becoming acute. I realized I had only a little time. I looked around for Dan and Mortimer again but they had disappeared. I pushed through the excited people in the aisles, but I could not find either of the two men.

I had an urgent desire to see Dan again immediately.

There seemed to be no sense in the desire, no reason in it. But see him I must. I went out into the cold and ashen day. The sun had disappeared, and by the thick massing of the clouds I was sure that snow was coming. The streets of Ripley were wider and had more traffic than South Kenton, and due to the fame of the case and its horrible details, these streets were thronged from curb to curb with buggies, buckboards, and carriages. All sounds merged into a prolonged uproar in my ears. I did not see anyone I knew intimately; everyone from South Kenton had vanished.

The only thing I can do, I thought, is to go to Dan's farm. He will return there, of course, and was probably already on the way. Mortimer would most likely be driving him home. If I hurried on my horse I would no doubt overtake them. I mounted and rode away. Every step of the horse made a separate agony in my aching bones. I stopped for a moment at a saloon, and, shivering violently, I drank two or three glasses of whiskey to warm up my chills. The saloon was crowded and everyone was vociferously discussing the inquest. I went out and got on my horse. I had some difficulty in leaving the town due to the crowded streets, but eventually I was on the open road. I circled around to the south, and soon found the road that meandered obscurely over the hills in the direction of Dan's farm. It was comparatively empty, for I was taking the long route again. I thought it most likely that Mortimer would take that route, but though I rode rapidly I did not sight them, though I expected to over each hill. But the road stretched away, gray and desolate and silent, past lonely farmhouses and copses of bare woods.

Due to my illness and the whiskey, my mind was at once preternaturally acute and dulled. My thoughts, secret, inner, obscure, had the acuteness, but all awareness of outward things had the dullness. I seemed to have been absorbed into the very center of my brain, and thoughts that in health and soberness had always been a little vague and unformed suddenly took on sharpness and color and significance. I could hardly endure them; they seemed like a sort of anguish, and I began to wonder if it were not for the best that our senses are a little calloused and numb with familiarity. It would not be possible for a man to live in such a state of acute awareness; it would be like living without a skin, every nerve exposed, every brain center unprotected, quivering with reflexes and assaults. For one moment I actually seemed to see a brain so denuded; every gray and glistening fold was visible to my eye, shivering and shrinking, suffering and defenseless.

"I wonder if that isn't the way the soul is, when it is stripped of its protecting flesh," I said aloud, "attacked on every side by a thousand impressions, every thought and every touch magnified countless times, every vague emotion like a wasp with a red-hot sting."

The thought made me feel physically ill. I tried to focus my eyes objectively on the country through which I was passing. But a transparently dim shadow seemed to have fallen over it, through which every object was at once intensely intrusive and immensely distant and formless. For a little while I forgot who I was, where I was, and where I was going, and I'll never forget the anguish I endured for that brief while as I struggled to recapture my identity and reason.

The road continued to be empty. Surely some of the people from South Kenton must have come this way, if only to avoid the heavy traffic on the main road. For a few moments I thought I did see a group of horsemen and two or three buggies ahead, but when I looked closer, either because it had been a delusion or the day was becoming too dark, or the road wound too much, I did not see them again.

Suddenly I thought of Beatrice, and she became the acutest thing in all the world to me. She is not dead, I thought. She is more alive than we are, more mobile, more comprehensive, and more vicious. The whole atmosphere seemed to become charged with her personality; she was the heavy sky, smothering and cold and close; she was the iron earth, rigid with frost; she was the barren stretches of the colorless countryside and the gray smoke of the hills.

She imbued everything with desolation and death, with decay and hatred, with emptiness and sterility. She did not seem to speak to me again, but her presence oppressed me, weighed me down with a sense of horror. I rode on, bent double in my saddle, shivering.

And then I seemed to see Livy's face, the steadfast eyes, the resolute mouth. I could see the fine white honesty of her, the lack of hypocrisy, the clear courage. She was like a light breaking into darkness, and Beatrice seemed to recede, to be swallowed up, to retreat into fathomless places. The sharpness of my perception faded; everything lost psychic and terrifying significance, became friendly and concrete again, earthy and familiar. I was again only a sick man hurrying home. With the fading of the perception came physical exhaustion.

I began to wonder about Dan. For the thousandth time I turned the whole matter over in my mind. He had left at nine o'clock; he could, by fast riding, have reached his farm within an hour, murdered his wife, left softly when old Martha had let herself in the back door, and then could have galloped back to town. When nearing the outskirts, at a little after eleven, he could have started back leisurely. He would have known that they would be looking for him, and he could have let them pick him up at a shrewdly calculated time, after midnight. During this time he could have planned his alibi, knowing that old Mortimer would not betray him, knowing that I would keep silent. But, did he do all this? Remembering him, I could hardly believe that he had planned to kill Beatrice without revealing to me some faint sign of what was going on in his mind. Or, perhaps, he had no intention of killing her when he had left us at or a little before nine o'clock, and only formulated his story when the thing was done. But, did he do all this? Was I never to know?

I knew that if I had been less his friend I still could not have betrayed him. Somehow, the thought that Livy had loved him, might still love him, did not seem important. It was just a sad incident which I could not make real. My mind then was preoccupied with the old puzzling

wonder as to why Dan was hated so. "Socialist?" It
sounded ludicrous to me. I knew more than did anyone else
the hatred and disgust in which Dan held the shiftless and
the stupid, the improvident and the illiterate. If he had
defended a few of these people it was because he could not
endure to see suffering. He had an impartial sense of justice.
But these things did not account for the active animosity
and detestation in which he was held by almost all who
knew him. He had never been aggressive, he had never
forced himself anywhere, he had always retreated, always
shut doors behind him. He had rarely spoken. He had not
been manifestly peculiar, obstrusively distinctive. He had
not been a great genius, thus arousing envy and scorn.
Why, then?

I still do not know. It was not because of his obscure
beginnings, for one of the young men of whom South
Kenton was most proud had been the son of a miserable
farmer, then Ezra King had taken the lad into his bank to
do errand jobs and sweeping. But he had shown application
and intelligence and was on the way to becoming manager.
South Kenton was democratic in its way.

And then, perhaps it was that very aloofness, that very
impersonal withdrawal, that very indifference to everyone
that had set hate barking after Dan. He had lived among
us, but not with us. He had been a stranger who had made
no effort to learn our language, not from superior contempt,
but from utter indifference. Because he really had not seen
us. Yes, perhaps that was it. Mankind can endure any
affront except not being noticed.

"Look and pass." He had looked at us, had seen us only
impersonally, had passed and left us. Just as he had looked
at life and passed it. It was without color and point and
significance to him. Whether he was right or wrong I do not
know. Even today it seems a bloodless and alien way to look
at life. He probably could not help it. His inner eye could
not focus on anything about him; he was preoccupied with
the secret and vivid life he lived in himself. Perhaps, I
thought suddenly, he was that exposed and quivering brain
that I had seemed to see objectively. Perhaps he had woven

an artificial covering for it to protect it from the onslaughts of a fanged reality, and through that covering he could neither see nor feel. He was a prisoner in a small house with shuttered windows, but what went on in that house, none of us would ever know.

The next turn in the road brought me in sight of Dan's farm. I could see the dark greenness of the line of pines, the little valleys and hollows in the fields, the familiar hills. I spurred up my horse thankfully. Then as I came closer I saw that a group of about twenty men stood in the narrow and rutty roadway that led to Dan's house. They had hitched their horses to saplings and gateposts. Five or six buggies stood emptily on the bleached grass.

When the men heard my horse, they surged together in a mass and waited. There was an ominous air about them, a held menace. I could see the smoke of their pipes now, and the whips in their hands. A dull mutter came from them. But evidently they had mistaken me for Dan, for when they recognized me the mutter died down; they spat into the gray dust of the roadway and exchanged glances. I recognized several of them as being members of the lesser townfolk and country folk, but among them were Dave King, Willie Williams, and Jack Rugby. I pulled up my horse.

"Hello," I said uncertainly.

"Hello, Jim," muttered Jack Rugby with visible and sullen uneasiness. "What're you doing here?"

"I can ask the same thing of you," I replied. My vision became clear with apprehension. "I came to see Dan."

"So did we," said Dave King, and a hoarse and sinister chuckle rose from the other men.

I got off my horse slowly. "Look here," I said to my friends, "I hope you fellows aren't going to make any trouble. Dan's been freed of any suspicion in this business. I hope you aren't going to make fools of yourselves. There's law, you know. Surely none of you are asses enough to think he did that. He wasn't even around."

"That's the story," said Jack significantly. "But all of us

think there's something fishy about the whole business. Why, there's not been a tramp in these parts for months. No one else could have done it." He looked at me without friendliness, a stocky and sturdy young man with a red face and a cold and alert blue eye.

"If you were down in Ripley today, you know the whole story," I said angrily. "He didn't do it. I know he didn't do it. Not that I would blame him if he did. She deserved killing. But, that isn't the point. Why, Jack, he was with your father. Your mother saw him, heard him. Do you think they are liars?"

He shrugged. "I shill think there's something fishy about it." He surveyed me with contempt. "Don't get het up, Jim. We aren't going to hang or even to whip your damn friend. All we're going to do is to tell him to get out of here, leave the country. We don't want him around. Of course," he added casually, "if he doesn't see things our way we're going to persuade him."

I looked around at the surly and threatening faces of the others in despair. I put my hand on the side of my horse to steady myself.

"Expect you'd better go along, Jim," said Willie Williams, not unkindly. He laughed a little. "I'm a lawyer, ain't I? I'm here to protect the interest of my clients. I'll not let them get into a hanging matter. But anyway, we're going to see that Mr. Dan Hendricks leaves these parts, personally. I can even be his lawyer; I'll offer to close up all his business for him. I guess we can make him see reason."

The others burst into loud laughter, and looked at me derisively.

"There's law," I began.

"Yep, there's law," agreed Jack, flicking his leg significantly with his whip.

I glared at the nondescript men behind my friends. "Say, you, Jack, Dave, Willie, you aren't going to head this mob, are you?" I pleaded. "Where's your pride, getting mixed up with them? This—this is anarchy." My tongue felt thick.

"Oh, that's all right," said Dave easily. "Don't mind the other boys, Jim. We didn't invite them; they just came along with us, to see the fun."

"Now, be a nice little fellow and run home," urged Willie, coming forward languidly. He towered over me some six inches, being a lanky and spindling young man with a good-natured and almost perpetually grinning face. Despite his profession, he seemed a yokel, with his big, clumsy feet, shock of light yellow hair, and small, narrow eyes.

"No," I said quietly, "I'm staying." I looked at them all significantly. "I may be needed as a witness. Besides, I think I'll go into the house and telephone for the sheriff. You can argue it out with him."

I started for the house, but Willie, his good nature wiped from his face, seized me by the arm.

"No, you don't," he said, and his voice was no longer languid; it was grim. "We can't drive you off, if you insist on being a fool, but you're not going to get us into any trouble."

At that instant we heard the sound of approaching wheels in the clear and motionless air. Willie dropped my arm. We all swung in the direction of the sound. A buggy had turned into the roadway and was approaching slowly. Despite the dim light I could see that it was Mortimer's vehicle, and that he was driving. Dan sat beside him. A thick silence fell on the men. The buggy came on, then one of the men ran forward a few steps, snatched the reins from Mortimer's hands, and stopped the horse. Instantly the buggy was surrounded. I could not work my way through the press.

"Hello," said Jack quietly and slowly. I saw Mortimer's old face, thin and ghastly in the gloomy light, his eyes blinking. I saw Dan's face, passive and indifferent and removed. He merely glanced from one to another of the men. He was smoking his restored pipe placidly.

"Jack!" cried Mortimer shrilly. "What is all this?"

"I'm sorry you're here," said Jack regretfully. "Come on, Dad, get out. We want to talk to Dan Hendricks."

Mortimer clenched his whip, looked about himself desperately.

"I don't know what this is all about," he exclaimed loudly. "But I'd advise you fellows to let us pass. I can't believe this of you, Jack. I thought you had sense. We'll have a talk about this when we get home."

"Of course we will, Dad," said Jack gently. "But now, please get out. Here, let me help you."

"Get out, Mortimer," said Dan very quietly. "I'll handle this." He looked at them with profound contempt.

"No," said Mortimer resolutely, clutching his whip. He looked about him wildly, saw me, and for moment I read the sudden terror in his poor old face. I saw that he believed in that moment that I had told everything. I felt hot with humiliation and fear, and shook my head at him fiercely. He sank back a little on his seat. "Jack, let us by. This is no time for any nonsense. Call off this pack of dogs, and we'll talk it over in the house."

Jack hesitated, and glanced at his two friends. They looked irresolute. But the "pack" would not be deprived of its holiday; they did not believe in genteel palaver. They were out for blood and would not allow the "classy" fellows to take it from them.

"No, you don't go into that house!" shouted one of them, a burly farmer, as he pushed himself forward. "We're a-goin' to settle things right here and now! That so-and-so's got to leave town, and right away! We're a-goin' to be the bodyguard that's goin' to take him to the cars. You other fellas can do what you want, come with us or not. What you say, boys?" and he turned to his companions, who roared in answer.

I looked at Jack and Willie and Dave with grim bitterness. "Well, you started something you can't finish, boys," I said. Jack gave me an evil look. But he was plainly disturbed. He tried to placate the men.

"Yes, he'll get out today," he said unemotionally. "But, there're things to settle. He's entitled to take what he wants with him. We'll go in with him, and you others can wait outside for us."

"No!" shouted the mob. "We're goin' to be right here, and so is he, and you, too. And if he don't hurry up, we'll drag him out of that buggy and hang him, in spite of your yellow guts and the old man there!"

They crowded around the buggy, pushing my friends roughly aside. Several hands reached up to seize Dan, who had sat in silence during all this, seemingly not connected with the matter at all. He was still smoking.

The word "hang" threw poor old Mortimer into madness. He sprang to his feet, crouching. He raised his whip, struck the men violently in the faces with it, then lashed at the held horse. It leaped into the air, slashed out with its hoofs, scattering the men for an instant, then sprang forward. Someone grasped for the reins, but the buggy leapt ahead; the reins were caught again, and the buggy was brought to a violent standstill.

Old Mortimer had been standing up, lashing about him; the sudden leaping forward of the vehicle had caused him to stagger. Its violent stopping threw him off his feet, and like from a catapult he was hurled out of the buggy, over the heads of the men, and thrown crashingly into the roadway.

It had all happened in a few seconds. It had taken eternities of slow and ponderous motion. I stared at all this, stupefied, at the trembling horse, at Dan leaning forward to see, at the suddenly silent men, at the crushed and motionless figure in the roadway. Mortimer's head had struck a sharp rock, and had been hurled grotesquely aside. I knew in one instant that his neck was broken, and that he was dead. And over all, the men, the buggy, the thin black figure sprawled on the ground, the pale dim light of the November evening fell. I even remember seeing the far pricking of the new stars in the sky.

And then, I don't remember just what took place next, but I found myself in the press of men, striking out madly at bobbing faces. I kicked and punched, I screamed and yelled and sobbed. Oh, in all the world there is no such delight as this, the feeling the soft and yielding pulp of a mouth under one's knuckles, the feeling the brittle crumbling of resistant teeth! There is no such delight, no such exquisite pleasure! The grunt of a man as he goes down is better than any music, any other sound in all the world!

A dimness had fallen over my eyes; I tasted blood in my mouth. It seemed the most delicious taste of all. I was conscious only of bodies that tried to elude me, of scattering figures, of faces that went down. It was some moments before I became aware that someone had seized me, was shaking me violently. Through spaces and aeons and centuries I heard a loud voice in my ears, stern and harsh.

"Jim! Jim! Stop it! Keep still! Hear me? Stop! Stop, damn you!"

I was literally swung off my feet. I found myself glaring up into Dan's face, panting. It was very white, and there was a bloody drop on his lip. His eyes were commanding.

"Jim! Can you hear me? Stop it. Help me with Mortimer. That's the only important thing now. Mortimer. Mortimer!"

He dropped me so suddenly that I reeled. I stared about me, blinking. In the dim distance I saw running figures, scurrying toward the main road. I felt the evening wind on my face. I looked toward the house, disoriented. Jack and Willie and Dave were carrying Mortimer up the stairs. While I watched, they bore him into the house. Dan took my arm, more gently this time.

"Jim. Listen to me. Mortimer's hurt. You know that. You're a doctor. We need you."

I broke down, began to weep wildly, staggered against him. "He's dead," I sobbed. "Didn't you see that, your-self? He's dead. It's no use."

He was shaking me a little, abstractedly, mechanically. Then I heard him groan. He turned away, began to stumble back to the house. I followed him, choking.

≈≈≈≈≈≈≈≈≈≈≈≈≈≈≈≈≈≈≈≈≈≈≈≈≈≈≈

Chapter Twenty-Eight

Mortimer had been laid upon the sofa in Dan's beautiful living room, the very room in which Beatrice had been killed. Jack, Willie, and Dave stood about the couch as I came in; blank misery was on all their faces. Jack kept squeezing a few hard tears through his red eyelids. Dan stood at the head of the sofa and looked down at Mortimer, silently, apparently unmoved.

I handled the old man as well as I could, but he was already dead. I pressed down his eyelids and laid down his arms. His neck had been broken, and he must have died instantly. It is strange how platitudes, how the things one has learned indifferently, rise like bits of wood to the surface of a disturbed and running mind, but I repeated to myself mechanically: "Greater love hath no man—"

I looked at them all slowly, unconscious for the moment of my own abrasions and bruises.

"Well," I said with great bitterness, "you can thank yourself, Jack. You killed your father—"

Jack's dry lips fell open with a harsh gasp. Dan lifted his head and looked at me with stern annoyance.

"Don't talk like a fool, Jim. This is no time for dramatics. 'Killed your father!' You use words too loosely, always did. This is a very terrible accident, and might not have happened if Mortimer hadn't lost his head. No one is to blame."

Jack turned his eyes to him slowly, and his expression became piteous, almost humble.

"Do you really believe that?" he asked, beseechingly.

Dan nodded, and turned away. But my anger flared up.

"Whatever you want to say about this, Dan, it's murder! And I'm calling the sheriff, now! They aren't going to get away with this, not if I have anything to say about it. You can smooth it over if you want to, but the fact remains that these fellows here were heading a mob set on violence. The violent thing happened, though not the way they expected. It's manslaughter, at the least."

I sat down, trembling, unable to stand. I looked at Mortimer lying there, supine, and quiet. Already the wry and satirical lines seemed to be fading, and his expression was becoming remote and majestic. The sudden thought came to me that this was best, that he was at peace now. But my hatred for his killers did not become less. I went to the wall telephone to call the sheriff at Ripley, and tell that astounded gentleman the facts. But before I could speak a word Dan snatched the instrument from my hand and calmly replaced it.

"Listen to me for a while, Jim," he said quietly, and forcibly led me back to the others, who were standing in silence with drooping heads. Jack kept mopping his eyes with his handkerchief. I could see his red hands tremble.

"Listen," Dan repeated, looking straight at all of us. "This can be kept quiet. That is, if you all have sense. That hangdog mob you had with you, Jack, won't talk. They're probably having diarrhea over it now. You won't need to talk, either. We were all together, met on the road. I was with Mortimer. The horse bolted, he was thrown out, and killed instantly. Jim, here, can testify to that. You can all testify to it. The other little—facts can be kept quiet. I'm not interested in knowing why you came or anything. It was all an accident, and the least said the better.

"I don't bear any of you any animosity. Not because I'm noble or anything, but just because I'm not interested in you or anything you have to say. I'm staying here. None of you could drive me off. This is my home; I bought it and paid for it. I want you to understand that, now. I'm staying. It is only when you have interfered with me that there has been trouble. I never interfered with you; all I have ever asked of any of you was to leave me alone. I hope I can expect that now.

"In the meantime, you have the story. I am sure that no one will question any of you—"

"I'm sick of stories!" I cried violently "I'm sick of smoothing things down, and lying, and keeping quiet!" I turned to Dan; he was studying me curiously, almost thoughtfully. "Yes, look at me, Dan. But this time there's going to be real trouble. I'll have these three rescals in jail before night, and I'd like to see anyone stop me!"

I glared at them. They returned my glare dully, as though their thoughts were elsewhere, as indeed they were.

"You haven't an ounce of pride, Dan Hendricks," I resumed. "They might have hanged you or beaten you up if this hadn't happened. Now, you've got them where you ought to have gotten them. Jack can have it on his mind all his life—that he murdered his father; he can look at Williams here, and King, and know they helped him kill him. They can have a nice little sojourn in jail, too, to think things over. They can have it to think about all their lives. You can ruin them. Even if you don't want to do that, I will do it. I will make this town too hot to hold them. Damn it, I never thought that you, Dan, would have a spell of Christian love all of a sudden!"

My words aroused the three young men, and they stared

at each other, affrightedly, drawn away from remorse and grief to consideration of immediate danger and themselves. They next looked at Dan, instead of at me, and under other circumstances I could have laughed at their imploring faces, their silent cries for help to him.

Dan smiled slightly at what I had said. "Will all that bring Mortimer back? Do you think, Jim, that he would want his son to suffer for an accident, that no one intended? Do you think he would be grateful to you for that? Don't you think you owe him a little consideration?"

I was silent, fuming. Jack bent over his father, touched the dead forehead with a trembling finger. He began to weep, silently. He stood up.

"Poor Dad," he said, his lips shaking. "No one ever had a better father. He always seemed to understand things other folks didn't." A sudden thought seemed to strike him, and over his father's body he looked intently and for a long time at Dan. There was surprise, wonderment, and shame on his face. He stood up.

"I don't care what happens," he said listlessly. "I expect we were all wrong. We won't bother you again, Dan. Seems like we always bothered you about something. I guess we can't be friends, but if you need help at any time we fellows want to be told about it."

Dan said nothing. I felt I had been excluded from serious consideration.

"Very pretty," I said contemptuously. "But I'm not moved at all. The sheriff is going to hear all about it."

Dan turned to me and again regarded me thoughtfully. It was one of the last times I ever saw him alive, and I can remember so vividly his tall thin figure, his steady brown eyes, his ugly yet somehow beautiful face. He began to speak slowly, his hands in his pockets, his rough shock of hair falling over his forehead. He spoke to me exclusively.

"Jim, you've always been reproaching me that I wouldn't let you be my friend, that I never asked anything of you, wouldn't let you come near me. Well, now I'm asking something of you. I'm asking you not to do what you seem to intend doing. I'm asking you, again, to keep quiet.

"I'm not asking this for anyone's sake but Mortimer's. It is what he would have wanted. I don't think he is bearing any ill will now, if he lives. I think he would be amused at you. He would want you to do as we will all do: shut your mouth. So, I'm asking you this for him."

Our eyes locked across Mortimer's body. A thousand mysterious and mournful things were in Dan's eyes—compelling, stern, tired and melancholy. I turned away.

I put my hand to my swollen face, let it drop heavily.

"Hell, all right," I muttered. "I expect I can keep quiet once more."

~~~~~~~~~~~~~~~~~~~~~~~~~~~~~

Chapter Twenty-Nine

There was no inquest over Mortimer's death. His funeral was very quiet, and for the first time everyone seemed to realize what he had meant in the life of South Kenton. Everyone was genuinely grieved and shaken. Mrs. Rugby took to her bed after her husband's death and never rose from it again. Jack's cockiness vanished for all time; he became subdued and abstracted and less bellicose.

I told Livy the facts, bitterly. But again she seemed to have a deeper understanding than I did.

Mortimer's death removed the public eye from Dan for a while. It was like a cold cataract of water on a furious fire. For a time he was almost forgotten. Then, just when that eye began to turn back to him, two weeks after Mortimer's tragic death, Sarah Faire died.

She had not really recovered consciousness since the

dreadful night of Beatrice's murder, and she died very quietly without speaking again. Dan did not come to her funeral, neither did he send a single flower. What he thought of the death of the only woman he had ever loved I do not know. I still do not know. He lived on his little farm and no one ever saw him, except at a distance.

Sarah was buried beside her daugher. Somehow, I felt this was wrong. But I could say nothing.

For a long time South Kenton lived in a gray apathy. Too many things had happened for it to assimilate them quickly. A listless search was made for possible murderers, such as tramps. No one remembered seeing any strangers in the country. No one was known to have any animosity towards Beatrice Hendricks. It was all a dark mystery, and the only one who could have enlightened us was dead. But perhaps the one who could have enlightened us was living, out there on his hidden little farm. Who knows? I never knew. Somehow, it doesn't seem important to me.

After three or four months, agitation for the forcible removal of Dan Hendricks from the country was begun. But it died down quickly. I am sure that Jack Rugby and Willie Williams and Dave King had something to do with that. They never spoke of Dan to me. As for myself, I avoided them for a long while. It gave me no pleasure to see them, to see their hangdog looks, their flushes, their uneasiness.

They put up an imposing monument to Mortimer in the graveyard. "Whom God endowed!" But they did not know how deeply God had in truth endowed him. That was a secret that only a few of us knew. The grave was kept vivid and bright with flowers, but the graves of Sarah and Beatrice lay in obscurity.

Months went by. I had become very ill with influenza on that terrible day and was prostrated for a long time. I heard of what was going on only at second hand. I was exhausted mentally and physically, and nothing impinged on me too acutely. Livy nursed me with devotion. Looking up in her smiling face, so quiet and firm and tender, I felt a deep content. I was only too glad not to speak of many things.

ZZZZZZZZZZZZZZZZZZZZZZZZZZZZZZZZZZZZZZZ

In the spring my father died of apoplexy. As I looked at him in his casket I had the strange thought that I had never really known him, that he had died in mystery. Yes, we all live in mystery, and die in mystery. We see each other's comings and goings, each other's faces and gestures, hear each other's voices. But we never know each other. What is behind those walls of flesh, those glimpses caught behind dark wickets, those thick garments? I know this is an old thought, not new, but it does not lose its poignancy and wonder. It strikes one afresh each time it is thought. To me it is the greatest grief of all: that we never in reality see those who are closest to us. Perhaps, seeing them after death, we would not recognize them.

My mother became less stately and sure after my father's death, and Livy and I were both pressed, I with the taking-over of all my father's patients and she with the care of the household. For the first and last time I regretted that I did not have a son to take my place.

South Kenton settled down into its warm and shining apathy and slowness. Life moved sluggishly, easily. Voices had the clear and languid sound of voices heard in deep and motionless silence. Though I was still in my early thirties I felt that I was growing old. You took root in towns like the South Kenton of thirty-five years ago, became steadfast like its trees, rough of bark like those trees, standing complacently in old gardens. The early years of the century were very quiet and peaceful. I knew I was getting stout, and was glad that all my disquieting thoughts had begun to sink beneath the loam at my roots. I refused to let anything disturb me: old dreams, old desires, and restlessnesses, and discontents. I congratulated myself that I was at last free of the fever. I know now that it is a poor congratulation, a sort of self-betrayal, a subtle treachery. Now it seems to me that men live completely only in their dreams and subtle anguishes, and that peaceful years are years lost.

Only one thing disturbed me. Livy was quiet, but not peaceful, I knew. She moved softly, spoke gently and honestly, smiled, touched everything tenderly. She was active in church affairs, was at the head of sociables and bazaars, but in some way I knew that she had not taken root as I had. I could not speak to her of this; I could no more approach her than I had been able to approach Dan. Now that I am older I wonder if we don't all of us live like that, unable to touch anyone else. It has always seemed wrong to me, but then, I had always been a prober. I congratulated myself that I had lost the desire to probe, that I had become willing, without question, to accept things that were offered for my acceptance.

I never saw Dan. I did not forget him. He was like a dim mountain in the background of my mental landscape. But eventually I grew used to that mountain, did not see it objectively. He never came to see me, and I never went to see him. I passed his farm, and once or twice I thought I saw him in his little fields. But I got no closer. Eventually even

South Kenton forgot him, or remembered him with only a dim hatred. Whatever business he did, he did it in Ripley. I never had any desire to see him. I did not wish to be disturbed again, to have the placid calmness of my life broken up into fragments, revealing the dark and mysterious things underneath.

Sometimes Livy and I took trips to New York, to Baltimore and Chicago. We bought a little motor car, the first in South Kenton, and enjoyed it immensely. I always came home satisfied and happy to return, but Livy, though she said nothing, seemed abstracted for a long time afterwards. I have never asked her, but I think she detested South Kenton.

ᴄᴄᴄᴄᴄᴄᴄᴄᴄᴄᴄᴄᴄᴄᴄᴄᴄᴄᴄᴄᴄᴄᴄᴄᴄᴄᴄᴄᴄᴄᴄᴄᴄᴄ

Nineteen-six. A beautiful, quiet, slow-moving, and tranquil year. I have never known life since to be so sweet and full of peace. It was like a prelude, soft, gentle, sonorous, and majestic, to the turbulent drama of the years to come, the years that were already like low and thunderous drumbeats under the placid gaiety. Life will never be the same, never so stately and peaceful and rich with individual lives. Today I can't keep up with things, and they bore and distract me.

The spring of that year seemed especially lovely to me, opulent and warm and full of comfortable laughter. I had not been disturbed by any thoughts for a long time. The peace and slowness of South Kenton were like a golden web in which I, a complacent beetle, was caught and was content to be caught, swinging sleepily under thick vines. I had all the work I needed to do, a comfortable income, a fine old house, a good wife, friends and contentment. It was all I wanted.

One morning I had a call to attend some farmwoman and set out under golden-green trees glittering in cool, shining air. After I had made my call I turned back to town, riding slowly, singing aloud, my hat removed to the fresh, bright wind. I passed Dan's farm.

I had passed it scores of times during the past few years, with only an abstracted glance such as one gives a familiar painting, without experiencing any personal emotion or interest. But today, as I passed, I looked intently at the house behind its pines, at the red, low roof burning ruddily in the spring sunlight, at the blaze of early flowers in the great gardens, at the dazzling whiteness of the newly painted picket fence. A faint gray umbrella of smoke hung over a red chimney, and I could hear the drowsy cluck of chickens and the lowing of a distant cow. The little fields belonging to the house were vividly green and sprouting, the hills on the horizon lavender and jade. I stopped my horse, and then, almost without thinking, I turned in the rutty little road that led to the house. I opened the white gate that led to the garden; I had seen a stooping figure there. It was only when I had closed the gate that I regretted the impulse that brought me here, and if the man in the garden had not raised his head and looked at me intently I would have departed more swiftly than I had come.

I hitched my horse to the gate post and went towards the man slowly and reluctantly. Another look reassured me that it was Dan, for all the thick short beard, old clothes, and broad bowed shoulders. The eyes were the same, dreamy yet intent, mournful yet indifferent.

"Hello, Dan," I said awkwardly.

There was a moment's silence. "Hello, Jim," he said quietly. He looked at his hands; they were coated with wet brown mud. He dropped his trowel and simply rubbed his hands on the legs of his overalls, then offered one hand to me. His clasp was warm and dry, firm and strong. The very touch of him made me acutely conscious of life and vitality. We stood staring at each other for a few moments.

He had grown old beyond his years; he might have been thirty-five or forty-five or more. His face was sunburned and parched with wind, but a deep sadness and peace lay on it. I had always connected peace with happiness and fulfillment, but I knew now that sadness can also become peace, a real peace that expects nothing and asks nothing.

"You have a nice garden here," I said, becoming aware of my own scrutiny.

He turned and regarded the garden thoughtfully, as though trying to see it with my eyes. He turned back to me with a smile of real and simple pleasure.

"Yes, it is, isn't it? Nice. I've worked hard on it. You should see it in June, when the roses are out. I've got over two dozen varieties. Hardiest flower there is. Other flowers are beautiful, but not the way roses are beautiful." His voice was a little rusty, as though he did not use it much. He looked at his leafing bushes; I wondered if he were thinking of Sarah's old garden, sunken in roses. They had been her favorite flower, also. He turned to me.

"Shall we go in for a minute?" he asked.

"Yes, I'd like to," I answered with his own simplicity. Oh, it was easy to do, if one wisely forgot the years and all the things in them, if one could regard events as trivial, no matter how noisy, and one's own thoughts as the only real and important things. I had a sudden insight into this philosophy of Dan's; or rather, it was not definite or deliberate enough to be a philosophy. It was just himself.

When we entered the great old hall with its shining floors and the reflection of the sun bright on them through the fanlight, I saw a youngish woman busily dusting there. "Old Martha's daughter," said Dan casually, nodding at her in a friendly manner. She looked a little surlily at me, as though she thought I was intruding.

We went into the long, low sitting room, the beautiful and comfortable room where Beatrice had been murdered. The sunlight glittered on the little windowpanes, burned richly on the polished furniture, brought out into intricate detail the pattern of the old rug, mingled with the fire, and picked out the red or bright blue of a book binding. I saw that another immense bookcase had been built on one side of the room, and it was thick with volumes.

I had had a moment's shrinking about entering that room. I thought it would be haunted by memory of Beatrice. But instantly I felt that she would never haunt this place, even though she had died here. She had not belonged in this room; her presence could not permeate it. She haunted, rather, the gay new house in South Kenton, which had stood empty and desolate all these years, unwanted. Her presence could enter this place no more than a dark cloud in the sky could enter into the substance of a deep pool.

We sat down before the fire. The youngish woman brought us, at Dan's request, a bottle of brandy and two glasses. She peeped at me furtively and with bewilderment; it was apparent that she was amazed that Dan had a visitor. He told me that her husband helped him with his small farming. He spoke of his farm and the little daily happenings on it, the breeding and flourishing of his small stock. And he talked casually, as to a pleasant, though not very intimate, acquaintance.

I sipped my brandy. I had been uneasy and embarrassed, but it was not long before the slow peace and calm of the place and the man seeped into me. Time had no status here; it was not something to be feverishly followed, a whip-master with a loud and imperious voice. It was a meek slave who served and was not intrusive. I found myself relaxing; I had been at peace for a long time, but now I realized that my own peace had been static and unprofitable, a mere not-thinking, while here was a peace that realized everything and endured because of that knowledge. I was not aware that a silence had fallen between us until I spoke, and then I remembered that neither of us had said anything for a long time.

"You are very happy here, aren't you, Dan?" I asked.

He looked at me meditatively, as though a little, but not too much, actively surprised.

"Happy? What is happiness? You don't know. I don't know. We all look for it. I looked for it here, alone. I don't know whether I'm happy or not. I only know that I'm not wracked with voices I don't want to to hear, faces I don't care about, eyes that hide nothing and are greedy for everything. I'm not troubled about anything. Nothing at all. Perhaps that is happiness."

"Not troubled!" Didn't his memories trouble him, haunt him, stand about him? I looked at him sharply. He was not looking at me; he puffed on his old pipe and gazed tranquilly into space. And then I knew all at once that they didn't trouble him. He had been an unwilling and very tired spectator of everything that had occurred, even when he had participated in it. He had "looked and passed," and found the passing happy. But could it be happy, I thought, troubled? It seemed like a life in death to me.

"You ought to have been a monk, a Trappist," I said listlessly.

He smiled, took his pipe out of his mouth a moment, then returned it.

"No, Trappists are too concerned with trivial things. Sins; the wickedness of the world." He smiled again. "Their silence and isolation are too active. Postive negations. Now, I'm not concerned with anything, not even with myself. I am free. You can't have an ideal, an ambition, a hope or a dream, and be free."

I searched my memory for old things I remembered from my schooldays. "Oh, you're a sort of Buddhist," I said, pleased that I could dredge this up from the hot and cluttered years that now seemed so exciting. "Looking at your navel. Don't they believe in Nirvana or something, where one is absorbed into the Infinite, even while alive, if one persists in looking at the belly button and not hearing or seeing anything?"

He smiled again. "Nirvana. I don't think Western religions could understand that. They think it means oblivion. But it doesn't. It means that it is only when the individual lives in himself completely that he is free. You can't be free when you let a thousand hands pull you in a thousand directions. Only a man who is absorbed in his thoughts is free. If you let the world in, you are like this bottle of brandy here; everyone takes a drink from you, becomes excited by you, is comforted by you, angered by you, or made drunk by you. And after the world is finished with you, then you are just an empty bottle with a label on you: your name, to let everyone know that once you were a full bottle or had a name."

"I'd like to see a civilization conducted under your ideas," I said somewhat irately.

He laughed. The laugh came reluctantly, as though it found its natural channels clogged.

"Oh, I'm not advocating anything for anybody. If a bottle of brandy craves drinkers, let it be drunk. But I prefer not to have anybody drink me. A bottle that stubbornly keeps its cork makes everybody mad; it's a selfish bottle that won't give up its blood for some noble cause or family or society. I'll keep my cork."

"Sometimes a bottle that keeps its cork gets smashed," I said.

"Well, it still keeps something inviolate. Nobody can drink spilled brandy," he answered.

Talk! Talk! And the years ran like a dark river between us, carrying strange cargo which we could not ignore even while we kept silent. I drank some more brandy.

"You don't want anything, Dan?" I asked suddenly.

He shook his head. "Nothing," he repeated gently.

I hitched myself closer to him. "Dan, didn't you ever think about going away, about living? About leaving this place? This isn't all the world. You could start out new somewheres," I finished lamely.

"Where? Why? Wherever I went, Jim, I would take myself with me. I couldn't get away from myself. I'd still be the same person in New York or Afghanistan. There's no point in getting away if you can't get away from yourself." He smoked a moment in silence, then he turned his distant yet penetrating eyes on me. "I know what you mean, Jim.

You think I could 'forget.' Look at it from your point of view, not mine. Suppose you were a man who had been suspected of killing his wife, and was not quite cleared in everybody's eyes. You would go away, far away. But news spreads. Someone, anywhere, would have heard about it. They would look at you and think: there's a man who might have killed his wife. Here, everyone thinks it. It is no news to them. They are used to the idea. I am used to their idea. But to go away, to start again, would be to expose myself to curiosity, to eyes that demanded, to mouths that everlastingly talked. It is horrible to me to think of strange faces, strange voices and towns. It is horrible to think of strangeness, of starting again, as you call it."

For one moment I remembered my feverish vision of the exposed brain again, quivering, unprotected, always trying to shrink from curious and alien fingers, always trying to grow a shelter for itself.

"Even if nobody ever heard," he continued thoughtfully, "I could never forget. And that is the only thing that matters."

Ah, I thought, with exultant sadness, so you do remember!

"Have another drink," he said, and filled my glass.

"Dan," I said slowly, "I expect I've never really known you. When we were kids together, I thought I did. But I didn't. And I've always wanted to get close to you. I never really had another friend. But I see it's my fault; I should not have probed into you, demanded anything of you. That's all you asked of me, to let you be yourself in peace. But none of us did that, until—until recently. We all demand something from each other. You neither demanded nor asked. I wonder how many people there are like you in the world. Quite a few, I think. Some of them try to 'adjust' themselves, either because of circumstances or because of some stupid idea of duty. I imagine many of them end up in insane asylums, or commit suicide when they can't stand the tearing hands any longer. You are what we call a 'solitary.' God knows why we consider that abnormal. I always did until now. We know that variations from the norm aren't really abnormal, but a different species. I don't know why they think that men who refuse to submit to mental and social cannibalism are abnormal or dangerous. Mass civilization doesn't seem to me to be so very splendid or valuable. It doesn't do away with exploitation and cruelty and war and stupidity. Perhaps you are right; perhaps it is only the individual that is valuable or precious. I can't see why a heterogeneous stew, where everything has lost its identity, is so palatable. I think you've had lots of courage; you've kept yourself for yourself, yet there have been times when you have come out and done something really vital, when necessary. Men without identities are men without flavor or keenness. Yet, civilization's first effort is to rob men of flavor and keenness. It calls it 'mass effort,' 'collectivism'; something or other about everyone surging forward in a body to accomplish something magnificent. But it never does."

I looked at him timidly, expecting a smile of indulgence for my groping difficulty in expressing myself. But I was amazedly gratified to see that he was listening, that his eyes had dilated a little with wonder and pleasure, that he seemed eager and released.

"Yes? Yes?" he said impatiently.

I pondered, excited myself. My brain, stirred up from years of peaceful lethargy, moved painfully with new life.

"It's funny how 'civilization' absorbs, or tries to absorb you. It eats you alive. It constantly demands. 'Give me your hand, your eyes, your heart, your soul.' And if you do, you have nothing left. You have to fill the empty places with mass ideals or gestures in unison."

"God is a poor substitute for personal integrity," Dan broke in. And smiled. His teeth glimmered through his beard.

All at once I felt unhappy and wretched, as though I had wasted something precious. But who did not? Except Dan and Livy. God! He should have loved her! What a horrible waste. When I came to die, what would I have? Nothing. I would be a disintegrated individual. But here was a man who would be integrated, strong in inviolate personality. Yet this too seemed very sad to me, I don't know why. Was he right or wrong? Was anything right or wrong? It was exhausting to think about it. I wanted to get away again, where I would not have to think. I stood up.

"Life's a damn mess," I said.

"Seems to me I've heard that before, Jim," he smiled. He stood up, also. He did not ask me to stay.

"But there must be something—meaning," I said helplessly from the depths. I did not quite understand why I said it, or what I really meant. He regarded me with something like compassion, but made no comment. He went with me to the door, and outside. I unhitched my horse and walked beside it down the rutty road. Dan went with me. An unbearable depression gripped me. It did not do to expose one's self even to one's self. It was profitless, like hungry teeth tearing at its own flesh. Hadn't someone written somewhere that much thought is much weariness, and an abscess in the soul?

I shook hands with him. Again I was conscious of the warm, strong vitality in his hand, earthy and free, of the kind and remote steadiness of his eyes. But I saw again that he was a stranger, would always be a stranger, that I could never really touch him.

I got on my horse. I looked down at him.

"I can come again, Dan?"

"Yes, of course," he replied heartily. "Soon, too."

I rode away. After some little distance I looked back. He was leaning on the low gate, smoking, watching after me. I waved. He waved in answer. It was like someone waving from a ship that was leaving harbor. A stranger waved.

Chapter

~~~~~~~~~~~~~~~~~~~~~~~~~~~~~~~ *Thirty-Two*

It was not until I got home that I realized that we had
not talked of the years between, that he had not asked me
any questions of how things were with me, that he had
shown no interest in what I was doing or what I was thinking. He had not asked of Livy or of anyone that we both
knew. Events, years, death and life, were equally insignificant to him. Locked in the cell of himself, he had not even
known that the world had gone by.

I had no desire to see him again. I kept promising myself
that I would, but I noticed that I half-subconsciously
avoided the road that went by Dan's farm. Once, at a distance, I saw on horseback a man that might have been he,
and I rode hurriedly down a side road to keep from meeting him. I don't know why I did this, at first. I was heavily
wretched and unhappy. Everything had become tasteless

and tedious, futile gestures while the tired feet walked in a circle. My thoughts, though vague and pointless, were exceedingly painful. Curse these people who made you think, anyway! They walked through the gates of your garden without permission, tramped over your careful little flower-beds, looked contemptuously at your ancient, sleepy trees, pointed out that your invulnerable walls were built of sand, and that your house would not weather a storm. Their voices broke up your quiet and contented reveries; their remarks demolished your peace. They either beat drums that you did not wish to follow or killed all your little goals with gentle laughter. No wonder the world hated its reformers, its saviors, its saints, its poets, and its heroes. No wonder it killed them, burned them, beat them down, or exiled them. And it did all this, not because it did not believe them, but because in its heart it did believe them, and hated them for the agony of thought they brought to murder its peace.

So I did not go to see Dan. If I saw him I would be unhappy, because I would be released from unthinking and pleasant peace for a little while, and I did not wish to be released. I preferred my warm prison.

I had not told Livy of my visit to Dan. We never mentioned his name. But it was always between us like a river of fire that we pretended was not there. Gradually, as time went on, I thought less of him. Our little hospital was badly in need of funds, but finance was getting tight, and even our largest donors were giving piddling sums. If this went on, I thought desperately, we would have to close the hospital that had saved so many lives. I gave my services gratis, and a great part of my income. But still we lagged far behind. We also needed new equipment and beds. We had to hustle out patients who needed further care, and because a farmer's wife had an incurable case of cancer which would probably take several months to kill her, we had to refuse her a bed. It was disheartening. We held bazaars, fairs, parties, and dances to obtain cash, but though these were great successes socially they barely covered expenses.

In the fall Livy had an attack of appendicitis, and we had

to rush her to Ripley because of lack of facilities in South Kenton. I had many bitter and terrified thoughts on the way to Ripley with her. If she died, it would be the fault of South Kenton. But we removed the appendix just before it ruptured, and I returned to South Kenton more than ever determined to raise funds if I went bankrupt myself. For the first time I fully realized our deficiencies; we had no circulating free library for the young people; we had no decently equipped hospital. For entertainment we had our own tight homes, the church, and the saloon. It was very bad, though no worse than other small towns of that period. I felt something should be done about it. Something was done, but in a way I did not dream of, and even though the benefits were enormous I would have gladly sacrificed them not to have had the thing happen.

Spring came, a desperate spring for the country. It was nineteen-seven. No one who remembers that time needs explanation. I feel it was the beginning of that great cycle of social adjustment which has culminated in our present demoralized state, and that it was not, as some claim, merely a customary phenomenon, a natural ebb and flow in the tides of men.

I was hard pressed. My patients, half of them, could not pay me anything, and even those who could pay held back as long as possible. One of the banks in Ripley, one in which I had a good portion of funds, failed. A heavy gloom settled over the whole country, and dire prophets rose then as now.

The spring seemed depressed also, cold weather lingering well on into months that should have been warm. The roads ran with a particularly sticky and loathsome red mud, so that it sucked down my horse's hoofs, and the prints he left brimmed with water immediately. The atmosphere hung thick with unprecipitated drops, and the sky seemed full of gaseous clouds.

I finally went to Willie Willams in desperation, and I told him that I wished him to write letters to my more affluent patients demanding payment. He looked at me with surprise.

"Well, sir," he said slowly, in his yokel's voice, "this was never done before, Jim. Your dad never did it. After all, all these folks are your friends. We don't send duns to our friends. Why," he added, astounded as he thought about it, "you'll lose every patient you had. Folks won't even speak to you."

"I can't help it," I said recklessly. "We need money for the hospital; I need a new roof on the house. Damn it, I haven't even paid Dr. Winslow for Livy's operation yet, and the last letter I got from him wasn't too delicate. In the first place the old rascal had talked about professional ethics and what not, and refused payment. But when I insisted, for he isn't too flush himself, he didn't say anything. Now he assumes I owe him the money. I've got to do something. So, get after these people."

"I wish you'd reconsider this, Jim," he said hesitatingly. "It means a lot to you. Folks don't forget. Wait a few days."

"Oh, all right," I said wearily. "I'll send them a few dozen more letters and waste stamps, and hound them like a peddler whenever I see them. Then, if they don't cough up—"

I had a call from an arthritic patient in the country one late afternoon, when a slow, heavy rain was falling and the air was like liquid ice. The man already owed me fifty dollars, but he was an old patient of my father's, and I had to go. He was a farmer, poor and hopeless, living on a stony little farm six miles out. I would have to pass Dan's farm or take another route adding more than a mile. I could let no personal delicacies stand in my way today; the weather was too foul. The air was so heavy with water that my horse began to wheeze as he plodded over the roads like soupy rivers. A little wooden bridge over a creek rumbled and shook as I went over it, and I looked down into a stream livid and dirty and swollen. Every farmhouse seemed isolated in liquid mud; every tree, with thin, belated foliage, dripped down a cold, wet burden on me. I passed Dan's farm, but I was too sunken in my own personal misery to give it more than an abstracted glance.

When I turned homeward, evening was rapidly falling. The lowing of cattle rolled in hollow waves over the watery and desolate earth, and the hills had vanished in moving fog. In the west was a dull and sullen gash of gold which threw a faint saffron tint on the tops of the palely green trees and the tops of farmhouses. I shivered in my raincoat.

Eventually I became conscious that the saffron tint seemed to take on a shade of orange, then red, that it was rising higher into the gray, dark sky. I looked bemusedly at the phenomenon, and it was not until I saw the red mounting higher, flickering, that the truth rushed in on me. Somewhere, someone's house was burning. I spurred up my tired horse. A fire in the country was a frightful thing. There was not much anyone could do about it. The only thing one could hope was that no one was caught in the conflagration. Well, it was still daylight, and no one would be in bed; that was a thing to be thankful for, at any rate.

I turned a bend in the road, and a terrible sight shone on me across the acres of gray and sodden fields. The valley here was smooth and level, and set in the midst of it a house in the distance was furiously burning, already a pyre of orange, scarlet and yellow flames. I could even hear the faint rumbling of it. It colored the mist that roamed over the valley; it lighted the sky, it quivered in a thousand small and shattered lakes on the earth so that they too seemed burning. What made it the more appalling was the utter silence of the evening skies and the earth, the lack of motion and voices. It was Dan's house that was burning. There it stood, alone, a gigantic bonfire on the silent floor of the valley.

Oh, my God! I thought dully. I pushed my horse to his limit. I passed a farmhouse, and shouted. A woman came to the door and shouted back at me that her husband and sons had already gone to the fire. I ran on. Now I passed one or two madly running figures who bellowed unintelligible things to me. By now I could hear the hoarse and prolonged roaring of the flaming house and could see the heavy columns of smoke that rose from it straight into the livid sky. So fierce were the flames that the hills in the near distance flashed out into vivid view at moments, stark and motionless, then fell into darkness as the flames sank. The whole countryside was lighted as the night fell, and I could distinctly feel the hot breath of the fire as it was carried to me on the wind.

I arrived at full speed at the little road that led to the house, and galloped up it. I saw now that a dozen or more men were standing futilely near the house, staring at it blankly. A woman was pleading and gesticulating to each and everyone, but they stood stolidly as though they had not heard her. They turned to me as I came up, and every face was carved in bright orange against the dimness of the evening.

The woman recognized me immediately. It was old Martha's daughter. Before I was out of the saddle she was clutching me, her face running with tears, her cheeks smeared with soot, her hair hanging disheveled about her shoulders.

"Doctor!" she cried desperately. "Mr. Dan's still in there! Get him out! He'll be burned to death!"

"In there?" I shouted, starting to run towards the house.

"Yes, sir!" she sobbed, running, panting, beside me. "I had the little dog upstairs, locked in a room, and the fire started, and I ran out, and Mr. Dan ran out! It seemed to start a hundred places—at once— And I told him—little dog still in the house, and—he ran back in—and didn't come out again—! Don't know how it started— Hundred places at once. Tried to get them to go in for him, but they won't!"

The house was gutted. Already the upper floor had crashed in, and black fragments, like burned bones, protruded against the orange flames. I told myself it was hopeless. Flames were pouring out like flaming waters through the sitting room windows. Hopeless. Hopeless.

I turned in frantic despair and hate to the stolidly watching men.

"You swine!" I screamed. "Standing there while a man burns to death! I'm going in for him! Is anyone here man enough to go with me?"

A heavy-faced farmer shook his head. "Doc, you can't go in there! House like a bonfire! No use goin' in."

"I'll go with you, Doc," said a younger man suddenly, coming forward. "Mr. Hendricks paid my mortgage last year." His face was sickly white. We went to the door, wrenched it open. Instantly black smoke poured out upon us, blinding us, choking us, overwhelming us with hellish heat. We staggered back a moment while through coughs I instructed the young man to pull his coat over his head. We went in, tongues of heat licking our exposed flesh, singeing our clothing. The uproar of flame and falling timbers was like drums in our aching ears.

The hallway was a mass of thick smoke. The sitting room beyond flamed brilliantly with leaping and dancing flames, so violent that they lit the hallway. The stairway that led to the upper floor, burned halfway down, was smoldering, sending up showers of scarlet sparks. On the floor at the foot of the stairway lay Dan, face down, motionless, one arm thrown over his head. His clothing smoked. In the shelter of his other arm crouched a small fluffy shape, the little dog that had cost Dan his life.

We seized Dan, unconscious of the smoldering clothing that seared our hands. Our breath was gone; we were choking and gasping and weeping. I remember distinctly how the hot floor burned through our shoes, scarred our flesh. The little dog whimpered and coughed; I seized him by the scruff of his neck, and we dragged man and dog out upon the porch. Then there were sufficient willing hands to help us with our burdens, and in a few moments we carried Dan to a little distance and laid him on the wet earth. The little dog had not been hurt at all, except that his hair was singed and filled the air with an acrid odor.

Just when we laid Dan upon the earth, a hungry roar came from the house, and it collapsed in upon itself, the triumphant flames rushing skyward in a furious burst of crimson and yellow. So vivid was the light it made that for a great distance about the countryside was as bright as noonday.

Old Martha's daughter, sobbing frantically, brought me my bag, and I carefully cut the smoldering clothing from Dan's body. He lay unconscious, stark and silent, his face upturned to the sky. The little dog crept to him, whimpering, nuzzled him, finally crouched beside him licking his flesh, and whining. From the first exposure of Dan's body, I knew it was all over. Third-degree burns and worse. The fingers of his right hand were burned almost to the bone and hideously blackened. It was no use. The only thing I could hope for him was that he would die quickly, without gaining consciousness. However, to make sure he would not suffer too much I hastily filled my hypodermic syringe and shot a terrific quantity of morphine in the one unscorched spot I could find on his arm. I did all this mechanically, my hands not trembling, oblivious of the crowd of awed and frightened men that stood about us.

Because of the position in which he had fallen, his face was almost untouched. I gently wiped the soot from it, prayed again that he would not recover consciousness. I could not feel anything particular; I was numb. I accepted a horse blanket that someone gave me, and we laid Dan upon it, and covered him with a coat. The fire still flared with enormous fury, and the gutted timbers fell deeper into the pit of themselves with dull crashes.

Old Martha's daughter knelt down beside me, wringing her hands, sobbing incoherently. The little dog whined, looked at me despairingly when his master did not respond to his lickings, and finally crept around to me and licked my hands. That simple and humble touch, grateful and pleading, unnerved me. I began to sob as I knelt there, as yet unaware of my own injuries. When I looked again, Dan's eyes were open, unfocused yet, bewildered and groping. I bent over him.

"All right, Dan?" I asked shakily.

He stared at me intently for a few moments, then he smiled. "Good old Jim again," he whispered. A spasm of agony touched his face for a moment, and then it was tranquil once more.

"Dan, is it—is it all right?" I could hardly control my voice.

"Not—bad," he replied with a terrible effort.

"Doc," said a hoarse voice beside me, "I got my cart here. Can we take him to town?"

I shook my head without looking at the speaker. Though Dan had shut his eyes again he seemed to realize what had been said, and he smiled a little, ironically. Then he opened his eyes, and his lips moved. I bent over him.

"Jim—go—Ripley National—old Mr. Semple."

"Yes, yes, Dan! Don't talk."

My voice appeared to arouse him, and he stared at me for a long moment. I bent over him again.

"Jim. I want to tell you something—now."

"Yes, Dan?"

But instead of answering immediately, he looked intently and piercingly into my eyes, as though he were searching through the inmost refuges of my mind. There was something awful and fateful in that look. He moved his head slightly in a negative gesture.

"No. I won't—burden you with that—not now."

He was whispering through his seared lips. I almost touched them with my ear.

"Good—old Jim. Good—old Jim. I never—Want you realize—"

The whisper died away, then began for the last time again. "Dog—"

"I've got him, Dan. I'll take him home with me."

He smiled. A spasm of rigidity struck his face, passed

away. When it had gone he was dead, but the smile remained, ironic, sad, yet infinitely kind.

Then I began to weep uncontrollably, covering my face
with my own burned hands, while Dan stared at the sky
with dead and fearless eyes.

I had been burned worse than I knew, and had to stay in bed for two weeks while Dr. Winslow from Ripley took over my patients. I developed a high fever and was unconscious for two or three days. During my delirium I dreamed the dreadful scene over and over, a hundred times, and I could faintly hear myself screaming. And I heard Livy's voice, calm and gentle, soothing and tender.

Luckily most of my burns were first-degree, with only a few second-degree. My hands had suffered most. To this day my right hand is stiff and scarred, and I can no longer perform delicate operations. But I do not regret it; I can look at that hand and feel a deep content. It is the only thing in my life that has given me such soul-quietness.

Fortunately, I could feel nothing for a long time, until I was out of bed and getting around feebly again. I could think nothing clearly nor acutely. For this I was thankful. I knew a day was coming when I would feel again, and dreaded it. Livy told me gently one day that they had buried Dan beside Sarah Faire; Beatrice lay on her other side. I felt comforted even in my grief.

Livy gave me a letter that had come for me from Mr. John Semple, president of the Ripley National Bank, in which he expressed regret for my injuries and asked me to call upon him as soon as I could. I put down the letter and looked at Livy. She seemed ill, worn out, and piteously white. I leaned towards her and put my bandaged hand on hers.

"Livy," I began painfully. "Livy. Is it all right now?"

She smiled at me. Her smile did not waver, though tears ran down her cheeks.

"All right, Jim. Perfectly all right."

Again, I was content. She put her arms around me and pressed her lips into my neck.

One day I told her what Dan had said, about not burdening me, and wondered aloud what it was he had started to tell me. But Livy put her hand on my mouth as though in fright.

"Let it go, Jim. He wanted to let it go. Don't think about it anymore."

But I did think about it. I shall always think about it. I have an idea—

Six weeks after Dan's death I went over to Ripley to see Mr. John Semple of the First National Bank. He was a wizened, gold-bespectacled old man with a dry and pompous air. He received me in his private office and immediately got down to business. He importantly removed a thin sheet of paper from a blue envelope. I looked at it impatiently. He cleared his throat.

"You know, of course, Dr. Marcy, that Mr. Hendricks left quite an estate. Yes, if I may say so, quite an estate. His needs were small; he didn't use up his income from the wells."

"Yes. Yes," I replied.

He cleared his throat again. "I have here the last will and

testament of Mr. Daniel Hendricks. I will read it to you. It was made out three years ago. December eleventh, 1904, to be exact."

He began to read. I listened dully for a few moments, then with intensity.

"I hereby will to my friend, Dr. James Marcy, of South Kenton, New York, the sum of ten thousand dollars outright, for his own personal use."

"My God!" I whispered. Mr. Semple, unmoved, read on.

His property, containing the oil wells, was to be sold outright to the Ripley Gas Company, and the proceeds, which would amount to more than twenty thousand dollars, was to be given to our little free hospital. Dr. James Marcy was to be sole director as to how the money was to be used.

The gay and desolate house where he had lived with his wife, Beatrice, was to be torn down, and the land was left to the town of South Kenton on condition that upon the site was to be built a free circulating library. The sum of twelve thousand dollars was willed towards the building and stocking of the library.

He had left two thousand dollars and the farm to old Martha.

I was named sole executor of his estate.

I sat there, dumb and shaken, drawing my hand down over my face, and trembling. Mr. Semple, coughing, meticulously folded up the will. He tapped an arid finger on his desk.

"A very good will. A very kind will. Seems to me, Doctor, that you folks in South Kenton didn't—er—appreciate Mr. Daniel Hendricks. A very good man. Very fond of him, myself."

"We can't take it!" I cried wildly, starting to my feet. "They hounded him—they tried to kill him! Somehow, I feel they did kill him!"

Mr. Semple clucked. No doubt he found me hysterical and childish. He shook his head.

"Well, that's what the will says, Doctor. It isn't in your hands. The property and money was left to the town of South Kenton, and I doubt, I very much doubt, that they will refuse it. Of course," he smiled, "you are at liberty yourself to refuse your own specific legacy." He seemed to find me absurd.

I called a meeting a few nights later in the town hall. I looked over the crowded room, experiencing in advance a bitter satisfaction. I read a copy of the will to them all. For a long time they sat motionless, dumbfounded, then gradually eye sought eye and looked away again. There was no cheer from the enemies of Dan Hendricks, no stereotyped motion of gratitude and thanks to the dead man. They filed out in silence. But I had the acrid pleasure of seeing that many an eye was dim, and that many men coughed and went away in subdued groups. I hated them all passionately.

Many years have gone by. I am getting old now, and there are two new young doctors to help me and to take my place, the place a son will never take. They live with Livy and me. They argue incessantly, and think me an old doddering country doctor whose day and theories are done. No doubt my time and ideas are done. I bear these young men no malice. I like to see their smart bags, listen to their learned new ideas. I like to visit the hospital, where I am chief of staff, and I take immense satisfaction in its perfect equipment, its shining operating rooms, the starchy whiteness of the nurses' uniforms, its lines of white beds.

South Kenton has changed, become larger and very important. The old Baptist Church has been torn down, and a splendid garage stands in its place. South Kenton is on the main highway to New York, and that highway and our streets swarm with automobiles and interstate buses with their sonorous horns. The Great Depression has not hit us too badly, and our girls and young women dress as well as ever. Our evenings are noisy and hideous with the screamings of radios. Thick throngs of young people gather in ice-cream parlors along Main Street of summer evenings, and over the New York Store is a garish dance hall where our youngsters dance three times a week to the unreconciled disapproval of their elders. Change. Change. Not always a pleasant change, but then, I am getting old.

The younger people are only vaguely familiar with the name of Dan Hendricks. They are not really interested. They think their parents are bores when mothers and fathers speak of Dan. His life is a tedious story to them. They crowd the Hendricks Public Library night after night and day after day, without a thought for the man who had made it possible for them to have this neat white stone building. When they are ill they go to our hospital, free if they cannot pay, and for a small fee if they can pay, and do not think of the one who gave them comfort and care.

Most of my friends are dead or half dead. We rarely speak of Dan Hendricks. He is like a book that has been read, a tale that has been told, a strange song that has been sung and forgotten. If we do speak of him, it is with vague gratitude and a distant uneasiness.

No one but Livy and myself visits his sunken grave. There had been a halfhearted suggestion about putting up a prominent monument to him, but I nipped the idea in the bud. Dan would have laughed at it. I felt that such a stone would have weighed him down, imprisoned him. But Livy puts the first flowers from her garden on his grave, and we often spend an hour or two in the summer Sunday afternoons, I kneeling stiffly to clip intruding grass, Livy to sprinkle water on the potted flowers with a green sprinkling can. We rarely speak of him, even when we are alone, but he will always be the most vital thought in our minds.

Livy is getting old, too, plump and gray-haired and quiet, but with the old resolute glance in her eyes and with the old honest mouth. We do not need to speak often, for we know each other's thoughts.

I have no fear now of writing of my own part in Dan Hendricks' life. No one will be interested. I told Livy I was writing it, and she did not answer for a long time.

"What can you write that would take more than a few hundred words?" she asked at last, very quietly.

I explained, but she did not seem to be listening. It was as though she were looking inward into thoughts that I could not share.

My life is complete. But sometimes I wonder if it is as complete as Dan's was? There are so many things I might have done, might have said. I think we regret these things more than any "sins" we might have done, on the last day. I try not to think too much. I still think that saviors and heroes get pretty much what they deserve, for disturbing us.

No, Livy and I do not speak much of Dan Hendricks.

Yet, somehow, I think she could tell me a lot that I do not know, that I do not wish to know. I must have peace.

Taylor Caldwell

☐	NEVER VICTORIOUS, NEVER DEFEATED	08435-9	1.95
☐	TENDER VICTORY	08298-4	1.50
☐	THIS SIDE OF INNOCENCE	08434-0	1.75
☐	YOUR SINS AND MINE	00331-6	1.25
☐	THE ARM AND THE DARKNESS	C2627	1.95
☐	CAPTAINS AND THE KINGS	23069-4	2.25
☐	DIALOGUES WITH THE DEVIL	G2768	1.50
☐	THE FINAL HOUR	C2579	1.95
☐	GLORY AND THE LIGHTNING	C2562	1.95
☐	GRANDMOTHER AND THE PRIESTS	C2664	1.95
☐	GREAT LION OF GOD	C2445	1.95
☐	THE LATE CLARA BEAME	23157-7	1.50
☐	MAGGIE—HER MARRIAGE	23119-4	1.50
☐	NO ONE HEARS BUT HIM	Q2507	1.50
☐	ON GROWING UP TOUGH	23082-1	1.50
☐	A PILLAR OF IRON	C2418	1.95
☐	THE ROMANCE OF ATLANTIS	X2748	1.75
☐	TESTIMONY OF TWO MEN	C2416	1.95
☐	WICKED ANGEL	Q2740	1.50
☒	TO LOOK AND PASS	X3491	1.75

Buy them at your local bookstores or use this handy coupon for ordering:

FAWCETT PUBLICATIONS, P.O. Box 1014, Greenwich Conn. 06830

Please send me the books I have checked above. Orders for less than 5 books must
include 60c for the first book and 25c for each additional book to cover mailing and
handling. Orders of 5 or more books postage is Free. I enclose $_____ in check
or money order.

Name_____

Address_____

City_____ State/Zip_____

Please allow 4 to 5 weeks for delivery. This offer expires 6/78.   C-1